THE
SOMETHING
GIRL

JODI TAYLOR

HEADLINE

First published in Great Britain in 2017 by
Accent Press Ltd

This edition published in paperback in Great Britain in 2019 by
HEADLINE PUBLISHING GROUP

3

Cataloguing in Publication Data is available from the British Library

ISBN 978 1 4722 6437 4

Printed and bound in Great Britain by Clays Ltd, Elcograf S.p.A.

Headline's policy is to use papers that are natural, renewable and recyclable
products and made from wood grown in well-managed forests and other
controlled sources. The logging and manufacturing processes are expected
to conform to the environmental regulations of the country of origin.

MIX
Paper from
responsible sources
FSC® C104740

HEADLINE PUBLISHING GROUP
An Hachette UK Company
Carmelite House
50 Victoria Embankment
London EC4Y 0DZ

www.headline.co.uk
www.hachette.co.uk

I should say, right here, that anyone who feels that enormous, invisible golden horses are not for them should stop reading now, because Thomas is the most enormous, the most beautiful, the most invisible golden horse you will never, ever see. And he's very definitely real.

PROLOGUE

Three years ago, I was nobody. I was nothing. That's what they called me – The Nothing Girl. Because that's what I was. I had no life, no parents, and no friends and, when my stutter was very bad, I had no speech either.

Everyone around me seemed to have it all. My cousin Francesca was a successful actress/model and her brother Christopher owned and ran the local bookshop. Then there was Russell Checkland, the up-and-coming artist, setting London on fire with his work. My uncle, Richard Kingdom, one of Rushford's most successful solicitors, lived with his wife, Julia, in the best part of Rushford. They gave me a home after my parents died, but very little else. I lived in the attic. Solitary, friendless, and afraid of nearly everything.

Looking back, I don't know how I survived and there were two occasions when I very nearly didn't. When my story nearly came to a premature end.

The first was at what I thought at the time was the very lowest point of my life. I was thirteen. My road hadn't been very long but it hadn't been very smooth either. I was entirely alone and contemplating something awful and then I looked up to see an enormous golden horse standing in the corner of my bedroom.

No one else could see him. No one else could hear him. Only me. Sadly I wasn't transformed instantly into a fashion princess with a mobile phone that never stopped ringing or a queue of wannabe boyfriends but, with his help, I faced down the bullies at school. With Thomas standing behind me, enveloping me in his smell, like

1

warm ginger biscuits, I could string words together if I took things slowly. I could make my voice heard.

I grew up with Thomas always at my side. Advising, guiding, giving me the courage to face each long, dreary day as my life stretched out in front of me, going nowhere very slowly.

They said there was something the matter with me. That there was something wrong with Jenny Dove, as I was then, and I, believing this was true and grateful not to be sent off to one of those 'special homes', hid from the world, kept quiet, and did as I was told.

It was Thomas who pushed me to go the party where I met Russell Checkland again. We'd known each other since we were both children. I still don't know how Thomas managed to persuade me to accept Russell's ridiculous proposal of marriage, but he did. I married Russell, escaped the stupefying boredom of life with my aunt, and jumped straight from the frying pan into the fire.

Life became difficult again. I was completely out of my depth and there were people who wished me ill. My world grew darker and, just when I needed him most, Thomas left me. That was the second worst time of my life. I can see now that it was his version of tough love, because now that I was married I needed to stand on my own feet and move out of his shadow. I needed to realise that far from being isolated little Jenny Dove, I was now Jenny Checkland, and people were relying on me. People needed me. He had to do it, but at the time it nearly finished me. I couldn't comprehend a life without big, golden Thomas at my side. But of course, being Thomas, he didn't leave me quite alone. He couldn't stay – so he sent.

He sent another Thomas. A real horse. The first thing that was truly mine. Russell's birthday gift to me. A turning point in our rocky relationship. This Thomas brought me a different type of freedom. I can't describe the sense of achievement I gained from learning to ride. From finding that there was something in this world that I could do. And do well.

Sadly, my life wasn't peaceful for long. The people who wished me harm gathered for one last try and there was a dreadful night when our feed store was on fire and I thought I'd lost everything, including Russell. Matters were resolved, however, and we were left in peace.

For a while.

CHAPTER ONE

'Buff Orpingtons,' said Russell, bounding through the back door, shedding his jacket in one direction and a wellington in the other.

His household, familiar with his habits, regarded him without dismay.

'Braised Onions,' said Mrs Crisp, his housekeeper.

'Blunt Object,' said Andrew, his cousin.

'Blood Oranges,' said Kevin, his handyman.

'Black Olives,' said Sharon, his handyman's girlfriend.

'Blind Optimism,' said I, his wife.

'What?' he said, staring at us in puzzlement. 'What are you talking about? Jenny, what are they talking about?'

'Isn't it a game?' asked Andrew. 'I thought it was a game. Your turn.'

'Why are you here again?' said Russell, crossly, hopping across the kitchen floor with one welly on and one welly off. 'You're always here. Every time I look up you're sitting at my kitchen table, making eyes at my wife.'

Andrew winked at me and I grinned back.

'Stop that,' said Russell, finally divesting himself of his recalcitrant wellington. He tossed it out through the door into the mudroom and stared disapprovingly around, his gaze finally alighting on the cat, who sprawled on his back in front of the range, presenting something that Russell could legitimately complain about. Strictly speaking, the cat had been forbidden the house on several occasions, Russell stoutly maintaining he could stay only if he earned his keep by battling the rodent population outside. Typically, the cat ignored him for most of the time but, every now and then, he would underline his dominance by presenting Russell with a spectacularly gruesome dead rat, lovingly laid across his trainers in the mudroom. Job done, he would return to his spot on the old rug in front of the range, leaving Russell to deal with the disintegrating corpse.

Russell put his hands on his hips and frowned heavily. 'I've told you before Mrs Crisp, that cat is not an attractive sight in a food preparation area.'

Mrs Crisp looked at me. 'Do you think it would help if I covered him with a tea towel?'

Russell nodded. 'Excellent idea. Cover away.'

She draped a tea towel over Russell's head.

Sharon, mashing potatoes as if her life depended on it, giggled, and the rest of us fell about.

'Very funny,' said Russell, the tea towel puffing slightly with every word. 'Your sense of humour will be reflected in this month's wages. And may I remind you all – again – that I'm the head of the household and as such...'

The cat sneezed and woke up.

Russell, who had learned to keep his distance, pulled off the tea towel and stepped back.

His dark red hair flopped over his forehead as always. He pushed it out of the way and returned to his original grievance. 'So Andrew, why are you here? Again.'

'You invited me for Sunday lunch.'

'No, I invited the very beautiful Miss Bauer. You're just a by-product. Where is she by the way?'

'Shopping.'

'Well, she can still come to lunch, can't she?'

'In Berlin. With her mother.'

'Oh.' He scowled at his cousin. 'Well, we'll just have to put up with you, I suppose, but we're only doing it out of the goodness of our hearts. You're hardly an acceptable substitute for the lovely Tanya.'

Andrew ignored this comment. 'I have to ask, Russ, why are you crashing through the door shouting, "Buff Orpingtons"? Is that like a rural "Open Sesame"?'

Russell came to sit next to me, putting his hand over mine for a moment. His hands were warm and steady as usual. He smiled at me. Most people would say that Andrew, with his conventional dark good looks, was the more handsome of the two cousins. Russell's face was longer and thinner but I always thought him the better looking. 'All right, Jenny? Where's the young madam?'

'Upstairs, asleep after … her lunch.'

'Speaking of which…'

'Possibly ten minutes,' said Mrs Crisp, crashing things onto the draining board, 'but since it would appear I'm not being paid this month, who knows?'

'I pay you every month,' he said indignantly. 'I can't believe this ingratitude.'

'Mrs Checkland pays me,' she said calmly, emptying vegetables into a serving dish.

'Buff … Orpingtons?' I said, trying to get him back on track.

My stutter is much better these days. Sometimes it's barely noticeable. Especially when I'm with friends. There's the odd hesitation occasionally and I'm never going to be a chatterbox but – and I can't tell you what this means to me – when I speak, people listen. Only someone whose voice was not heard for years can possibly know the importance of that. I would struggle, hot with embarrassment, and embarrassing those around me as well, and after a while, people just stopped listening. Because, of course, if you can't speak properly then it follows that what you say can't be important. Conversations would wash around me. Any contribution I might make was always four or five sentences behind everyone else. After I while, I stopped contributing. A while after that, I stopped even socialising. The horizons of my life closed in around me. My world grew smaller and smaller and, in the end, it was just Thomas and me.

And then one day, Russell Checkland erupted into my life and listened to me. Actually listened to what I had to say. As if I was a real person. And he made the world listen, too. I married him. Of course I did. He was handsome, talented, charming and a complete idiot. Who wouldn't marry him?

Well, my cousin Francesca, for a start. She'd ditched Russell for someone more useful to her career and it had nearly finished him. I think he sees now that the two of them would never have worked but when I first met him he was enthusiastically drinking himself into a state nearly as dilapidated as his old farmhouse. As if that wasn't bad enough, no sooner had Russell married me than Francesca decided that she did want him after all. After a series of shattering scenes, the dust settled and they both realised that they'd made the right choice. Their relationship these days is usually Francesca wanting Russell to do something for her, and Russell making her work for it. It had been a rocky road for all of us, but Russell and I were now the proud owners of a rundown farmhouse, Frogmorton; a daughter, Joy; a donkey, Marilyn; two horses, Russell's Boxer and my Thomas, currently on loan to the Braithwaites up the lane. And the cat with no name.

Quite a large menagerie, and if Buff Orpingtons were what I thought they were – it was about to become even larger.

Russell turned to me, restlessly fiddling with his cutlery because he can't sit still. 'Chickens, Jenny. We should have some chickens.'

'Why?'

'Why not? The benefits are endless. Fresh eggs every day. And Joy can help feed them and look after them. It'll be good for her. All this will be hers one day. She should start to learn responsibility.' He gestured expansively but inaccurately at the downstairs toilet.

'She's eight … months old,' I said.

'Given her father,' said Andrew darkly, 'the sooner she starts taking a run up at responsibility, the better.'

Russell ignored him. 'Picture the scene, Jenny. Half a dozen pretty little chicks scratching around the yard making those comfortable clucky noises. You and Joy standing together scattering…' he paused, a victim of his own ignorance. '…some sort of chicken food for them, doing your bit for the rural economy. Mrs Crisp will collect the eggs every morning and we'll all sit down to a golden-yolked miracle for our breakfast.' He glowered at Andrew. 'Well, those of us who actually live here will.'

'Where will … we keep them?'

He sat back. 'I shall build them a hen house.'

'You?' said Andrew, incredulously.

'Well, not actually me, obviously.' He held up his hands. 'These are not hen-house building hands. I'm an artist.'

We all looked at Kevin, who helped out with odd jobs around the place and who almost certainly was going to discover he had hen-house building hands.

He grinned amiably. 'Never made one of those before. What colour do you want?'

'Green,' said Mrs Crisp, banging down the roast potatoes.

'Purple,' said Sharon, following through with the vegetables.

'Blue,' said Andrew, spearing the biggest Yorkshire pud.

'Gold,' I said.

Kevin nodded, 'OK.' And before Russell could interject and issue instructions that his hen house was not to be any girlie pastel shade, but a manly, rufty-tufty, rural brown, Mrs Crisp brought the beef, which took his mind off things nicely.

All Sunday lunches at Frogmorton Farm are lovely and this one was no exception. We sat in the big kitchen, discussing football, the new people who had moved into the cottage further up the lane, the impending opening of Sharon's cupcake shop, and the pedestrianisation of the new shopping precinct: something to which Russell and I were greatly looking forward, because we were waiting for an offer on Christopher's old bookshop. He'd signed it over to us on instructions from his father, my Uncle Richard. Uncle Richard had done it to keep us quiet. It's a long story and we don't talk about it.

The sun shone through the windows, highlighting the plates on the big dresser along the back wall and sending shafts of light across the warm terracotta tiles. We were gathered around the old kitchen table and sitting on mismatched chairs, but the cloth was spotless, the cutlery gleamed and the atmosphere was happy and friendly.

I remembered the first time I had seen this room, and reflected on the change. Yes, that day had been dark and rainy and today the sun was shining, but it was more than that. There had been an air of hopelessness about the house then. Of unhappiness. The rooms were dreary and empty. Like my life. Like Russell's too, at the time. Neither of us had a future to look forward to. Nor had Mrs Crisp, lost in a maze of guilt and cooking sherry. Our plans to do up the house had so far come to nothing and most of the rooms remained almost as I'd first seen them, but these days the house smelled of sunshine, furniture polish, home-made pot-pourri, oil paints and baby powder, not dust and despair. It was a proper family home now, filled with light and love and laughter.

It was only after Andrew had spooned up the last of his Eton Mess that contentious poultry issues raised their heads again.

'That was fantastic, Mrs Crisp,' he said, dropping his spoon into his dish. 'Why don't you give Russell the old heave-ho and come and live with me and Tanya.'

Mrs Crisp has been with Russell for ever. She brought him up after his mother died in a car crash. She's his Aunty Lizzie. She would never leave him and we all knew it.

'If only I could,' she said, 'but I couldn't possibly leave poor Mrs Checkland to struggle on alone.'

Poor Mrs Checkland grinned at her and got up to make the coffee.

'There's no poor Mrs Checkland,' said Russell indignantly. 'Jenny's lucky to have me and she knows it.'

Joking aside, I did know it. My life was lovely. Yes, we were still broke. Yes, the roof still leaked. Yes, Russell was still struggling to re-establish himself as an artist, but my life was wonderful and I never made the mistake of taking it for granted. I looked around the table, full of empty dishes and contented people and felt a small chill. Can life be too good? The gods dislike hubris and sometimes it pleases them to tear down what they have built up. I shivered, suddenly nervous. If anything were ever to happen to Russell. Or Joy. Or any of us. I don't know what brought on this sudden fit of heebie-jeebies. Was it that now, because I had a baby, I was vulnerable?

I carried the tray of coffee to the table where the conversation had reverted to chickens again.

'Well,' said Mrs Crisp, 'we've heard all about your plans for when they start laying, but what happens when they stop?'

'Stop what?' said Russell, spooning sugar.

11

'Stop laying. They don't go on for ever, you know.'

He paused in astonishment. 'Don't they?'

'No, they don't, and then...' she made a graphic gesture.

As one, his household stared at Russell.

'I'm the man of the house,' he announced. 'I'll take care of that.'

I personally was convinced that the man of the house would bottle out when receiving a non-laying chicken in one hand and a hatchet in the other. It seemed safe to assume that the man of the house would hide in the pub, along with his part-time handyman and his cousin. The women of the house, meanwhile, would be forced to hide the underachieving hen behind the barn and gallop into the village to buy the shrink-wrapped equivalent from Tom Kasap, Quality Purveyor of Meats etc., all ready for triumphant presentation to the probably quite unsteady man of the house on his return home.

I sat quietly while others voiced similar opinions and at the height of the debate, with a tap on the back door, Bill the Insurance Man walked in.

Bill the Insurance Man is Mrs Crisp's boyfriend. After our feed store caught fire, he turned up to assess the damage, and came back on so many occasions and with so many trivial questions, that Russell began to suspect the insurance company was trying to weasel out of the claim. Since it remains unpaid, this seems very likely. Russell's hostility was scarcely lessened by the discovery that it was Mrs Crisp and not the charred remains of our feed store that was the attraction for Bill and, for a long time, was barely even civil to the poor man.

With true heroism, Bill turns up every Thursday and Sunday, collects Mrs Crisp, and off they go. No one knows where they go or what they do when they get there. Russell is terrified he's going to have to do the 'What are your intentions?' speech.

'Hello Bill,' said Andrew, politely.

'Where did you come from?' demanded Russell. He turned to Mrs Crisp in sudden suspicion. 'Have you been chaining him to your headboard again? I thought I had instructed you to release all your lovers back into the wild. Must I remind you – all of you – of the presence of an innocent young child in our midst and the need to behave with decency and decorum?'

Andrew made a rude noise. 'There's only one person around here not behaving with decency and decorum.'

Russell ignored him.

Mrs Crisp disappeared to her own room to get ready. Bill seated himself in her chair and, apparently oblivious to Russell glaring at him over the blue and white striped milk jug, placidly said good afternoon.

'Nice to see you,' said Andrew.

'Again,' muttered Russell.

I asked Bill if he'd like a coffee.

He looked at his watch. 'I don't think we'll have time, Mrs Checkland, but thank you.'

Russell shifted in his seat. 'Busy afternoon planned?'

'Extremely.'

Silence fell.

I saw Russell take a deep breath to enquire what exactly, in relation to Mrs Crisp, a busy afternoon entailed, and said quickly, 'How … are you?'

'Very well, thank you.'

We sat in silence. Bill did silence very well.

'So,' said Russell, approaching from another direction. 'Where are you off to this afternoon?' and at that moment, Mrs Crisp came back into the kitchen, looking very smart and wearing lipstick.

Bill at once got to his feet. 'Ready?'

She nodded, snapped her handbag shut, said, 'See you

13

all later,' and the two of them disappeared out of the door leaving a very dissatisfied silence behind them.

'White slaver,' said Kevin solemnly, and Sharon nodded agreement.

'I have to say, Russ,' said Andrew, severely, 'I'm really not at all sure you should let Mrs Crisp waltz off with the first insurance assessor who crosses her path. They're a feckless bunch, you know.'

'Why are you still here? You've eaten. Now go.'

Andrew poured himself another coffee.

Russell pushed his chair back. 'Ready, Jenny?'

'Yes,' I said, excited, because Sunday afternoon is Driving Lesson Afternoon.

'Where are you going?' said Andrew. 'It's hardly polite to abandon your guest.'

'You're not a guest, you're only a cousin, and it's time for Jenny's driving lesson.'

'Oh, well done, Jenny. Who are you going with?'

'Me,' said Russell with dignity. 'I'm teaching her to drive.'

'Are you insane?'

'Which one of us are you talking to?'

'Well, both of you, actually. Isn't it well known that spouses should never teach each other to drive?'

'He's very ... good,' I said, with more loyalty than accuracy. 'And he says I'm doing really well.'

Russell had never actually said anything of the sort and we all knew it, but there is a time and a place for veracity and this wasn't it.

'This I must see,' said Andrew, getting to his feet.

'I'll go and get Joy,' said Russell.

'You're not teaching her to drive as well, are you?'

'Don't be an ass, Andrew. She can't reach the pedals yet. You can keep an eye on her while Jenny burns up the big field.'

14

We left Kevin and Sharon loading the dishwasher. Russell appeared with Joy who gurgled happily at the sight of her Uncle Andrew.

Yet another example of my good fortune. Some babies can be fractious, I know. Ours was an angel. Yes, she cried a little occasionally, but not with any great enthusiasm. She did tend to wake in the night, laughing and cooing to herself. Lying on her back holding her feet seemed to be her favourite pastime. She spent hours/ talking to her feet. According to Andrew, who was two years older, Russell himself had done something similar as a baby, and this did not augur well for Joy's future.

I picked up the keys and we all trooped out into the yard, currently occupied by a small donkey, loitering with intent to discover something she could eat.

We have a donkey. I don't know why I've taken so long to get around to talking about her. As anyone who has a donkey knows, they tend to be the primary topic of any conversation. And not always for the right reasons.

Our donkey is tiny. Her name is Marilyn. I chose her name because she looks like Marilyn Monroe. She's a lovely soft dun colour and peers beguilingly out from underneath her bushy forelock, batting huge eyelashes. People instantly fall in love with her friendly nature, not having the slightest idea she's only checking them over for something edible. She had a tough start – Russell discovered her, neglected and starving in a field, and stole her. Her deeply unpleasant owner turned up shortly afterwards and was seen off by Sharon wielding a Le Creuset frying pan. Just another day at Frogmorton Farm.

Seeing us crossing the yard, Marilyn came skittering over, confident that someone, somewhere would have something for her to eat.

Andrew shunted Joy to one hip and rummaged through his pockets. He's a vet. He always has something edible in his pockets. He claims his life was once saved by scattering Mars Bars in the path of a charging bull.

'A bit like Medea, scattering pieces of her brother in front of the pursuing ships,' said Russell.

'Exactly,' said Andrew. 'I was only sorry I didn't have a convenient cousin to hand.'

Most of our land is let to our neighbour, Martin Braithwaite, who uses it for his sheep. It's about the only regular money we have, supplemented occasionally by the sale of one of Russell's paintings and the income from what Tanya managed to salvage from the remains of my own money, but we've kept the two fields next to Frogmorton for our own use. The smaller was usually occupied by Russell's horse, the perpetually challenged Boxer, currently gazing in alarm at a butterfly; the other had a number of oil drums scattered around at strategic points. They're painted with letters of the alphabet. Currently, I could see a, b, c, f and then another f, because Russell hadn't been concentrating. Or had been drunk. Then there had obviously been some sort of oil drum-related catastrophe because from f we jumped straight to p.

The oil drums were laid out just as they were when I learned to ride, although I have to say I found driving slightly trickier. Russell's Land Rover was in no way as good-natured as a horse.

Russell flourished his clipboard.

'Good afternoon, Mrs Checkland. Please drive to b and then turn left.'

I ignored him, taking the time to adjust the seat and the driving mirror and fasten my seat belt. He twitched impatiently. 'In your own time, Mrs Checkland.'

I made him wait, making sure I was comfortable before starting the engine, and off we went. Conscious of the audience at the gate, I cut the turn a little close and we shaved an oil drum

'Sorry,' I said, flustered.

He leaned back and stretched his long legs. 'Not a problem – we have another five.'

I clipped another one. It went boing and fell over.

'Four.'

'Sorry. Sorry,' I said, crashing the gears.

'Stop panicking. Just relax and you'll find it all comes quite naturally.'

'All right.'

We bumped around the field while I took another few breaths, sorted myself out, and sought for relaxing conversation. 'When are … the chickens turning up?'

'Tomorrow.'

Boing.

'Three.'

'But what about the hen house? Where will we put them?'

This is typical of Russell. He'd agreed to the chickens – probably about three months ago, forgotten all about them, and then suddenly realised they were coming tomorrow and he hadn't told me.

'We'll stick them in the stable for the time being. They can roost in the rafters.'

'You're locking … them in with an omnivorous donkey and a … paranoid horse?'

'They'll be fine, Jenny. Stop worrying. Chickens are very robust.'

'What happens if they … drop an egg on Boxer.'

'They're too young to lay. He'll be perfectly safe.'

Boxer had been a racehorse in his youth and Russell had lost a great deal of money on him, which, he said, had created a bond. Sadly, although he runs like the wind, he's neurotic even by racehorse standards and is terrified of almost everything. Wind, rain, hostile telegraph poles, cats, threatening trees and, as I'd recently noticed, butterflies. His previous owners gave up on him and Russell, aware of the fate of some ex-racehorses, took him in. Having Marilyn has calmed him a little and the two of them are devoted to each other. I couldn't help but feel he wouldn't react well to having potentially life-threatening chickens living over his head and said so.

'He'll be fine. He's watching you now over the hedge. Look how calm he is these days.'

I craned my neck.

Boing.

'Jenny, you have to look where you're going.'

'You told me to look at … Boxer.'

'It was a figure of speech. Third! Third! Change down. You're going too fast. Brake for God's sake!'

We skidded to a halt.

'Well, will you look at that,' said the world's worst driving instructor, getting out to inspect the damage to his beloved Land Rover.

'What?'

'There. That dent. Look at it.'

I was spoiled for choice. 'Which dent?'

'The latest dent.'

'Told you,' said Andrew from where he was sitting on the gate. Kevin and Sharon sat alongside. They were passing Joy back and forth between them like an old parcel. She thought it was a wonderful game. Marilyn was peering critically through the bars. An astonished Boxer craned his neck over the hedge. I sighed. No one should have to learn to drive under these conditions.

'That's enough for today I think,' said Russell. 'A world-class instructor always ensures his students end on a high.'

'That … was a high?'

'Minor bumps happen, Jenny. You have to get used to

them.'

We both looked at the Land Rover – living proof that to Russell at least, minor bumps happened all the time.

'Can you … teach me to parallel park?' I asked Russell as Andrew pushed the gate open for us.

'Parking is dull,' he said, ushering me through the gate. 'I could teach you to do handbrake turns instead. Much more fun.'

'He can't park,' said Andrew, latching the gate. 'That's why he never bothers. He just stops and gets out. He doesn't pull over. Sometimes he doesn't even switch off the engine.'

'What about reversing? Can you … teach me to reverse?'

'I can try, of course,' said Russell, 'we world-class driving instructors never baulk at a challenge, but it's only fair to tell you that, as a female, you will have to prepare yourself for continual disappointment in that area.'

'Why?'

He remained silent. Baffled, I looked at Andrew, who said, 'He doesn't think women can reverse.'

'Indeed,' I said icily, and Sharon went to DEFCON 3. Fortunately, there were no frying pans to hand.

'No, no,' Russell said hastily. 'It's a proven scientific fact. Isn't it Andrew?'

'On your own, mate,' said Andrew.

We folded our arms and waited for him to dig himself deeper.

'Explain,' I said.

'Well, it's your ovaries, isn't it?'

I've been married to him for three years now and I thought I'd learned to follow his thought processes, but just occasionally…

We stared at him.

'Look,' he said patiently. 'Scientists have proved that

19

when women turn backwards to look over their shoulder to reverse, it twists their ovaries and they lose their sense of direction. It's not their fault, but that's why they can't reverse.'

At this point even Marilyn was glaring at him.

Sharon punched one arm and I punched the other.

'Ow,' he said, hurt. 'I was just trying to lighten the mood. As a good instructor, I didn't want you brooding on your latest failure to master the art of driving.'

'By making ... derogatory comments about ovaries?'

He grinned, his stupid fringe flopping down over his forehead. 'Should have seen your faces. Don't know about you lot but I could really do with a cup of tea.'

CHAPTER TWO

The next day, we – Russell and I – set off for Rushford.

'A bit of shopping,' said Russell, handing me the keys, 'and then off to Sharon's new shop for artistic advice and guidance from me, and brute labour from you. Come on – you know how you dawdle.'

He disappeared at his usual speed. I kissed Joy goodbye and told her I'd see her soon. She seemed completely unconcerned at the disappearance of both parents, sitting eggily in her high chair and watching her toast ooze through her fingers.

'Very like her father,' said Mrs Crisp, handing me the shopping list which Russell had, in his haste, left on the kitchen table.

I drove very slowly and carefully down the lane, mirrored, signalled and manoeuvred to an empty landscape, much to Russell's amusement, clattered through the village, and along the Rushford road. There wasn't a lot of traffic about as we drove down the high street and I made a cautious turn into the car park.

'Excellent work,' said Russell. 'You hardly hit anything.'

'I *didn't* hit anything,' I said, pulling the ticket from the machine and watching the barrier go up.

'A bit slow though.'

'Speed limit,' I said, pulling slowly forwards.

His lips moved as he strove to accommodate this unfamiliar concept. 'There. There's a space. Pull in there.'

I indicated.

'No, no. Pull past it and reverse back in.'

21

'Why?'

'It's easier.'

'No, it's not.'

'Yes, it is. Because all you have to do then is pull out. Forwards.'

'Always assuming I was able to reverse into such a … narrow spot in the first place.'

'Try it – it's much easier and quicker I promise you. Off you go.'

'No.'

'What?'

'No.'

'I can scarcely believe this defiance. I'm almost certain you promised to love, honour and obey me at all times. What happened to wifely obedience?'

'No … idea, but I can tell you what happened to our … parking space while you were wasting time … telling me to reverse.'

We both stared at the car now smugly nosing into our space. Forwards.

'Hmmm,' said Russell, reaching for the door handle.

'There's another one,' I said, pulling forwards quickly before I was instructed to ram the intruder.

I did try. Changing gear in Russell's Land Rover is a bit like stirring porridge in a pot, but I found reverse eventually. I see-sawed backwards and forwards, in and out, confused, lost, and unsure which way the wheels were going. Eventually, sprawled diagonally across the space, I gave up.

Russell leaned out of the window. 'A couple more goes, Jenny, you're not quite straight.'

'I don't … care,' I said, switching off the engine and resolving never to reverse again. I would just keep turning left until I arrived at my destination. However long that took.

He grinned at me. 'Sorry – it's a man thing. We just have this compulsion to reverse unnecessarily – like salmon returning to their spawning grounds – we just can't help it.'

He forced his way out of the Land Rover with some difficulty – 'Good job I'm skinny!' – squeezing himself between us and the correctly parked car alongside. Together, we surveyed the results of my labours. I drooped despondently.

Russell patted my shoulder in what he thought was consolation. 'Ovaries like Hampton Court maze. Never mind. Come on, a quick bit of shopping first – then Sharon.'

Sharon's new shop was at the bottom end of the High Street, near the medieval bridge. There's a little pedestrian lane off to the right with the car park at the end, so it's a good location. Sooner or later, everyone has to walk past.

The sign over the door read Half Baked, which according to her business advisor was just asking for trouble, but I thought it was just right. Russell had painted the name in flowing letters – purple on green.

Inside, the colour scheme was still purple and green, except for the far wall where Russell had gone mad one rainy afternoon, and painted the Mad Hatter's Tea Party. We'd all had to pose. Sharon was Alice in her pretty blue dress. A muttering Andrew was the Mad Hatter, complete with the price tag on his purple hat. The March Hare looked just like Kevin, if Kevin had enormous ears and teeth and a green checked coat. The sneezing baby, muffled in a lilac blanket was Joy, and the sleeping dormouse had more than a hint of Bill the Insurance Man about him, but that was probably just a coincidence. A scruffy, one-eyed, one-eared Cheshire Cat lay under the table, belly up and grinning mischievously. The tablecloth was painted in the same green and purple stripes that Sharon had selected for the cafe and, in the centre of the picture, the Mad Hatter and the March Hare were exclaiming in delight over a plate piled high with Sharon's sumptuous wares. As a piece of art it was wonderful – as an advertisement it was superb.

We paused to look at it.

'It's lovely,' I said, as I always did.

He grinned. 'It's not bad, is it? I enjoyed doing that.' He stood for a moment, his head on one side. 'I miss doing portraits,' and then disappeared into the back area, where Sharon and Kevin were arguing over the placement of mixers, ovens, working areas and the like. There was a great deal of banging and, because Russell was there, some shouting, too.

I stayed out in the public area, swept and washed the floor, cleaned out the toilet and then, when the floor was dry, began to unpack the colourful crockery and set it out on the big dresser.

It was very peaceful out here in the shop. Just me, making sure all the cups and teapots pointed in the same direction. Certainly more peaceful than back in the kitchen where apparently some sort of war was being fought. I ignored them to concentrate on what I was doing.

Sharon emerged, brushing her hair off her face.

'You don't want to go in there, Mrs Checkland.'

'No,' I agreed. 'Where do … you want the tablecloths?'

'Can you wipe down the tables and lay a cloth on each one. The rest will be stored in the bottom drawer of the dresser so I have cutlery, crockery, and cloths all together. If you don't mind,' she said, suddenly polite.

'No, of course not. Good thinking.'

And it was. This was not the Sharon of twelve months

ago, shy, clumsy and overweight. Sharon is Mrs Crisp's niece and had worked briefly at The Copper Kettle, further up the High Street. She hadn't been very happy there, so she came to work for us at Frogmorton, where she'd met Kevin. Well, I say 'met Kevin', because that makes things sound normal but, actually, she'd come in through the gate, smiling her beautiful smile, and Kevin, trundling his wheelbarrow across the yard, had been unable to take his eyes off her. He'd walked straight into the water trough, wheelbarrow and all. She'd blushed and smiled even more. He'd blushed and been unable to speak a word. Obviously at some point he'd regained the power of speech and they were hardly apart these days.

Anyway, this new Sharon had cut her hair, gone to college, acquired her qualifications, badgered the bank, and was about to open Rushford's first cupcake shop and cafe. We were so proud of her.

There was a prolonged clatter, followed by a sudden, worrying silence from the back. We looked at each other.

'You go,' I said. 'I'll put the kettle on. Tea in five … minutes.'

She disappeared to investigate.

I filled the kettle and pulled out a tray. I thought we could sit at the window table, where people could see us as they passed, because it would be good publicity for her forthcoming opening. Carrying the tray to the table, I began to lay things out. I smoothed the cloth and made sure it hung straight, polished up the gleaming teaspoons, and began to set out the cups and saucers. I was concentrating hard and making sure everything looked pretty because this was, literally, her shop window.

I don't know what made me look up, but something did.

I looked up and there was a man on the other side of the window. Less than twelve inches away. Looking directly at me. For a moment, I couldn't believe my eyes. If I hadn't known he was abroad, I would have sworn it was my cousin Christopher. The sun was shining on the glass and I couldn't quite make out his features. It couldn't possibly be him. I hadn't seen him since the night Russell threw him out. Out of our house and out of our lives for ever. Or so I'd thought. I took a step to one side, trying to see through the 'dekaB flaH' lettering on the window. Was Christopher back? Was he right here, right now, and staring straight at me? I squinted some more, trying to see his face. The man inched forwards, still staring straight at me and I stepped back in a hurry. It was him. I was sure of it.

If his face had been contorted with rage or he had been screaming threats then I think I would have been less frightened, but his blank, empty-eyed look took away all thought and movement. I stared back, paralysed.

Long, long seconds passed and still he stood motionless, his face pressed up against the window. He wasn't a tall man and I was standing on a raised area, which meant we were eye to eye. I could see the individual hairs in his eyebrows. In my imagination, I saw him draw back his fist, punch through the window, and reach for me…

The cup fell through my fingers and shattered on the tiles. I heard the pieces skitter across the floor as all the old nightmares came flooding back. His bullying. His casual cruelty. His single-minded dedication to getting his own way at all times and what he could do to anyone getting in his way. My heart-stopping terror when I thought Russell was burning to death. The things he would do to ensure that whatever happened, he, Christopher, would always be all right.

I've always thought Christopher was the wrong way around. Most people protect their soft interior with a hard

26

shell on the outside. In his case, his core was solid rock, but people usually only saw his soft, spongy exterior and judged him accordingly. How could I have been so stupid as to think he would give in and quietly leave the country? Of course he wouldn't. Of course he would come back. What he thought he could do was a mystery to me, but that was Christopher all over. Long on self-interest but very short indeed on intelligence, which made him dangerous. People would be hurt. People I loved.

I heard Russell shout, 'You all right out there, Jenny?'

I'm sure I only looked away for a heartbeat, that I only glanced over my shoulder towards the sound of his voice, but when I looked back again, the window was empty. Just normal people hurrying past with their shopping, chatting, calling their children, scrabbling for their car keys. Christopher was gone. If he'd ever been there in the first place. How could anyone vanish so quickly and so completely? I leaned forward and craned my head to right and left, trying to catch a glimpse of him hurrying away, but there were too many people around to make him out clearly.

I let the table take my weight. My heart was pounding and I felt sick. I stared at the cloth, concentrating on the green and purple pattern. Following the stripes. Struggling for calm. This could not be happening. Not again. Only yesterday I'd looked around the lunch table and felt that first faint shiver of premonition? Like wind ruffling the surface of a lake. Was I imagining things? After all, I'd spent years talking to an invisible horse. Old fears I thought long buried began to claw their painful way to the surface.

'First breakage,' said Russell, emerging from the kitchen. 'And not even open yet.'

I tried to speak, to say I was sorry, but the words wouldn't come. To hide my face, I knelt down and started

27

to pick up the pieces.

'I'll get the dustpan,' said Sharon and, fortunately, everyone was too busy milling around pouring tea and sweeping up the broken cup to notice that I couldn't speak. Even if I could, what would I say?

Yes, I know. Normal people would say, 'Hey, you'll never guess who I just thought I saw,' but I'm not normal. I've spent too many years being poor little Jenny Dove who had something the matter with her and counted herself lucky not to be packed off into some sort of home. As Jenny Checkland, I had a stake in the real world now, and I wasn't going to risk losing it, so I stayed silent, because – take it from an expert – it's much better to be thought clumsy than mad.

I chose my seat carefully making sure I had my back to the window, while everyone else chattered away about how much work there was still to do.

Eventually, Russell looked at his watch. 'Sorry to drink and run, but Jenny and I have chicken responsibilities.'

'It's not today, is it?' said Kevin, in alarm. 'I haven't built the hen house yet.'

'No problem, we're sticking them in the stables until they have a proper home. They'll be fine,' said Russell, the eternal optimist.

'Rats,' said Sharon.

Even Russell stopped in his tracks. 'I beg your pardon?'

'You'll need to watch out for rats. Chickens attract rats.'

'Do they?'

'Well, not the chickens as such, the chicken feed and water. You mustn't leave it out at night.'

I could see Russell thinking furiously.

'Kevin, how long to build a hen house?'

He shrugged. 'With help, about two days I should think. But I have to finish here first.'

'Don't knock yourself out. I've just had rather a good idea.'

Someone groaned.

'Yes,' he said, leaping to his feet. 'Come on Jenny, they've probably already arrived and we don't want them imprinting on the wrong person. Say goodbye politely and try not to break anything on the way out.'

They both do this – Andrew and Russell. It must be a Checkland family thing. They've finished their business, so they assume everyone else has too. Tanya, the love of Andrew's life, deals with it by ignoring them both, calmly finishing whatever she's doing and getting up in her own time. Today, however, I was too flustered. I just wanted to be home, so I gulped down my tea and rose to my feet. There are many advantages to being married to Russell Checkland, not least that he can talk for England, so no one noticed that in the flurry of goodbyes, I wasn't able to get a word out.

Russell swept me out of the shop and we set off towards the car park while I tried to think of a way of telling him I really didn't feel up to driving back to Frogmorton, without mentioning why.

I needn't have worried.

'I'll drive,' he said, whisking the keys from my hand.

We pulled out into the high street to the usual accompaniment of hooting horns and squealing brakes. Russell is not a good example as a driver – he's a horrible warning.

He spent the journey home chattering on about chickens, Boxer, the finishing touches to Half Baked, his latest work, and whether Joy was teething again. I kidded myself he hadn't noticed anything, sat back and let the comforting words wash over me.

We pulled into the yard with his usual toot on the horn. I jumped out and Russell went to park behind the stables.

Mrs Crisp appeared at the back door, waved, and disappeared again.

I stood in the yard and looked around me.

Frogmorton is not a beautiful farmhouse. There's no thatched roof or half timbering. It's a long, low, rambling building in a kind of stone and red brick patchwork. Random windows are scattered haphazardly around the facade and strangely shaped chimneys sprout from the roof. The kitchen leads into the mudroom which leads into the yard, which itself is surrounded by various higgledy-piggledy outbuildings. The barn and stables are opposite the gate and the big water trough sits against the wall. One big five-barred gate leads out into the lane, another opens into Boxer's field, and the third into our big field, currently the scene of regular Sunday afternoon dramas.

It's all a bit ramshackle. There never seems to be enough money to make it look pretty – a pot of geraniums by the back door is usually the best we can do. It's not even completely waterproof – But Russell loves it and I do too. It's our home.

I stared around. Everything seemed normal. The door to the stables was open, the boxes were swept clean. Boxer and Marilyn were grazing quietly together in their field. All the windows were letting in the summer breeze. The open back door gave a glimpse into the cluttered mudroom. Apart from the odd flapping curtain, everything was silent and still. There couldn't be a more peaceful scene.

It didn't last.

Russell's chickens had arrived in our absence. Two sturdy boxes had been delivered and were being regarded with deep suspicion by Mrs Crisp.

I'd looked up Buff Orpingtons on the internet and was therefore expecting big, golden-brown birds. These were much smaller; some had fluff still showing between their feathers, and they all had that mad dinosaur look.

'Pullets,' announced Russell incomprehensibly.

I must have blinked at him.

'Under a year old.'

'Ah.'

He reached down and gently scooped one up.

It screamed. I thought chickens clucked. Surely this wasn't right. True, no one who owns a donkey is a stranger to decibels, but this was ear-splitting. Eyes squeezed tight shut, it inflated its feathery body and screeched. How could so much noise come from such a tiny creature? And this is Marilyn's owner asking that question!

Presumably showing solidarity, the others screamed back.

Russell hastily replaced it and eventually the noise subsided.

The cat stalked over to have a look, tail in bottle-brush mode and ready for anything.

'Oh yes, right,' said Russell, trying to edge him away. 'Now you wake up.'

The second, as yet unopened, box began to shuffle its way across the kitchen floor under its own steam.

Mrs Crisp seized her security tea towel and backed up against the range.

The cat moved into attack mode.

'The … magic … moving … box,' I said.

'The cockerel,' said Russell, proudly.

'Russell, you don't need a cockerel,' said Mrs Crisp.

'You do if you want baby chickens,' said Russell, putting his arm around her. 'Let me explain to you how these things work. When a daddy chicken loves a mummy

31

chicken…'

She swiped him around the ear with the tea towel.

'Ow. Does Bill the Insurance Man know you're prone to these sudden fits of aggression?'

'You're not too big to go over my knee,' she said, grimly.

'Not in front of the girls. We don't want traumatised poultry running around the place, so please make an effort to curb your violent impulses.'

'The … cockerel,' I reminded him, before he got the tea towel around the other ear.

'Not in here,' warned Mrs Crisp.

'No indeed,' said Russell. 'Sadly, my plan to house them in the stable is not the brilliant idea I thought it was. Fortunately, I have conceived another. Wife, bring the other box.'

I scooped up the surprisingly heavy box, nearly dropping it again as whatever was inside shifted its considerable weight. Russell had the other box and was already heading towards the stairs.

'You're not keeping them in one of the spare bedrooms,' shouted Mrs Crisp.

'Of course not,' he said indignantly. 'That would be unhygienic.'

With considerable misgivings, I followed Russell up the stairs to the family bathroom. He shouldered the door open. 'In here, Jenny,' and proceeded to decant the hens into the bath where they puttered up and down, their claws making funny scratchy noises on the enamel.

'What do you think? Brilliant, eh? They can't get out. Rats can't get in. A couple of days while we get their living quarters sorted out. And we can hose it down with the shower each morning – practical *and* hygienic. Do you know, sometimes, I amaze even myself?'

'You're keeping the chickens in our bath?'

'Well, we could hardly keep them in someone else's, could we? And let's face it, we've already had a donkey in here, so chickens aren't going to make a great deal of difference. Let's have a look at Big Boy.'

I handed over the box and retired to a safe distance. He unfastened the box and an indignant comb-covered head stuck itself out and glared around, rather like an angry submarine periscope. Scrambling free of the box, it flapped its wings, left the ground, perched on the taps and took stock of its surroundings.

His harem gazed adoringly at him.

'Women used to look at me like that,' said Russell, nostalgically.

The cockerel leaned forwards slightly and released something greasy and unpleasant.

'Russell!'

'It's a bathroom, Jenny. Where could be more appropriate? And all we have to do every morning is lift them out, hose everything down and put them back again. We'll put their feeder up at the blunt end, their water at the other, and with a bit of straw on the bottom to give them grip they'll be absolutely fine.'

'But...' I said, convinced this wasn't right, but unable to pinpoint the huge flaws I knew must be there somewhere.

He patted my shoulder. 'It's the family bathroom – no one uses it. There's another bathroom off Joy's room and a shower in our bedroom. Tell me honestly, have you ever used this bathroom?'

'I ... threw up ... in ... it once.'

He regarded me severely. 'Are you considering a repeat performance over the next couple of days?'

I shook my head.

'Then we're good to go. I'll go and get their bits and pieces. You stay here in case they panic at all.'

What action I could possibly take should six chickens and a cockerel take it into their heads to panic he didn't say. I lowered the toilet lid and made myself comfortable. They looked at me. I looked at them.

'So he's a ... madman,' I said. 'Live with it. The rest of ... us have to.'

He was back minutes later. I heard his footsteps galloping up the stairs and along the landing. He opened the door gently. 'Everything OK?'

I don't know what catastrophe he thought could have occurred in the five minutes he'd been gone. 'Of course.'

'Great.' He poured chicken food into the feeder and gently lowered it into the bath where it disappeared under a mass of milling chickens. Feed flew in all directions, pinging off the sides of the bath. I was glad to be out of range.

He filled the water dispenser, which immediately disappeared under a mass of milling chickens. Water flew everywhere.

'Russell, there's ... water everywhere.'

'Not a problem,' said Frogmorton's resident genius. 'Just leave the plug out and it'll drain away. It's a *bath*, Jenny.'

I did briefly contemplate braining him with the toilet brush, but there was no need. Once Mrs Crisp discovered he was keeping chickens in the bath, he had only moments left to live anyway. I could wait.

'Do they have names?' I said, watching six excited chickens rushing from one end of the bath to the other under the mad, despotic eye of their overlord. The cockerel kept an eye on them, too.

'They certainly do,' he said, pulling a crumpled sheet of paper from his jeans. 'Let's see. Yes, the smallest one – that one there. That's Agatha. Boadicea is slightly darker than the others – see. Cleopatra is more yellowy. Desdemona keeps nodding her head all the time. Elfriede has that funny white patch and Francesca has hairy legs.'

I couldn't believe my ears. 'You … named a … chicken after Francesca? The one with … hairy legs? How … much trouble are you in when she … finds out?'

'She'll see the joke.'

I said nothing.

'You don't think she'll see the joke?'

Franny's a lot better these days. She is at least aware of the existence of jokes. She's just not aware of them in relation to herself. The news that she'd given her name to a hairy-legged chicken would not go down well.

I let the silence linger.

'You don't think she'll see the joke.'

'I *know* she won't see the … joke.'

'Oh. OK then. Well, I don't want to upset her. How about Fifi la Foo?'

I closed my eyes.

'And for the cockerel – what do you think of Cogburn?'

I opened my eyes. 'Cogburn?'

'As in Rooster Cogburn. Clever, eh?'

'I've … married … an idiot.'

'You have indeed, but you knew that anyway, and at least now the idiot can see that his wife no longer looks as if she's seen a ghost.'

This is typical Russell. People think he's just a noisy idiot who can paint, and he is. He breezes along, apparently blind to everything around him and only later do you realise that, sometimes inconveniently, he doesn't miss a thing.

'Sorry about … that,' I mumbled. 'I was … so upset at dropping that … cup. Sometimes I'm so … clumsy.'

He looked at me thoughtfully for a while. 'OK,' he

35

said. 'Shall we go and scrounge a cup of tea and I'll tell Mrs Crisp about the chickens.'

'Rather ... you than me.'

'I'm the man of the house, Jenny. Responsibility for the welfare and well-being of everyone under my roof devolves upon me. An onerous burden, but I shoulder it with courage and resolution.'

We entered the kitchen where Mrs Crisp was just pouring the tea. She looked up suspiciously. 'What's going on up there?'

'Jenny's keeping chickens in the bath,' said Russell, helping himself to the biggest piece of cake.

CHAPTER THREE

Kevin did his best, but it was over a week before the hen house was completed, even though he was being urged on with word and gesture by Mrs Crisp, who had received the news that seven chickens now lived in the family bathroom in complete silence, much to Russell's relief. I think he genuinely believed he'd got away with it until we sat down to dinner that night. A steaming plate of her special lamb and apricot stew was gently placed in front of me, with instructions to eat it all up. Russell was presented with a piece of toast.

'Hey!' he said, indignantly, looking up.

She remained unmoved. 'I said nothing when your snake escaped...'

'I was six. Let it go.'

'I hardly said anything when your gerbils ate each other.'

'That wasn't my fault.'

'I barely even remonstrated when I discovered you had a rat in your top drawer.'

'I never understood why you were in my top drawer anyway. Who does that sort of thing?'

'I was putting your socks away.'

Their voices were beginning to rise.

'If you had just left them on my bed I would have put them away for myself. A useful life lesson for me, and you'd never have come face to face with Boris. You frightened the wits out of him. His tail nearly fell off with shock. That happens you know.'

'When have you ever put your socks away?'

I nodded.

'Or your shoes?'

I nodded again and reached for a bread roll. Russell never puts anything away. Apparently, it's the artistic temperament. After his first sale – says Russell – he'd had to sign up to The Code of Professional Artists. None of us have ever actually seen this famous Code, but it definitely exists – says Russell – and he quotes great lumps of it when faced with doing anything he doesn't particularly want to do. Like putting his socks away. Picking up his shoes would, apparently, put paid to his artistic creativity for all time and we wouldn't want that, would we? No real artist would ever pick up his own shoes – says Russell.

Now he became cunning. 'If I'm reduced to just toast then I'll never have the strength to finish their house and they'll have to live in the bathroom for ever, slowly pining away for the feel of sunshine on their backs and the gentle breeze on their little faces. Spending their declining years mournful, imprisoned and eggless. Really, you know, keeping them in the bath like that is little better than factory farming. And you – you, Mrs Crisp – possessed the means to save them, to give their lives purpose and meaning, and you withheld it. Fortunately, it's not too late. A really big bowl of stew, a bread roll or two – if Jenny leaves any – and I'm set up for tomorrow. House completed. Chickens gone. Happy ending. And only you, Mrs Crisp, can make this happen.'

'Chickens! In the bathroom! It's not safe!'

'Oh, come on. They're not going to get out and eat you in your sleep, you know. That hardly ever happens these days.'

I thought he was lucky he wasn't pulling bits of lamb and apricot out of his hair, although she did smack down the bowl with some force.

He smirked, looked up to find us both watching him, and rearranged his features. 'Mm-mm. Delicious.'

From the very first, it became apparent that performing chicken ablutions every morning wasn't anything like as easy as Russell had thought it would be. Despite all his efforts, the routine was as unchanging as it was exciting, noisy and unsuccessful.

Outraged screaming would announce their removal from the bath.

A succession of anonymous sounds and bad language would indicate he was sweeping the bath, considerably impeded by young female chickens, who were vociferously indignant at being removed from their home and straining every sinew to get back in there. We would hear the shower being turned on and then, for Russell, everything would really go downhill.

I was emptying the washing machine one day. Joy was in her high chair, playing with her bricks, and Mrs Crisp was getting lunch ready. By mutual consent, we were ignoring the outraged shrieks, the cries of pain and the crash as the bucket went over. Whatever was going on up there, the man of the house could manage for himself.

Ten minutes later, he strolled into the kitchen, pulling feathers out of his hair and wearing some very interesting stains on his T-shirt.

'Well,' he said cheerfully, investigating the contents of the pantry and pulling out an enormous slice of date and walnut cake. 'Now we know the origin of the phrase, "Madder than a wet hen".'

'How much longer?' said Mrs Crisp in the tones of one pushed beyond endurance.

'Tomorrow,' he said soothingly. 'They'll be gone tomorrow and you'll never have another chicken in the house again.'

'I should never have had a chicken in the house in the first place,' she said, peeling potatoes with terrifying vigour and hurling them into the saucepan. 'I wouldn't be at all surprised if we haven't all gone down with bird flu by next Tuesday.'

He patted her shoulder with one hand and lifted another piece of cake from behind her back with the other. 'You never used to be this timid. I blame the influence of the insurance industry. When I think back to the laughing carefree Lizzie Crisp, running barefoot through the meadows … What has he done to you?'

She heaved a martyred sigh. 'What do you want Russell? Why are you in my kitchen?'

'Oh. Yes. Good point. I'd forgotten. We've had a bit of a thing upstairs. Not a big thing – more a kind of accidentette. A bijou catastrophe.' He stuck his head in the pantry again. 'Where do you keep the mop?'

'Where it's always been.' She stamped off.

I watched it dawn on him that he had no idea where that was and, before he could involve me, I seized the linen basket and went to hang out the washing. As I left, I could hear him banging around the kitchen. There was a faint cry as something fell on his head.

Ten minutes later, he reappeared in clean clothes, helped himself to another slice of cake, kissed me crumbily, and said he was going out.

'Did you … find the mop?'

'What? What mop? Oh. No. Doesn't matter. I used the bath towels. Did the job just as well. See you later, Jenny.'

The construction of the hen house was achieved in typical Frogmorton fashion. Boxer peered over the gate, snorting at the noise, while Marilyn, carefully observing through the bars, shouted advice and comments. The cat, awoken from what Russell always swore was a coma, strolled outside to see what was going on and somehow managed to get himself built inside. He was subsequently discovered in one of the nesting boxes.

Mrs Crisp, bringing tea and biscuits said, 'I thought it was going over in the corner by the stables.'

'It is,' said Kevin, helping himself to a big handful of biscuits. His excuse is always that he's a growing lad, which he certainly is: if he doesn't stop soon, he's going to be entitled to his own postcode. Looking at the rather good-looking and confident young man he is today, it's hard to believe this was the skinny, sickly boy who so inexpertly tried to mug Russell and me in the alley behind the post office. What a long time ago that seemed now.

'But you've built it here,' she said, 'in the middle of the yard.'

'Yes?'

'How will you move it?'

It takes more than an awkward question to faze Russell.

'Successfully,' he said, sipping his tea and daring her to argue.

She nodded, and went to sit on the old seat by the back door. I joined her a moment later with Joy. We waited patiently for events to unfold.

Of course they couldn't move it. It was far too big and heavy. They strained unsuccessfully for about ten minutes and, in the end, they had to take the roof off again.

Mrs Crisp and I said nothing.

They moved it to its new location, put the roof back on, and stood back admiringly.

'Aren't you … going to paint it?'

'I thought you might like to do that.'

'OK,' I said. 'Yes, I would.'

'There's some dark brown paint in the outhouse. Top

41

shelf. I bought three tins. Can you do it tomorrow while I'm out?'

I nodded obediently.

Following instructions, I painted it brown and it looked dreadful. Brown is not a good colour for anything, especially a hen house. According to Russell's many books on the subject, hen houses should be light and airy. This one looked like a Dickensian workhouse. I looked at it for a while and then wandered back into the shed and rummaged around among the old paint tins on the shelf. I found some nice pastel shades, blue, green, yellow, and a bright orange. It was so orange it was almost neon. I had no idea why on earth Russell would have a can of neon orange paint. Kevin, stacking the remainder of the wood neatly, turned to look at me.

'There's not enough there to repaint the whole thing,' he said.

'No,' I said thoughtfully, my mind wandering towards Sharon's shop, 'but I could do stripes.'

'Stripes are difficult,' he said. 'You should have heard Russell's language when he did Sharon's.'

Everyone had heard Russell's language when he did Sharon's stripes.

He frowned. 'What about spots?'

'Spots?'

'Yeah. Dead funky. In different sizes and different colours.'

We grinned at each other and trailed into the kitchen. Mrs Crisp was just retiring to her own room with a cup of tea. And it was tea, these days. The cooking sherry was safe. The reforming influence of the insurance industry.

'We need cornflake packets,' said Kevin, rummaging through the cupboards.

'You've just had lunch,' she said, indignantly.

42

'For stencils. Any packets will do. We can have different-sized spots. Mrs Crisp...?'

'I have to put up with this from Russell. I'm not paid enough to put up with it from you two as well.' She left the room, muttering.

We sat at the kitchen table and drew around dinner plates, saucers and egg cups making stencils of differing sizes.

'This is going to be so cool,' said Kevin. 'The girls will love it.'

I could hear Joy stirring upstairs. 'You get everything ready. I'll get Joy.'

Leaving the kitchen, I ran through the lounge. The French doors were open into the garden and I could hear the sound of birds and insects. The curtains billowed gently into the room, bringing the smell of cut grass and roses. I loved this room. This was where Russell and I sat in the evenings, watching TV or just reading. The fireplace was empty because it was summer, but in winter, with the logs blazing away and the lights down low, you couldn't see the shabby furniture, or the worn carpet, or even the stains on the rugs. Most of these had their origins in the time Andrew had lived here with Russell. Heaven knows what the two of them had been up to.

The big table under the window was cluttered with unpaid bills (there always seemed to be rather a lot of those, the sooner we got the bookshop contract signed the better), paint catalogues, Russell's sketches and notes, my laptop, a few paperbacks, a tape measure, a spare mouse, an assortment of pens and pencils, and Mr Edward, Joy's teddy. The bookcases around the walls were stuffed with paperbacks and one of Russell's wonderfully colourful abstracts hung over the fireplace. I never entered this room without counting a blessing or two.

The staircase was at the far end, disappearing up into

the gloom. As a safety measure, we'd had it carpeted. I'd once fallen from top to bottom and that wasn't something I ever wanted to do again. During my pregnancy, Russell, displaying the calm, sensible good judgement for which he was famous, had insisted on escorting me personally up and down the wretched thing, claiming I had form. He became particularly paranoid towards the end, wanting to install one of those stairlift things. You know the one I mean – they used to be advertised by that famous actress. Sadly, Ms Hird is no longer with us, but Russell claims to have had an enormous crush on her as a young boy and wanted to install one in her memory. I steadfastly refused to have any such thing. One night he became so insistent that I was forced to telephone Andrew for help. He turned up an hour later, scooped up Russell and took him to the pub.

Alas, for all his good intentions, Andrew's capacity is nowhere near as great as Russell's, and he had to be brought back to Frogmorton to stay the night. He was still considerably unwell the next morning, so Russell offered to drive him home, unfortunately clipping the water trough on the way out, although, since it wasn't his own vehicle, he said it didn't count. Andrew, surveying the damage to his car and suffering the mother of all headaches, maintained that it very much did count. Happily for me, in the subsequent torrent of cousinly abuse, the idea of the stairlift had been quietly forgotten.

There's a dogleg at the top of the stairs. Turn left for our bedroom at the end of the corridor and Joy's room is next door. The right-hand landing leads to the family bathroom, the spare bedrooms, and right at the very end, Russell's studio, where he hides the pizza boxes he doesn't want Mrs Crisp to see. Mrs Crisp, of course, is perfectly aware of their presence and sometimes, in a spirit of revenge for the 'lovers chained to her headboard' comments, offers to go in and dust, and then, with the air of a connoisseur, sits back and watches him panic.

I raced up the stairs, shouting, 'Not long … now, ladies,' to the chickens in the bathroom and into Joy's room. This had been my room once upon a time. The bed still stood between the two windows, but pride of place now went to her cot, up against the wall, with the little chest of drawers nearby for her bits and pieces, and her Shaun the Sheep mobile overhead. She was awake and shouting at her feet. Sometimes she reminded me of Russell so much. I lifted her from her cot, held her up high, sniffed her bottom, recoiled, whipped on a clean nappy, and took her back downstairs where she could watch the proceedings.

We sat her in her playpen in a shady corner of the yard with a selection of her favourite bricks, toys and teddies and she immediately rolled onto her back and began to play with her feet again.

'She does that a lot,' said Kevin, assembling brushes and pouring paint.

'It's a sign of great intelligence,' I said loyally, and then ruined my argument by saying that apparently Russell had done it too.

There was a thoughtful silence and then we changed the subject.

Kevin held up the stencils. 'We just paint the holes,' he said. 'It's easy. And I've mixed some blue and green together so we have turquoise as well. I think one of us should hold the stencil steady while the other one paints.'

'Agreed.'

As anyone who has ever done this sort of thing will know, restraint flies straight out of the window. People say less is more. They don't know what they're talking about. We soon had different-sized blue, green, lemon, and turquoise spots all over the hen house. We had quite a

45

few over ourselves, as well.

'Ready?' said Kevin, picking up the fluorescent orange. I nodded.

'Not too much,' he warned. 'A little of this goes a long way.'

And it did. But it looked so good we thought we'd add a bit more. And then there was a gap over there. And maybe we had room for another few spots just there...

We ran out of paint.

'Wow,' said Kevin, stepping back to admire the effect.

I blinked. 'I think it ... might be a hazard to low ... flying aircraft.'

'Never mind that. I think it might be a hazard to shipping. What's Russell going to say? He wanted brown.'

I had no idea what Russell might say. He might regard it as a work of art. And then again, he might not.

'Not important,' I said firmly. 'If he feels that strongly then he should have painted it himself. And anyway, you know what he's like. He probably won't even notice.'

We surveyed the multi-coloured structure reflecting the sun's rays.

'True. Although it will be a bit of a giveaway if you don't have a shower before he gets back.'

I wandered over to talk to Joy who was clashing two bricks together and laughing, while Kevin put away the empty cans.

His voice drifted out from the shed. 'Is it OK to let Marilyn out now?'

'Yes, fine. I'll put the kettle on.'

I brought tea for us and juice for Joy, and we sat peacefully together, admiring our handiwork. Marilyn skittered over to check us out for custard creams. I snapped a carrot in half and handed her a piece. She took it gently, as she always did, her soft lips tickling my palm.

46

Kevin gently fondled her ears, which she loved. Joy clapped her hands and squealed. Marilyn was too short to look over the side of her playpen, but lowered her head and peered in at her.

'It'll be great when Joy can walk,' said Kevin. 'The two of them will be running around the yard together.'

'Mmmm,' I said dubiously.

'They'll be fine,' he said. 'She's in no danger. And even Boxer, big though he is, wouldn't hurt a fly.'

True enough. Boxer is amiable, dim, and far from hurting a fly is regularly terrorised by them. Russell swears he once saw him strafed by a butterfly.

'And the cat will stay well clear in case she wants to dress him up in doll's clothing or whatever. Really Jenny, she'll be fine. She'll get horribly dirty, of course, but that's not a problem. And you have to remember it was running around this place that made Russell what he is today.'

I stared at him suspiciously as he sipped his tea.

A clatter rather similar to that of three hundred sewing machines in an echo chamber announced the arrival of Russell and his Land Rover. He swung into the yard, did a double take, and missed the water trough by inches.

Swinging open the door, he turned off the ignition and leaped out. The engine continued running for some time afterwards. Kevin says it's not supposed to do that.

Russell was regarding his wonderful new hen house with less than wonder.

'What the hell…?'

He had to break off to attend to Marilyn who knew on which side her bread was buttered. Or carrots in this case. He found one from somewhere. I have long since accepted that I am married to a man who, in times of crisis, can always produce a carrot. He fended her off. 'No. Just the one. You're getting fat. Go and bully Boxer.'

Next, of course, he had to greet his daughter who was laughing and lifting her arms to be picked up. 'Hello you. How's my gorgeous girl? One of my gorgeous girls,' he added belatedly, realising too late he possibly hadn't given quite the right impression there.

He sat beside me on the bench, jiggling Joy up and down. Marilyn, for whom the word 'no' did not exist, pestered him for another carrot. Joy wanted to play with the zip on his jacket and what with one thing and another, he was fully occupied for some time.

I waited quietly. Russell has the attention span of a door hinge. It was very possible that he would forget the multi-coloured extravaganza standing in the corner of his quiet farmyard.

'What the hell have you two been up to?'

Or not.

'Surely you haven't … forgotten. It's your hen house. Really, Russell, I … know you're busy, but you must … try to concentrate more.'

'But what happened to it?'

'I painted it.'

'How are they ever going to lay in that? All the articles I've read say that a peaceful environment is essential for optimum egg production. I was going to play them Mozart and you're housing them in something that looks as if it came last in a paintball competition, while simultaneously suffering some dreadful skin complaint. Why is it glowing?'

'It's the orange. Yes, it's a little … bright at the moment, but I'm sure it will … weather.'

He stared at me. 'Orange paint? Off the top shelf?'

I nodded.

'No!'

'What's the problem?'

'It's glow in the dark paint.'

'What?'

'It's paint that glows in the dark.'

'Why?'

'Well, you wouldn't see it during the day, would you?'

'No,' I said patiently, because I had no choice, 'I mean why did you ... buy ... glowing paint?'

'I was going to paint the corner of the water trough. You know, after Andrew fetched it a wallop last year.'

'No, you fetched it a wallop when you were ... driving Andrew's car.'

'Not important. The point is I thought I'd paint the corner of the trough to prevent it happening again. As the most responsible person on the premises, it's up to me to prevent these little accidents occurring.'

'That ... particular little accident occurred last year.'

'I would have got around to it quite soon. It's on my list of things to do.'

'You should ... probably take it off again. I used all the ... paint.'

Noting my heroic use of the word 'I', Kevin got up quietly and prepared to slope off.

'You stay put,' said Russell without even turning around.

'I don't see the ... problem,' I said.

'Well, it won't be a problem for us. We'll be inside with the curtains drawn in self-defence. For people using the lane at night or low-flying aircraft, it's going to be a big problem.'

Mrs Crisp appeared briefly in the doorway, summed up the situation, and disappeared, reappearing seconds later wearing sunglasses.

'That's ... really not helping,' I said and turned back to Russell. 'I think you're overstating the ... problem. The only people who could ... possibly see it are the ... Braithwaites and they're not ... going to say anything. They'll think it's a good joke.'

'What about the new people?'

'They're … new. They won't say anything,' I said, rather relishing the novelty of being the one in trouble for a change.

I honestly don't think Russell was that bothered. I think he was more annoyed he hadn't done it himself.

His phone rang. He dragged it from his pocket, glanced at the screen, looked at me, and stuffed it back again. Francesca, I guessed. I'd noticed he often wouldn't speak to her in front of me.

Joy was bouncing up and down, demanding attention. I looked at my watch. 'Time to start … dinner. Is everyone hungry?'

We trailed inside to find that the cat, despite being fast asleep all afternoon and not going outside in any way, had managed to get orange paint all over himself.

'Oh great,' muttered Russell. 'We have a cat with a glow in the dark arse.'

CHAPTER FOUR

I made sure I wasn't around when Russell finally released the ladies – as he persisted in calling them – from their imprisonment in our bathroom and into their new multi-coloured abode. I wasn't anticipating any difficulties with the chickens, you understand, but I'd been married to Russell for three years and, not only are there some situations it's best not to be involved in, I also had a very good idea who would be lumbered with restoring the bathroom to its pre-chicken standards of cleanliness.

Accordingly, I strolled up the lane to have a chat with Monica Braithwaite and check out my horse, Thomas.

It was a lovely day. The summer had been good this year and even though we didn't have long until September, the hedgerows still looked green and fresh. It was going to be a good year for blackberries. I took Joy with me and we stopped to look at flowers, point at birds and wave at passing clouds.

The afternoon was quiet and peaceful and after the last few chicken-crammed days, I was able to use the slow stroll up the lane to have a good think about Christopher. Which was worse? Actually seeing him or only imagining I'd seen him? Was I in any sort of danger or was I just mad? These were not easy questions to answer. There were several occasions when I'd drawn breath to tell Russell what I thought I might have seen, but my family, Christopher included, had very nearly ruined his life. We'd put all that behind us and I really didn't want to bring it up again. I didn't want anything to mar this perfect summer. His work was going well – he said – and it was true that no half-completed canvases had come flying out of his studio window recently, so I was inclined to believe him. I had no idea where Sharon and Kevin were heading but they seemed happy together. Mrs Crisp no longer peered blearily at the world through a bottle of sherry, and I had a happy family life. I'd stopped being slightly odd Jenny Dove living in her aunt's attic. Now, I was Jenny Checkland, with a family who loved me and listened to me. There was no way I would do anything to jeopardise that. I decided I would remain silent and keep my eyes open. Quite honestly, I had already half convinced myself I had imagined it. That a man who *happened* to bear a close resemblance to Christopher had *happened* to peer in through the window and his expression *happened* to be a trick of the light, no more. He'd probably been as taken aback as I was to find a strange woman staring back at him and had made off as quickly as he could, which was why I hadn't been able to see him leaving. I told myself this was a very reasonable explanation.

The Braithwaites lived further up the lane. There was Martin the sheep farmer, his wife Monica, and their two sons, one at school locally and the other currently at agricultural college. Their one daughter, Fiona, had been looking after my horse for me while I was pregnant. I'd wanted to continue riding throughout my pregnancy and Russell had objected strongly, even to the extent of having one of his fortunately very rare hissy fits. The whole thing had coincided with Fiona's last growth spurt, when she finally and reluctantly had to admit that she'd grown out of her own much-loved pony. He was now pensioned off and living a fat and contented life doing almost nothing, and Russell had offered to lend her Thomas.

'It's the least we can do, Jenny. They looked after our animals for weeks after our fire and they wouldn't take anything for it. I know times are tough for them at the moment, and they can't afford a horse for Fiona. It'll do Thomas good to get regular exercise and she's a cracking little rider. It's an ideal solution.'

I was unconvinced. Thomas had been Russell's birthday present to me and I adored him. Thomas, I mean. And Russell too, obviously. He – Thomas, not Russell – was calm and sensible and placid, and we don't get a lot of that at Frogmorton.

'It's only for a year.'

I think some of my anxiety must have bled into my voice. 'Suppose he forgets me.'

He was sweeping the yard at the time. He put down the broom, took my hand, pulled me into the empty mudroom and cupped my face with his hands.

'No one who has met you could ever forget you. I certainly can't.'

I felt tears well up.

'Why are you crying?' he demanded, slightly panic-stricken. 'What did I say?'

'Something nice.'

He seemed indignant. 'I say nice things all the time. I'm famed for it.'

I chuckled into his old, holey sweater, he put his arms around me, and we stood quietly for a while, just enjoying the moment. As usual, he smelled of fabric conditioner, linseed oil, and horse. A unique combination that was typically Russell.

He pulled back. 'You're very affectionate this morning. Don't think I don't appreciate it, but are you quite sure this is the time and place? Mrs Crisp is only feet away.'

We looked down. A small donkey had soundlessly entered the mudroom and, taking advantage of Russell's momentary distraction, had seized the opportunity to

53

investigate the few areas she could reach on the off chance he might have something edible tucked away.

Hearing her name, Mrs Crisp appeared at the doorway. She looked from me to Russell, back to me and frowned at my wet eyes.

'Yes?' he said, haughtily. 'Can I help you?'

'Is there a problem?'

I nodded. 'He's being wonderful.'

She sighed. 'I hate it when he does that.'

Anyway, here we were, Joy and I, wandering up the lane, singing snatches of songs and generally enjoying the day. The cat followed us part of the way and then turned off for sinister purposes of his own, which was just as well, because we were drawing near what Russell always referred to as The Chocolate Box Cottage – and not in a good way.

Once upon a time, this had been a tumbledown cottage hiding from the lane behind a jungle of overgrown garden. The roof sagged, the windows had been removed and the door hung askew. Russell said no one had lived in it for years.

And then, about eighteen months ago, we'd woken to the sound of men and machinery. Someone had bought it and, having bought it, proceeded to hurl money at it on an unprecedented scale. The original little cottage disappeared under the weight of gables, extensions, half-timbering, a new thatched roof – 'They'll regret that,' said Russell, in full Cassandra mode – and twee little diamond-paned windows. It was as if someone had said, 'I want a country cottage – the full works. Here's a lot of money – get on with it.' The garden was levelled and landscaped in what an expensive London designer obviously considered to be 'Country Garden' style, with hollyhocks, roses, lavender, the complete works, all carefully positioned to give that casual 'just grown' look. Kevin, a trainee landscape gardener himself, could barely bring himself to talk about it. Oh, and they called it Pear Tree Cottage. Not a pear tree in sight, obviously.

Once the work was completed, a couple of enormous furniture vans had roared up the lane, and become wedged under low-hanging branches. Their drivers came knocking at the door for permission to lop them off. Russell refused, quite politely for him, they forced their way through somehow, damaging the trees anyway, a quantity of expensive, carefully chosen 'country furniture' was disgorged, they drove away again, and silence fell.

'Weekenders,' was the general verdict in the pub that night. We finished our drinks and forgot about them. The hope was that they might never appear at all. And then, one day, about a month ago, I'd seen smoke curling from their twisted chimneys. I hesitated for a long time about going in and saying hello. I'm never sure about the etiquette for this sort of thing, but I think the responsibility rests with the locals to make the newcomers feel welcome. I kept putting it off and putting it off, and then I tried to get Russell to come with me. I did think his nosiness might overcome his hostility, but he hadn't forgiven whoever it was for the trees and refused.

I'd walked past several times, but even the thought of calling uninvited made my blood run cold. I imagined the inhabitants opening the door and then shifting from foot to foot with impatience as I struggled with 'Good morning'. And probably going on to die of old age while I tried to comment on the weather. Russell never has these problems – he talks to anyone and anything – but I'm not Russell. I wish I was, but I'm not.

Opinions as to who the occupants could be varied considerably. Sharon and Kevin plumped for a deposed despot, fleeing his vengeful subjects and hiding out in the depths of the English countryside. We vetoed that one because of the lack of black helicopters. Russell plumped for mafia money. Mrs Crisp was of the opinion it was the headquarters of a coven of witches dedicated to cursing the village and its inhabitants. On what grounds she remained a little vague. I had my money on a famous film star whose plastic surgery had gone wrong and, too grotesque to face the world, had retired to a life of isolation. As you can see, the winter nights are sometimes quite long in the countryside, and if there's not much on the TV and it's too wet to get to the pub, there's not a lot to do.

Having said all that, their garden really was very pretty, and Joy and I lingered, staring over the carefully built dry-stone wall (there'd been an old wire fence there before) and admiring the colours. Well, Joy, her father's daughter, admired the colours. I took the opportunity to have a good stare at the windows on the off chance I might catch some movement inside. Nothing.

After a minute or so, we continued on our way up to the Braithwaite's farm.

Monica was crossing the yard.

'Jenny! How lovely to see you. How are you?'

'Very well, thank you. Everything … OK here?'

'Everything's fine, thank you. Have you come to see Thomas? Fiona's taken him up onto the moors. They should be back in an hour or so. Come in. You can be my excuse to put the kettle on. Hello, you beautiful little girl.'

I had long since realised that no one meant me when they said that.

I plonked Joy on the sofa where she played with the tassels on the cushions for a while and then fell suddenly and deeply asleep.

'Lucky thing,' said Monica, pouring the tea.

She looked tired and I remembered what Russell had said about times being tough for them. Seeking to distract her, I asked if she had met our new neighbours yet.

She smacked down the teapot. Anyone meeting plump, cheerful Monica Braithwaite would think she was one of the nicest people in the world. And she is, but then I remembered the Nativity play last year when she and Fiona had stitched up the Virgin Mary with a pregnant sheep. She'd given birth on stage. The sheep, I mean, not the Virgin Mary. She'd screamed and fled. The Virgin Mary, I mean, not the sheep. Leaving Fiona Braithwaite as the Angel Gabriel victorious on her celestial hay bale. Life in the countryside is considerably more brutal than town dwellers often realise. Anyway, the vicar, dear Mr Wivenhoe, had had to lie down afterwards, prior to writing a careful letter to the bishop, and now it seemed our new neighbours had managed to get themselves on the wrong side of her as well.

'Obviously you haven't.'

'No,' I said, puzzled by her reaction. 'I haven't.'

'Well, I have.' She scowled into her tea.

'Yes? And?'

'Her name's Balasana.'

I blinked. 'Is there a Mr Balasana?'

She swallowed the rest of her tea. 'No one knows. Certainly no one has ever seen him. Not in these parts, anyway.' Her eyes twinkled. 'The children say she's probably murdered him. That's why she's come to live here. He's walled up in the cottage somewhere. Or buried under the new garden.'

By children she was referring to her two sons – both enormous. One was still at school, and the other who was at agricultural college had arrived home for the summer holidays suspiciously early.

'Let's face it, Jenny, where better to conceal a body than a building site?'

'So have you met this Mrs Balasana? What's she like?'

57

'I haven't seen her face to face but we've had her on the phone, bitching about everyone and everything. We've had complaints about the noise, the mess, moving the sheep up and down the lane, all sorts. Has she not been down to see you about Marilyn?'

'No,' I said, startled.

'She will. And you just wait until Cogburn learns to crow.'

'But you're a farm. Noise ... and animals happen.'

She shrugged. 'Not in Ananda Balasana's world.'

I paused with my cake half way to my mouth. 'Ananda Balasana?'

'Obviously an alias, don't you think? To escape justice. Although I have to say, if I was running from the law I'd choose a better name than Ananda Balasana. Wouldn't you?'

'Where on earth ... did she get Ananda ... from?'

'No idea. Sounds like a yoga pose, don't you think?'

'So have you actually seen her at all?'

'No, but I can imagine what she's like, can't you? You see it all the time these days. People retire and think they want to live in the country because it's pretty, and when they get here, they hate it. They think it's going to be like a giant theme park with pretty lambs and calves and orchards and thatched cottages and actually it's all muddy fields in winter, manure in the spring, flies in the summer, and rain all the time, and the entire agricultural community lurching from one crisis to the next, and moaning their socks off down the pub.'

She paused for breath and more tea.

'Do you know anything at all about her?'

'She pursued a career in advertising, met and terrified Mr Balasana into marrying her, then sold her agency and came to live here. Rich, successful, and determined to mould us all into her idea of "the countryside".'

58

I sat quietly and thought about this. Can there be anything sadder than achieving a dream and then wishing you hadn't. I gave a little shiver.

Monica hadn't finished. 'And you just wait till she turns up on *your* doorstep whinging because the sky is the wrong colour or there's too much grass. You won't feel so sorry for her then.'

'No! Seriously?'

She smiled and continued more calmly. 'Well, not quite, but you get the drift. It's a working farm, for God's sake. Does she expect me to waft around like Little Bo Peep?'

I laughed. I couldn't help it. She scowled at me for a moment and then joined in, and we laughed so hard we woke up Joy.

Mindful that Russell had probably dealt with the chickens by now and it was safe to return, I stood up to go.

'I had better warn Russell.'

'Oh, he knows all about her. They had a bit of a set to about his Land Rover.'

'When?'

'About a fortnight ago.'

'He didn't say anything to me.'

She hesitated. 'I hope I'm not speaking out of turn but he did ask me if you were worried about something. He probably didn't want to upset you. Is there anything wrong?'

'No,' I said, being careful not to be too bright and cheerful. 'Nothing at all. Apart … from the roof, of course. And I think Joy's teething. And we … still haven't signed that stupid contract. But otherwise…'

She smiled. 'These things will work themselves out, Jenny. Signing the contract will give you the money for the roof and everything will be easier after that. Try not to worry too much.'

She looked so kind that I did hesitate for one moment and wonder if I should tell her what I thought I'd seen. What would she say? Was it better or worse to imagine I'd seen Christopher or know that I actually had? Once upon a time, I'd had someone to whom I could tell everything, but my beautiful golden Thomas had left me. He still came to visit me from time to time, but not recently. I sighed. I really missed him.

Joy and I drifted back down the lane singing 'Ten Green Bottles', only to discover that not only were our chicken difficulties far from settled, but during my absence, a whole new raft of problems had emerged.

It would seem that the ladies had become accustomed to their bath, and they had taken a very dim view of being removed to the great outdoors. Russell was sitting on the bench by the back door, a can of beer in his hand, eyes closed, ignoring the appalling racket coming from the hen house as six ungrateful chickens and a rooster protested vigorously at this supposed improvement in their housing conditions. There was no sign of Mrs Crisp. She had, apparently, been collected by Bill the Insurance Man and they'd gone out.

'It's not Thursday, is it?' I said, confused.

'No, it's Tuesday. I think the noise might have been getting her down. She did shout something, but I couldn't hear over all the racket. What on earth is the matter with them,' he said gloomily, raising his voice over the din. 'They're out of the bath, aren't they?'

'Why are they so unhappy?'

'I don't know. Their food is in there with them, *and* I gave them some golf balls so I don't know what the problem is.'

I mentally replayed that last sentence.

I was determined not to ask but it didn't make any difference because he told me anyway.

'For the ladies.'

I had wild visions of him trying to teach them golf.

'They're never going to let them … into the golf club. Not until … Francesca shaves her legs at least.'

'What?' He stared at me. 'What are you talking about?'

I shook my head wearily. 'I don't know.'

He stared at me for a moment and then said, 'You look tired, Jenny. You should take things more slowly.'

'I've just spent the afternoon with … Monica, lolling around, playing with Joy and eating … cake. I don't think I *could* go any … more slowly. Golf balls?'

'What? Oh, yes. To make them lay.'

'Do you throw golf balls at them until they … produce eggs in self-defence?'

'Well, I haven't ruled that out, but hopefully it won't come to that. No, you put a few in the nesting boxes and they think they're eggs and start laying eggs of their own.'

I couldn't think of anything less likely, but held my peace, plonking Joy on his lap and sitting down beside him. She was immediately attracted to his empty beer can. He tilted it backwards and forwards for her, showing her the colours.

'Red. Go on, Joy, say, "red". The thing is, Jenny, there weren't any perches in the bathroom.' He paused and brooded on the lack of basic roosting amenities offered in the Frogmorton abluting facilities. 'They need to learn to roost. We might have to show them how.'

'How?' I said, with more visions of Russell crouched on a perch every night, folding his wings and lowering his undercarriage. He ignored me. I suspected he didn't know.

'And we have to keep their food and drink inside at all

times. Say, "green". Rats, you know. And then after a week or so, we can let them out to scratch around in the yard. Although we might have to teach them to use the ramp.'

'How?' I said again, with yet more visions of Russell walking a series of buxom hens up the ramp three or four times a day. He ignored me again.

'Say, "Carling".'

The cat strolled across the yard to investigate the noise from the hen house; and Marilyn was nearly dislocating her neck trying to see what was going on in her yard.

'I had to put her back in the field,' said Russell, following my gaze. 'She does tend to regard the yard as her own personal domain so I thought it would be easier for everyone if she wasn't traumatising the ladies by sticking her head through their door or chasing them around the yard or standing on them or trying to eat them...'

He trailed away, leaning back and closing his eyes. It's not really in his nature to be despondent. I took his hand.

'Russell, what's the problem? What's wrong?'

He sighed. 'I'm waiting to hear whether I've got some exhibition space at a place in London. There are several people being considered, apparently ... and I should have heard by now.'

'You will,' I said, 'I know you'll ... struggle with this, but try to be patient.'

'Do you think I should ring them?' he said, a note of anxiety in his voice.

It wasn't like Russell to suffer a lack of confidence. I knew, suddenly, that I'd been right to keep quiet about thinking I'd seen Christopher. The whole thing had been just a trick of the light. Russell had enough on at the moment – unruly chickens, exhibition anxieties, Francesca and whatever she kept ringing him about, to say nothing of the fabulously named Ananda Balasana and her possibly murdered husband living only just up the lane. Monica had told me she'd complained about his Land Rover and he hadn't said anything to me, so we were both sparing each other anxiety.

I leaned back as well, and the three of us sat in the sun together while Russell showed us the colours on his can of lager.

And then we entered a period of … turmoil.

Marilyn objected to sharing the yard. She has the run of it for an hour or so each day to keep her hooves in good shape. She was starving and neglected when Russell stole – sorry, rescued – her, and her hooves were dreadfully overgrown. Through weakness and bad feet, she could barely walk. They're better now, but regular walking on a hard surface is essential to keep them that way, so she spends at least an hour a day in our yard.

'They're going to have to work it out,' said Russell, raising his voice over the sounds of outraged chickens and a territorial donkey. And when Rooster Cogburn took up his favourite perch on the water trough he and Marilyn were eye to eye.

He was doing his best to crow but he hadn't quite got the hang of it yet. Consulting his chicken book, Russell had announced that, contrary to fairy tales, cockerels don't always say 'Cock a doodle doo'. Cogburn's best effort so far was a kind of AAARRRDLEAAARRRDLE URG, to which Marilyn would respond with EEEEEEAAAWOOOOAAARGHHH, pause as the sound reverberated off the far hills, and then follow through with EEEEEEAAAAWWWWEEEEAAAAWWWOOOOORRR GHHH just to show him who was boss around here.

Boxer, terrified but loyal, would snort and stamp his feet in support.

'It's like bloody *High Noon* around here,' shouted Russell, slamming doors and windows shut. Mrs Crisp, ostentatiously wearing headphones would lift one ear up and shout, 'What did you say?'

'I said it's like bloody *High Noon* out there,' he would bellow.

'I can't hear you,' she would bellow back.

And Joy would clap her hands and laugh.

Andrew and Tanya refused to come anywhere near us.

The cat, accustomed to being master of all he surveyed took huge exception to a cockerel with squatting rights on the water trough and we endured several unpleasant encounters with fur and feathers flying while territories were disputed and boundaries imposed.

I don't know why Russell thought our chickens would all stay quietly in the yard, either. There were only six of them and yet they were everywhere. Nor did they stay together, either. Agatha, Elfriede and Cleopatra would head for the garden. Considering it was walled and gated we were mystified as to how they got in there, but get in they did. Kevin swore that every time he dug a hole to plant something, he would turn back again to find it occupied by a fat chicken, squatting in the bottom, wings spread, enjoying the dust and the sun. Even turning over the soil led to him being enveloped in a golden-brown crowd of excited chickens frantically hoovering up grubs, insects and God knows what, and he was terrified of accidentally beheading one of them.

They made one – just one – attempt to perch on the washing line but Mrs Crisp, jaw jutting, seized her tea towel and stumped out into the yard and they never did that again.

As for roosting on their nice perches in their nice hen house, two of them, Boadicea and Desdemona, preferred to sleep underneath it, and every evening had to be dragged, squawking, from their refuge and forcibly plonked on a perch where they ruffled their feathers and sulked.

Francesca – that's the chicken, not my airhead cousin – failed to get the hen-house idea at all. I have no idea what was going on in her mad little brain – or the chicken's either – but every afternoon she flew/lumbered onto the stable roof, posing elegantly against the sunset in full view of every fox in the western hemisphere; and every evening Russell – and Kevin, too, if he was available – would clamber up there and attempt to chivvy her back down to terra firma. Invariably she refused to budge and one of them would have to carry her, smirking complacently, and thoroughly enjoying the attention. Russell fell off the roof twice, the second time bringing Kevin down with him, leading to Mrs Crisp to enquire:

a) Were there any eggs yet?
b) Should he have a safety net?
c) Were there any eggs yet?

Leading Russell to enquire:

a) Why wasn't she in the kitchen where she belonged and what did she think he was paying her for?
b) Where did she think he was going to get a safety net at this time of night, for God's sake?
c) What was this sudden obsession with eggs anyway?
d) Was there any chance of one of her special shepherd's pies that night?

Eventually, however, the final chicken would be propelled, squawking vigorously, into the hen house, with a protesting Rooster Cogburn bringing up the rear, and hurling challenges at the cat, who would be hanging around in the shadows, gloating. Russell would slam the door and peace – or as near as we could get at Frogmorton – would descend. Realising the show was over for another day, Marilyn would consent to re-enter her stable to check whether anything edible had materialised during her absence. The cat would finish his milk and push off for the night, to get up to whatever he got up to under cover of darkness, and Boxer, reassured that the tiny, mad, feathered horses had disappeared, would negotiate the terrors of the yard and return to the safety of his box.

As Russell said, while I anointed him with something for his bruises and handed him a glass of something alcoholic, you didn't just decide to go to bed at Frogmorton, because if you didn't start shunting animals into their bedrooms at about half past two in the afternoon you'd never be finished before midnight.

On several occasions, I was the recipient of embittered complaints about him struggling on alone, and I would have to point out that during the time it took him to shut up seven chickens and lead one small donkey and one ex-racehorse to their stables, his wife had bathed his daughter, dressed her for bed, fed her, read her a bedtime story, found Mr Edward from wherever he'd been hiding, washed her own face and hands, laid the table and served up the evening meal. He would become very deaf and change the subject.

Putting the hens to bed was a little bizarre but not too bad by Frogmorton standards. More to the point, it was nothing compared with letting them out again the next morning. Russell would open the hen house, escort his ladies down the ramp and then have to divert them from their single-minded endeavours to return to the land of their golden youth, the family bathroom.

Marilyn would stand outraged, watching carefully as seven chickens plodded determinedly across the yard towards the back door, jealous because she thought they were allowed into the house and she wasn't.

'I don't believe this,' muttered Russell. 'We have the world's first homing chickens. Quickly, Mrs Crisp. Don't let them into the kitchen.'

Mrs Crisp, who would have died, tea towel in hand, rather than let a chicken into her kitchen, would slam the back door, locking and bolting it for good measure. Russell would then be forced to re-enter the house through the kitchen window.

Andrew frequently threatened to film the whole thing and post it to YouTube.

Mrs Crisp and I endured, in the hope that things would sort themselves out eventually.

Russell was out in the yard one morning, directing operations, when his phone rang. I took it out to him. He paused with his arms full of buxom chicken. 'Can you get it?'

I looked down at the display. 'It's Francesca. Again.'

He looked down. 'No, it's not – it's Agatha.'

I told him men had been divorced for less and handed him the phone. Clamping Agatha firmly under one arm, he reluctantly took it. 'Hey, Franny … I've always called you Franny … Yes, I have … Why don't you like it? … No, never mind, I don't have time. Make it quick before this chicken shits on me … Hey, did you know that chickens can shit and wee all at the same time because they only have one…? No, it's true. It's called a cloaca and … What? … Well *I* think it's interesting … All right, all right … Did you want something because I really don't have time to just stand around chatting, you know…'

It was time to intervene. I rescued Agatha because it

doesn't take much to traumatise a chicken and left him to it.

When I came back he was just uttering 'Yes, yes, yes, *all right*' before snapping his phone shut.

'What did she want?'

'Don't know,' he said. 'I wasn't really listening.'

'Russell...'

'Well, you know what she's like. She bores on and on, and after a while your ears start to bleed, and then your brain turns to cottage cheese and trickles out of your nose. She wants something or other.'

'How do you know if you weren't listening?'

'Why else would she ring me?' he said, evasively.

Why indeed?

CHAPTER FIVE

Of course, all this sound and fury was bound to attract attention. Martin Braithwaite walked past our gate one day, ostentatiously wearing furry ear-muffs. Russell laughed at him and the two of them ended up in the pub, but not all the complaints we received would be so amicably resolved.

Shortly after his return, I was sitting at the kitchen table with Russell, watching him feed Joy with one hand and juggle his phone with the other, when someone knocked at the door. The *front* door.

Life stopped.

'There's someone at the door,' said Mrs Crisp, in wonder.

No one comes to our front door. For a start, it doesn't open properly. Everyone walks around, opens the gate into the yard, assumes the position so Marilyn can frisk them for foodstuffs, negotiates the chickens, kicks their way through muddy shoes, wellies and old coats in the mudroom, sticks their head around the door and, having made it this far, says 'Hi,' and demands a cup of tea. Or something stronger.

We all stared at each other. Even the cat woke up. I think the last people through the front door were my Aunt Julia and Uncle Richard on the night Russell threw them out of my life for ever. I think that thought must have been what brought Christopher to my mind. Surely, he wouldn't dare … Russell looked at me, handed me Joy's spoon and said, 'I'll go.'

He shot into the sitting room, and seconds later, I

could hear him shouting, 'You have to push from your side. No, harder. That's it. Give it some welly.'

I exchanged glances with Mrs Crisp. Who on earth could it be? Even on the several occasions we'd entertained the police, Sgt Bates had known to come around the back.

Eventually, with a dreadful scraping sound that set everyone's teeth on edge, the door was dragged open. Out in the yard, Rooster Cogburn immediately set up his own response and then Marilyn, not one to brook opposition of any kind, trumpeted her own window-rattling retort. Between the livestock around the back and the door at the front, there wasn't a great deal of difference.

Mrs Crisp muttered something and went out to deal with Marilyn. I wiped off as much of Joy's egg as I could and tried to look like a responsible householder.

Russell bounded into the kitchen, trailing a strange woman behind him.

'Jenny, it's our new neighbour. Come in, come in. Mind you don't stand on the cat. He'll have your leg off as soon as look at you. Let's see if we can find you a chair. Jenny, chuck those paint catalogues on the floor, will you? No, not that one – the leg's wonky. Here you go. If you sit down slowly, you'll be fine. Now then, let me introduce you. The one covered in egg is my wife, Jenny, and the one covering her in egg is our daughter, Joy. Mrs Crisp is ... not here for some reason ... for which dereliction of duty she will have her pay docked, and I'm...'

'I know who you are, Mr Checkland.'

'Jolly good,' he said brightly, 'but I'm afraid I don't.'

She blinked. 'Don't what?'

'Know who you are,' he said cheerfully, and I could see immediately that he didn't like her

'You have just introduced me as your new neighbour.'

70

'Yes, but I don't know your name. I know we spoke on the phone but you were so busy complaining about something or other, that I forgot it. Do sit down.'

'No, thank you. I shan't be staying long.'

She stood in the middle of the kitchen and my first thought was that she must be related to Aunt Julia. They were the same type. She was tall and immaculately presented, and completely accustomed to getting her own way. She looked around our untidy kitchen. The cat was sprawled, upside down, in front of the range. The table was littered with Russell's paint catalogues, today's unopened post, quite a lot of Joy's breakfast egg and a large biscuit tin. Through the open door, we could hear Mrs Crisp shouting at Marilyn, who obviously wanted to come in and meet our guest.

I sighed, remembering what Monica had said. This was obviously the legendary Ananda Balasana and here she was, dressed for Country Walking. Or Country Visiting. Or Country Shopping. Country something, anyway. Her Barbour jacket was top of the range and immaculate, belted tightly at her narrow waist. It was easy to see her pockets weren't stuffed with tissues, carrots, odd bits of string, or lumps of sheep's wool pulled out of the hedge and forgotten. Her Hermès scarf was knotted around her neck in the casual way that only top stylists and French women seem able to achieve. Her cord trousers had a crease down the front, for heaven's sake, and her quilted wellies were mud- and dust-free. She couldn't possibly have walked down our lane. She must have driven. Her cottage was only a quarter of a mile away. I tried to tell myself she might be going shopping afterwards. In the West End, perhaps. She looked like someone who had opened a catalogue entitled 'Country Clothes' and placed a blanket order for everything. I remembered the overdressed cottage up the lane. Like

71

cottage like owner, obviously. Suddenly, Monica's joke about too many sheep and the grass being the wrong colour made perfect sense. And something told me this wasn't a social call.

I woke up to find everyone looking at me, obviously expecting some sort of response. I wiped my hands and stood up. 'How do you ... do? Would you ... like some ...'

'Tea?' she said briskly. 'No, thank you.'

I saw Russell's lips tighten. He hates it when people do that. I'm not keen on it myself.

'It's Mrs...' Dammit. The word wouldn't come out.

'Balasana. Yes. Ananda Balasana.'

To be quite fair, I don't think she was being deliberately rude. I think she was one of those people who moves through life as speedily as possible. Always hurrying from one moment to the next. As if the current one is never quite good enough.

I heard a slight sound from Russell who was spooning down the last of Joy's egg as fast as she could go. She was still chewing the last mouthful as he yanked her out of her chair, saying hastily, 'I'll change her upstairs, Jenny.'

She was already changed, but in the interests of neighbourly harmony, he was better off out of the way. Russell has no filter and he can be quite impolite to people he doesn't like. And he didn't like Ananda Balasana.

Neither did I, but with Russell upstairs and Mrs Crisp abandoning her post, it was all up to me. I gestured regally to our big living room. Shabby, yes, but shabby chic in a good light.

Typically, of course, the bright sunshine only emphasised the faded curtains and carpet, and the scratched table. She glanced briefly at our shelves of paperbacks, sniffed and came back to me.

'I shan't keep you long, Mrs Checkland. I can see you're very busy. I wanted to say…'

She was interrupted by Russell clattering back down the stairs, the light of battle in his eye.

'Well, Mrs Balasana, we meet at last. Always nice to put a face to a voice, don't you think? And I have to say you look exactly as I imagined you would. It's always gratifying to be right, as I'm sure you will find one day. So do tell us – what's today's complaint? Wrong sort of sunshine? Too many trees around the place?

She did not, for one moment, allow this to throw her. 'Actually, Mr Checkland, that's for another day. Today's complaint is about that garish monstrosity.'

His face was a picture of blank incomprehension. 'Sorry – not with you. Which garish monstrosity are we talking about here? Yours or ours?'

'Mine?'

'OK. Thanks for making that clear. Well, I wasn't going to say anything, but since you've brought up the subject – I hope you shot your architect afterwards. I mean – all those gables – and that rat-ridden thatch – and those stupid little windows. It's not as if life in the countryside isn't tough enough without some lunatic with more money than sense dropping a chocolate-box fantasy on our doorstep and frightening the living daylights out of Martin Braithwaite's sheep.'

In the silence that followed, I could hear Mrs Crisp pressed up against the door, listening … She could have had my ring-side seat with my goodwill, because I had a sudden feeling that Mrs Balasana was a more than worthy opponent. I thought – hoped – she would rise up in wrath and stalk from the room, but I'm not that lucky.

'Strange though you may find this, Mr Checkland – and I do beg that you at least make an effort to struggle with a difficult to understand concept – but my cottage received full approval from all the appropriate planning committees which is, I am convinced, not a claim that you can make.'

'Why would I want to? The obscure and irrelevant policies of local government are of no interest to me. I can, however, understand the appeal they might have to a certain type of person.'

'I think you will not be so dismissive when you receive the first of a barrage of complaints I intend to file with the appropriate authorities.'

'While I am sure you can imagine the reluctance with which I feel compelled to disappoint you, Mrs Balasana, I can assure you that even if the appropriate authorities are so misguided as to listen to such trivia, my dismissiveness will be enormous.'

I was lost. Completely at sea. I had no idea what this was all about and I rather suspected the two combatants had rather lost sight of the original topic of discussion as well. I said, turning to Mrs Balasana, 'I'm sorry, but I really … don't have any idea … what…'

'What this is all about,' she finished for me. 'Of course you don't, Mrs Checkland, since I haven't yet been granted the courtesy of being allowed to make my point.'

'Well, what is your point?' demanded Russell. 'We've been here for what seems like years and, so far, all you've done is maunder on about planning committees and the dire consequences of something or other.'

'The hen house, Mr Checkland. That bright orange, glow-in-the-dark monstrosity you have erec…'

She stopped suddenly. Russell's eyes were gleaming and I think she suddenly realised what she was opening herself up to. She turned to me, which did her no good at all, because I'd been struck dumb. This was all my fault. I was the one who'd decorated the thing with neon orange paint and brought us under the scrutiny of some sort of planning committee – or the Forces of Darkness as Russell would almost certainly describe them later – and rendered us liable to some sort of dreadful punishment.

I turned to him, anxiously. 'Russell, I…'

He smiled sunnily. 'It's all right, Jenny, don't concern yourself. Mrs Balasana is obviously completely unaware of the status of our so-called garish monstrosity, which, I think we can all agree, is astonishing coming from someone who lives in a pink rhomboid, but it's obviously up to me to explain, in simple terms, exactly how things work in the real world.'

He paused and she gazed at him expectantly. As, I have to admit, did I.

He glanced over his shoulder as if to reassure himself we could not be overheard, and then said in a hoarse whisper, 'Patagonian Attack Chickens.'

Oh God…

To give Mrs Balasana her due, she hardly blinked at all, saying frostily, 'Indeed? Patagonian…'

'Attack Chickens,' he finished for her, and I was pleased to see she didn't like it either. 'It all began during World War Two. As I'm sure you will remember, 1940 was our darkest hour.'

'Strangely, Mr Checkland, no.'

'Really? How astonishing. Well, never mind. To continue. The government was encouraging the country to prepare for invasion – you know, taking down signposts, blacking out the names of railway stations, setting up the Home Guard – you know the sort of thing. One of the War Office's many ideas was the utilisation of livestock as a kind of last-ditch defence. Dogs locally were trained to attack anyone who didn't speak with a Rushford accent. Geese, as I'm sure you know from your Ancient History, are excellent at defending buildings; and a poultry woman in Rushford hit upon the idea of training up her chickens.

She owned some twenty or thirty chickens recently imported from Patagonia, and had already noticed their extremely aggressive qualities. Certain that these could be utilised to good effect, she set about their training. I'm sure you know that chickens can fly, and it was the work of a mere weekend to teach them what was required. According to records, most of which you will appreciate are still sealed, many a fifth-columnist was rendered *hors de combat* by a Patagonian Attack Chicken coming at him out of the night, and beaking him soundly in both eyes.'

He paused for breath, which might have been a mistake.

'Seriously, Mr Checkland…'

But he'd hit his stride.

'Indeed, Mrs Balasana, very seriously, as I'm sure you can envisage. And they didn't stop there…'

'What has this to do with your hen house?'

'It's their home,' he said, as one explaining to the intellectually impaired. 'Painted in their regimental colours. The last remnants of the once notorious Patagonian Attack Chicken Battalion open brackets Rushford Regiment close brackets, living out their days in this obscure part of the world. Always watchful. Always vigilant. Waiting for the call…'

'I think you forget, Mr Checkland, that I pass your yard every day, and far from being an elite squadron of battle-hardened veterans, one of them always appears to be on the stable roof…'

'Parachute training,' said Russell, gravely.

'One perched on the water trough…'

'Diving training.'

'And the others are sprawled in the sun, fast asleep.

'Bomber squadron.'

She couldn't help herself and, quite honestly, if she hadn't asked then I would have had to.

76

'*Bomber* squadron?'

'They lie in the sun and it bakes their eggs.'

'What?'

'Hard-boiled eggs.'

'I hardly think…'

'I can see that, but trust me. A hard-boiled egg dropped from thirty thousand feet isn't going to do anyone any good at all. And they strive for pin-point accuracy, you know. It's a point of honour with them. It's their South American blood, I expect.'

He pushed his hair out of his eyes and seemed not to notice it flopping straight back down again.

'I take grave offence at…'

'Makes a change,' he said, cheerfully. 'I should imagine you're usually the donor rather than the recipient.'

She turned to go. 'You will be hearing from me again.'

'I never doubted it for one moment,' he said, gravely.

'I'll see you out,' I said, desperate to get her out before things got any worse.

I took her out through the kitchen where Mrs Crisp was making a great show of being very busy on the other side of the room before exiting into the yard. Mercifully, none of the Patagonian Attack Chickens open brackets Rushford Regiment close brackets, were in sight.

I said quickly, 'I'm not going to apologise for … my husband but I'm … sorry you didn't enjoy your … visit this afternoon.'

I thought for a moment her face softened. She paused, as if about to say something and I couldn't help wondering if she was lonely and like many lonely people couldn't help pushing others further away? Was this continual criticism and complaint the only method by which she could communicate? I couldn't help feeling guilty because I hadn't visited and welcomed her to the

77

village. I wasn't given an opportunity to think about his any further, however, because at that moment she said, 'There was another purpose to my visit today, Mrs Checkland. A man called at my door yesterday and asked after you.'

I stopped walking. I think I stopped breathing as well. 'Oh? Did ... he give his ...?'

'Name. No, I did ask him, but he changed the subject.'

I felt the familiar clenching sensation. Words were flying away from me. 'Perhaps ... you could ... describe him?'

'A little under medium height. Dark. I'm afraid I didn't notice him especially.'

No – that had always been Christopher's problem. No one ever noticed him especially. Not until it was too late.

'He did leave a message, however. He said he'd called here and that you had been out, but that he would see you again, very soon. Good day to you, Mrs Checkland.'

And, having demolished my carefully constructed edifice of self-delusion, she left.

CHAPTER SIX

I lost all track of time standing in the yard as a hundred thoughts whirled around my head. All right, the description – medium height and dark – could apply to a substantial number of men, but it was Christopher. I knew it. He'd come back.

I stared unseeing at my feet, trying to think sensibly, but there's always been something about Christopher that chills my soul. As a child, I avoided him whenever possible. Not always very successfully, because I remember Russell pulling him off me on several occasions.

I was roused by Russell shouting that he had to go out, and would I put Boxer in his field, please. I heard his Land Rover start up; he roared past, waving and hooting, and disappeared out into the lane.

I collected Boxer, opened the gate, and led him into the field. As always, he kicked up his heels at the feel of grass under his feet and broke into a canter. Tail kinked over his back, he stretched out his neck and increased his speed. It was a wonderful sight. He's a good-looking horse and he runs like the wind, but, as Russell says, not always in the right direction. Having galloped away his overnight tickles, he dropped his head and began to graze. Lucky Boxer. Not a care in the world. I sighed enviously, shoved my hands in my pockets, let the gate swing to behind me, and went off to see where Russell had left Joy.

She was fast asleep and there was no sign of Mrs Crisp, so I let myself into our walled garden. It's peaceful there and I wanted some time to think.

I sat on the wooden bench by the fountain, listening to the gentle trickle of water. At this time of year, the garden had a blowsy look that I quite liked. Summer was finishing and autumn was on its way. Yellow leaves were appearing here and there. A few already lay on the ground. There was a nip in the early morning air these days, and enormous dew-hung cobwebs stretched across the windows. Soon we would have the smell of bonfires and fireworks, and Mrs Crisp would be making our Christmas cakes and pudding. This would be our first Christmas together as a real family. Joy was born just before last Christmas and wouldn't remember any of it. I hardly remembered any of it myself. There had been the snow, and worrying about Russell being lost on the moor, and then she'd been born, and I'd been so happy, and now…

I have no idea how long I sat there in the warm sunshine. I can't even remember what I was thinking about, but I do know I was roused by the sound of Russell roaring back into the yard.

I got up stiffly and went to meet him.

He was peering into the field. 'Jenny, where's Boxer? Did you forget to let him out?'

Everything stopped. I stared, first at him, then at the empty field. Then at the empty yard. My whole body went cold. I forgot to breathe. They were gone. Both of them. Boxer and Marilyn. Their field was empty and the gate to the lane was open. There was no sign of either of them. Anywhere. I spun around. They definitely weren't in their field. Or the yard. Or the stable. They weren't anywhere, and the gate to the lane was open – as it always was.

Oh my God, they'd got out and it was all my fault. I hadn't shut the gate to their field properly and they'd got out and it was all my fault.

Russell was already running into the house, shouting

for Mrs Crisp.

By the time I caught up with him, he was on his phone talking to Andrew. Mrs Crisp was ringing the police on the landline.

He turned to me. 'Jenny, I have to find them. God knows where they are. I'm going to check the village. I'm sure they'll be there and someone will have recognised them and tied them up in a field or a garage somewhere. If not...'

If not, if they weren't there, they would be out on the main road somewhere, and neither of them had any road sense whatsoever. Russell never took Boxer that way. A horse who could be terrorised by an inanimate telegraph pole wasn't going to do well with traffic zipping past him. I tried to close my mind to what could be happening to them at this very moment. I saw them on the main road somewhere, huge lorries roaring past, horns blasting, missing them by inches. I saw Marilyn frozen with fear, eyes squeezed tight shut, because that's what she does. All donkeys do. They're cleverer than horses. In a crisis, they stand still. But horses bolt. I saw Boxer, terrified by the traffic, running blindly, until the inevitable moment when a lorry, brakes screaming, horn blaring, didn't miss him at all...

I struggled back to the present. Russell was talking to me.

'I've rung Andrew – he's putting the word out.'

Mrs Crisp replaced the phone. 'I've informed the police.'

'Thank you. Stay here both of you, in case anyone rings to say they've got them. Let me know at once if that happens.'

As he crashed out of the back door, his phone rang again. I heard him shout, 'For God's sake, Franny, not now.' The engine started, and he was gone again.

Mrs Crisp said, 'I'll ring the Braithwaites,' and I nodded because it was a good idea, and ran back out into the yard, just in case some miracle had occurred and they had come back home. I ran to look into our second field, just in case they had somehow got themselves into the wrong one. I ran around behind the stables, where Russell parks his Land Rover, just in case they had wandered around there by mistake. I ran into the lane and looked up and down, just in case they had only gone for a stroll, and even now were standing only a few yards away, grazing the grass verge. And all the time, a voice in my head said, 'You didn't shut the gate. You didn't shut the gate. You didn't shut the gate.' Because I hadn't shut the gate. No matter how hard I tried to remember, I just couldn't remember hearing the latch click behind me. I remembered pulling the gate to, sticking my hands in my pockets and walking away, thinking about stupid Christopher and not, not in any way, thinking about closing the gate behind me. If anything happened to them ... If anything happened to them, how would I ever be able to face Russell again?

Because Russell absolutely adored Boxer. Yes, he was hard work and cost him a fortune in vet's bills, but Russell was the only one who could do anything with him. By taking him in he had, quite literally, saved his life. Ex-racehorses don't always have much of a future, especially one with the brain capacity of a teapot, but Russell had brought him here to live quietly as a family pet. I remembered Mrs Crisp telling me that once you were taken in by Russell Checkland, you had a home for life, and that was perfectly true – Boxer, Marilyn, the cat, even me. All of us taken in and cared for. Only I'd repaid him by leaving the gate open and now we'd lost Boxer. And Marilyn as well. When I thought about what could be happening to them...

I was wracked with guilt. I just couldn't believe I'd been so stupid. And Russell hadn't uttered a single word of blame, which made everything even worse. How could I have been so ... so – I couldn't even think of a word bad enough to describe what I'd done. I put my head in my hands, crushed by guilt and despair and that's when it happened.

Childhood fears are the strongest of all and they never really go away. They can be deeply buried, or shut away out of sight, or forgotten, but they never truly go away, and now – with all the force of an explosion, from nowhere – an old thought punched into my brain, taking up its old position with an ease and familiarity that told me it had never really gone away.

Stupid Jenny Dove.

I'd heard it so many times. In the playground, in the street, at home, from Francesca, from Christopher – definitely from Christopher, and even, by implication, from Aunt Julia and Uncle Richard. The only person who had never said it was Russell Checkland, who had believed in me and helped me, and I'd repaid him by forgetting to shut the gate properly. Just a simple action, but obviously far too difficult for stupid Jenny Dove.

I became aware that I was still standing in the middle of the lane. I rubbed my eyes and tried to block out that awful, repetitive voice that just wouldn't shut up...

I took a deep breath. And then another. And then I looked around me. Russell had driven off down the lane and was searching the village. I looked up the lane – we'd heard nothing from the Braithwaites, who would have bundled the pair of them straight back home again faster than ... well, than something that was very fast. I couldn't, at that moment, think of anything. But, in between them and us was Mrs Balasana's place. No – if they were there then our telephone would have burst into flames, and she would probably have called out the army to deal with the situation, closely followed by every solicitor in Rushford demanding they be put down at once and claiming massive compensation. Our telephone remained uncombusted so they couldn't be there.

She might be out, said my internal voice, doing something useful for once.

I opened my mouth to call to Mrs Crisp to telephone Russell, and then had second thoughts. I might be wrong. I probably *was* wrong. He should stay where he was, searching the village. I could check this out myself.

I shot up the lane. Never before had it seemed so steep or stony. Or so long. I ran until I was breathless and then I trotted, until finally, lungs heaving, vision blurred, I arrived, panting and sweaty, outside Mrs Balasana's immaculate five-barred gate, painted in gleaming white and with the words, 'Pear Tree Cottage' picked out in black. Very smart.

I craned my neck to see over into the garden. Please God, let them be here. Please, please let them be here.

The relief made me stagger. For a moment, I had to hang on to the gate for support. They *were* here. Both of them. Actually, three of them were here and, far from indulging in an orgy of accidental destruction, Boxer was staring at the coal bunker – also painted in black and white, Marilyn was investigating a clump of Michaelmas daisies, and the cat was sitting on the wall nearby, blinking his one eye in the afternoon sunshine.

I looked up and down the lane. No one was in sight. I might get away with this. I wrestled with the latch, which was very stiff, and it took two hands to get it free. I pushed open the gate, and crept through.

Despite everything Kevin said, it really was a very pretty garden. The wide gravel drive on which I was standing led around the side of the cottage to the garage.

At the front, a small circular lawn was surrounded by beautifully maintained flowerbeds. The traditional summer favourites were just beginning to go over, but the dahlias, Michaelmas daisies and chrysanthemums were coming into bloom. A small sundial sat in the centre of the lawn, and a brightly polished horseshoe hung over the front door, quite unlike the rusty object hanging over our stable door at Frogmorton which, far from being a symbol of good fortune, frequently came adrift from its fastening and brained anyone unlucky enough to be passing through the door at the time.

To the side of the garden lay a small orchard, where ancient moss-covered apple trees stood in prim rows. The trees bore very few apples that I could see, and under Mrs Balasana's regime, I wouldn't give much for their chances of survival if they didn't sort themselves out soon.

I stood on the drive, still breathless from effort and relief, and said, 'And just what ... do you ... three think you're up to?'

Marilyn withdrew her head from the daisies and batted her eyelashes at me. Her nose was speckled with pollen. She looked like a picture on a chocolate box. Whatever was occurring here was obviously nothing to do with her, and she was completely innocent.

The important thing was not to panic them. Well, not to panic Boxer, who was perfectly capable of climbing into the coal bunker if agitated. Marilyn didn't do panic – unless you were trying to bathe her – and the cat was just a cause of it in others.

They looked at me. Well, two of them did. No, one of them did. Boxer resumed his inspection of the coal bunker, and the cat twisted suddenly, stuck a drumstick in the air and began a thorough wash of an area he should have attended to before he left the house. Marilyn and I stared at each other. I patted my pockets. I knew they were empty but she didn't. You have to box clever with Marilyn. As Russell has frequently discovered, you can't just walk up and grab her. We've never yet managed to work out how she does it, but one minute she's there and the next moment she's about thirty feet away. In his darker moments, Russell claims she can teleport.

Straining my ears for the slightest sound of anyone coming up the lane, I turned away as if I had something to hide, and I could tell by the sound of rustling foliage and snapping flower stems that she was fighting her way out of the border, almost certainly leaving a small trail of devastation in her wake. But, where Marilyn led, Boxer would follow. The cat could look after himself.

Not looking at any of them, and doing my best to pretend I had all the time in the world and I really couldn't care less whether they followed me or not, I took a few steps towards the gate, waiting ... praying for the sound of tiny donkey hooves on the gravel path behind me. Yes – with a final sound of expensively rending foliage, here she came.

The cat, private parts now spotless, jumped down from the wall and strolled towards me, tail waving like a bottle brush. Boxer, finding himself alone and unprotected in this strange new world, followed Marilyn. Straight through the border, obviously, and anything that might have survived the tsunami of Marilyn's passing, was submerged under his enormous feet.

We were fortunate that although he's a big horse, he's actually very gentle. He followed Marilyn down the path. Marilyn followed me. The cat followed the beat of his own drum.

I waited until Marilyn was pushing her nose into my pockets and then caught hold of her pretty red head collar. She's so small it's rather like taking a dog for a walk, but she consented quite happily.

I led her out into the lane, waited for Boxer to catch up, and then closed the gate and wrestled the latch back into place, breathing a sigh of relief. We were all on the right side of the gate. We were safe.

Oh no we weren't.

A figure appeared around the bend. Of course it did. Smart Barbour jacket, quilted wellingtons miraculously still unsullied, and with a small dog at her heels. The Wicked Witch of the West was back.

Marilyn, to whom all dogs are wolves, stopped dead and dug in her tiny hooves. Boxer also stopped and peered amiably over my shoulder. The cat moved fractionally into attack mode.

I said quietly, 'OK everyone. We've been on a pleasant … afternoon stroll. Indoor … voices. Best behaviour. Brace yourselves.'

She said, 'Good afternoon, Mrs Checkland.'

'Oh, hello … Mrs…'

'Balasana.'

I really wished she would stop doing that.

I said, 'I'm sorry, but our donkey … is frightened … of your … dog. We'll go back…' thus cunningly making it sound as if we'd come from further up the lane. Yes, I would tell her we'd been visiting the Braithwaites. All of us. A little odd, perhaps, but not completely unbelievable.

'No need.' She stooped and picked up her dog, tucking him under one arm. Marilyn pressed closer to me. The wolf was now taller than she was.

As we drew level, I said chattily, 'We've … just been up to … see the Braithwaites.'

'Really? I've just been speaking to them in the village.'

Why does this always happen to me? If Russell was here – and believe me, in a crisis Russell is never here –

he'd have another Patagonian Attack Chicken moment, but the best I could manage was, 'I know. They were out.'

Her gaze wandered over my entourage and she lifted an eyebrow.

'I have to take … Marilyn out … because of her feet.' I ran that sentence through my head and tried to make things better. I meant to say that because donkey's feet are always growing, they need to be on a hard surface daily, and of course it didn't come out that way at all. 'She's a…'

'Donkey,' she said. 'Yes, I can see that.'

I was hot all over. Every word just made things worse and any moment now she was going to notice that Hurricanes Marilyn and Boxer had touched down in her Michaelmas daisies. We would pay for the damage, of course, but I had planned to send her a cheque in the post – not actually to be present at the moment of discovery.

I sought for neutral ground. 'I … like your … dog.'

This time her face did soften. 'Her name is Bundle.'

The little dog looked up at the mention of her name and wagged her entire body. Mrs Balasana's face softened even further.

Russell would have called her a tree rat. The dog, I mean, not Mrs Balasana, although now I come to think of it … Anyway, Bundle was a tiny Yorkshire Terrier with her topknot tied up with a red ribbon in true Yorkie style. She wagged her tail again, gazing up at Mrs Balasana. The two of them obviously loved each other. Beside me, Marilyn shifted uneasily and I remembered I had only a head collar with which to hold her, and nothing at all for Boxer, should he take it into his head that this was actually a shoebox-sized wolf.

'She's … very pretty,' I said, wondering what on earth to do. In two minutes she would see her garden. The devastation wasn't massive, but one border was considerably less immaculate than the others. Some people might not even notice a few chewed flower stalks or trampled plants, but she would, I was certain. It would take her less than five seconds to put two and two together and descend on Frogmorton in justified fury. And if Russell happened to be on the premises at the time, things might not go well. I decided on a pre-emptive strike.

'It was us,' I blurted, because, as usual, the need to impart information was severely compromised by my inability to get it out in the first place. 'I'm ... sorry, Mrs Balasana ... but .... Marilyn has been in your front ... garden. She didn't ... mean any harm – it was my fault – and I'll ... gladly pay for the ... damage if you ... could let me know how ... much.'

She stared at me, saying nothing. Oh God, this was just awful. I battled on. 'And I ... wanted to say as well ... that if you would like ... one day ... I ... mean ... Russell is usually out in ... the afternoons and ... I don't know if you know many people...' I could feel sweat running down my back with the heat and the embarrassment and the effort. Gritting my teeth, I ploughed on, closing my eyes and imagining the words appearing over her head where I could read them, because sometimes that helps. 'Perhaps ... you ... would like to ... call in one ... afternoon. It would be nice ... Although I expect ... you're very busy...' And that was it. I was done. Exhausted. I stared down at my dusty trainers and waited.

Several lifetimes later she said, 'Thank you, Mrs Checkland,' although whether she was thanking me for owning up, the offer of compensation (which I could only hope wasn't too massive otherwise none of us would be eating for a month or so) or the invitation, I had no idea.

Behind us, further down the lane, I could hear the

89

familiar clatter of Russell's approaching chariot and the chicken dispersing toot he always gave as he pulled into the yard. It broke the spell.

'I … must … go.'

'Yes,' she said, briskly, 'so must I. Good day to you, Mrs Checkland.' She turned away but I did notice she took several strides away from Marilyn before putting down her little dog. I was still completely in the dark as to her intentions regarding prosecution, demands for compensation, or gaol sentences, but the important thing now was to get my flock home before Russell called out the Coastguard. And possibly Mountain Rescue as well.

He was so pleased to see us.

'Jenny! Oh, thank God. Where were they?'

I gestured up the lane. 'Mrs Balasana.'

'Shit. Does she know?'

I nodded.

'Did she see them? What did she say?'

'I told her. She was OK.'

Marilyn pushed past me to say hello.

As his wife, I stood, uncomplaining, as he first greeted Boxer, who amiably slobbered down his front, gently pulled Marilyn's ears, ignored the cat, and herded them both safely back into their field. With no idea of their narrow escape, they dropped their heads and began to graze. I opened my mouth to say something, but at that moment, his phone rang and he turned away. 'Franny? Look…' He began to walk away.

I stared at his back and then turned away myself. I went to check on Joy, who was fast asleep, but I could still use her as an excuse. I picked up her toys and tidied all her drawers, sorting and re-sorting her clothing, and doing all the other million or so tiny things necessary for the upkeep of an eight-month-old infant.

I went down into her bathroom, and rearranged all her

soaps and shampoos. I folded towels and hung her Shaun the Sheep bath scrunchie up to dry. I opened the windows to air the room and then closed them again. I heard Russell go by. He stuck his head around the bedroom door and said, 'Jenny?' but never thought to look in the bathroom. I stood still and he went away again.

The world fell silent. I guessed Mrs Crisp was in her room, Russell was in his studio, the chickens were doing chicken things, Boxer and Marilyn were continuing with their day, Joy was asleep, and that just left me. The odd one out. Again.

CHAPTER SEVEN

No one said anything the next morning. There wasn't even a pause in the conversation as I walked in with Joy.

Russell was on his phone. I heard him say, 'No. I'm not going upset Jenny over this. I'll talk to her about it in my own time. When the moment is right. You'll just have to be patient. That's all I'm saying at the moment so there's no point in going on at me.' He snapped his phone shut.

Mrs Crisp and Kevin were discussing our current egg-laying situation. Two cardboard egg trays lay on the worktop, conspicuously empty. Russell was ignoring them.

He smiled when he saw us and reached out for Joy.

'Hello, wife and daughter.'

'Cereal and toast,' announced Mrs Crisp. 'Because we have no eggs,' she added meaningfully.

'Early days yet,' said Russell, dismissively. 'And after our recent visit from Mrs Balalaika, we were lucky the milk didn't sour as well.'

I busied myself pouring a mug of coffee and waited, because the natural thing to do now was for everyone to discuss yesterday's little adventure and how they could possibly have escaped from their field. I watched my hands tremble as I stirred my coffee.

There was a short silence and then Kevin said he should be cracking on, and Russell plonked Joy in her high chair and began to shovel down her breakfast.

His phone rang. He looked at the screen, looked at me, handed me Joy's spoon and shot hastily out of the door,

93

but not before I heard him say, 'Franny, I told you...' before he closed it behind him.

Mrs Crisp put some toast in front of me and everyone else got on with their day.

Except me. I just couldn't settle. I wandered out into the yard and if I checked that stupid gate once, I checked it a dozen times.

Kevin passed me, whistling and wheeling his barrow. He glanced at me several times, but I wouldn't catch his eye, and I know Mrs Crisp was watching me from the back door. I wondered if they were making sure I didn't do anything stupid. Again.

I hung over the gate, watching Boxer and Marilyn grazing peacefully, with no idea at all of the repercussions of their little adventure yesterday, and I thought about just how fragile was the framework on which I'd hung my life.

I'd been living in a golden bubble. I led such a sheltered life that my deficiencies – for want of a better word – had passed unnoticed. Especially by me. But now I came to think of it, the brutal truth was that I'd been fooling myself. Teachers, relatives, everyone who knew me – those people couldn't all have been wrong. It just wasn't possible. And then along came Russell who decided that whatever was wrong with me he could live with it for the sake of the money, then discovered there wasn't any. But by then it was too late to get rid of me. To give him his due, he'd accepted it with good grace, but – and how could I ever have thought otherwise – there was something the matter with me – there always had been – and now the cracks were beginning to show.

I couldn't bear the thought that I'd let him down. That I'd nearly brought catastrophe down upon us, and all because, for a few fatal seconds, I hadn't been thinking about what I was doing. Before I married, I used to watch

94

myself all the time. I always had to concentrate. To make sure I got things right. That I said the right thing. Always keeping myself in the background where I couldn't do any harm. And now, after only a couple of years in the sunshine with Russell Checkland, I'd forgotten all that, and just look at the damage I'd almost done.

It's hard to describe how I felt. The nearest I could get was saying it was like standing in shallow water on a beach and feeling the sands shift beneath my feet. To know that all the things I had thought were solid and immoveable now were not. That my new life wasn't built on solid foundations after all. And worst of all, the old fears had come crowding back, thick and black and encircling me. Cutting me off from the outside world as they had always done. Once again, all the barriers I had thought were my protection would turn out to be my prison.

My thoughts were frightening me.

I went back to check the gate again.

Russell came back for lunch. Unable to face him, I took Joy up to her room, spending so long with her that he'd gone again when I came back downstairs.

It was only when Mrs Crisp asked whether I wanted any lunch that I realised I hadn't spoken all day. I took a breath but nothing happened. I focused on the pattern on the tablecloth, pale blue and cream checks – blue square, cream square, blue square – but it was useless. Like me. So I smiled and shook my head, and took myself back upstairs again to watch Joy sleep, and to think about what I had done. Or rather, what I hadn't done. And what had happened. I spent a lot of time thinking about what *could* have happened. I'd just reached the point where the pair of them had somehow reached Rushford and been hit by traffic, causing multiple pile-ups and widespread devastation when Mrs Crisp tapped on the door and called that she'd left some soup outside.

I waited until I heard her footsteps die away before opening the door. There was a pretty tray with a bowl of steaming soup, two bread rolls and an orange.

I did my best, because if I didn't eat then questions would be asked, but I really didn't want it so, feeling even more guilty, I threw the soup down the toilet and one of the rolls into the garden for the birds. I thought leaving the second roll on the plate lent a touch of realism, realised I was deceiving the people who loved me, and felt my self-esteem plummet even further.

It got worse. Well, I got worse. Fortunately – and I can't believe I said that – Joy developed a bit of a snuffle, which provided the perfect excuse for me to avoid everyone else and stay in her room. She slept most of the time which meant I had nothing much to do except wipe her occasionally crusty nose so, of course, I used the time to brood over the events of that day. Over and over again, I let the gate swing behind me. I could feel the cool metal under my hands, hear the faint squeak of the hinges, remember what I was thinking of at the time, feel the hot sun on my head, and not in any way hear the click as the latch engaged.

I wondered which of them had been the first to investigate this excitingly open gate. I was certain it would have been Marilyn, whose second home was our yard. And where Marilyn led, Boxer would surely follow. And then she would notice the gate into the lane – usually open so that Russell could roar, unimpeded into the yard, and make an entrance. There was never any danger of him hitting anyone – in his Land Rover you could hear him coming from miles away. Particularly if he was in third gear when the engine tended to sound like a cavalry

96

regiment clattering over a cobbled street. And these days, he always hooted when turning into the yard – to give the ladies a fighting chance to get out of the way, he said.

Out of habit, Boxer would turn left, up the lane towards the moors, because that was the way he was familiar with. And once out of the yard, off they would go. In my mind, I saw their rear ends disappearing around the bend and silence falling on Frogmorton. Until Russell returned and saw what I had done.

A sudden gust of rain on the window brought me back. Night had fallen. I hadn't realised so much time had passed. Where had the afternoon gone? And it was raining. A small part of my brain reminded me I should check the buckets up in the attic. I remembered it had been raining when I first came to Frogmorton. Had my life come full circle? Buying buckets had been the first thing Russell and I had ever done together. I sat very still, filled with superstitious dread. Was this it? Was the cycle complete? Did this mean everything was ended? Was this really all I would ever have? A few years in the sun and then, somehow, I would lose it all. Everything would be snatched away from me. And I would have to go back to the way things were before I met Russell.

Hoping it would make me feel better and because I was cold, I showered, changed into my pyjamas and dressing gown, and went back to check on Joy.

I drew the curtains in her room, switched on her little nightlight, and sat beside her cot and felt the hot tears running down my face. Because the next stage was that they would take her away from me. Because I couldn't be trusted with even the simplest task. Because I was exactly as stupid as everyone had always said I was. Except Russell who, yes all right, had married me for my money, discovered I didn't have any, but stood by me anyway …

'But only because he couldn't have Francesca,' said

the nasty little voice inside my head.

Words, never my friends, circled like vultures. 'He couldn't have her so he decided he might as well take you and your money, only it turned out there wasn't any, was there, but he kept you anyway, and this is how you repaid him, and you really are as odd as everyone always thought. There's something the matter with you, and now he's stuck with you, and you nearly killed his horse, and he spends a lot of time talking to Francesca these days, and how long before they decide you're not fit to have care of your baby, and …

'Jenny, stop it. Stop it now. This minute. Open your eyes. Look at me. No, look at me.'

The words seared a path straight through this sticky maelstrom of anguish. There was no question of my not complying. My eyes opened of their own accord and at exactly the same moment I registered the comfortably familiar smell of warm ginger biscuits. I caught my breath in a sob, soaring in one brief second from despair to utter joy. Soaring so fast it made my head spin.

Thomas was here. Thomas had come back. Now, exactly when I needed him, Thomas had come back.

I stood up so quickly that I knocked over the dressing-table stool.

There he stood, over in the corner of the room, just as he always did, his beautiful golden coat glowing slightly in the night light.

'Thomas. Is that you? Is that really you?'

'Really Jenny, how many horses do you regularly find in your bedroom?'

I ran across the room and he lowered his head to me in that gesture I knew so well. His huge dark eyes shone with love for me. For me – stupid little Jenny Dove.

'Jenny, my very dear friend, how are you?'

His familiar gentle voice was too much for me. I felt

98

fresh tears fall. 'Oh Thomas, I've made such a mess of things.'

'Really? That doesn't seem very likely. Perhaps you've just got yourself in a bit of a tangle, that's all.'

I shook my head. It was far worse than that. Part of me ached to tell him – to share the burden a little. The other part hesitated. Thomas never judged – never criticised, but if I told him how stupid I'd been...

'Why are you here?'

'Just passing through.'

'Can you stay?'

He shifted his weight a little. *'I expect so.'*

I snuffled and groped for a tissue in my pocket. Not finding one, I wiped my nose on my sleeve.

'I see I've come back not a moment too soon.'

I mumbled, 'I can't find a tissue.'

I could hear the smile in his voice. *'Jenny, this is a baby's bedroom. Every box of tissues in the entire western world is in here.'*

'I know,' I said, finding a box by her cot and blowing my nose. Hard.

'My goodness, what a very thorough girl you are.'

Russell had said that to me long ago, when he asked me to marry him and I had burst into tears on that occasion as well. It occurred to me, as I snorted into my tissues, that I wasn't a naturally joyful person.

'Don't I get a hug?'

I hung back. 'Thomas, I've done something terrible.'

'No, you haven't.'

'Yes, I have.'

'No, you haven't.'

'Yes, I...'

'Can we move on – we're beginning to sound like a Christmas pantomime.'

I took a deep breath and forced out the words. 'I left

the gate open and Boxer and Marilyn got out.'

'Did you get them back?'

'Oh yes, they hadn't gone too far. But they got into Mrs Balasana's garden, which was a complete disaster, because she's not very nice and complains a lot, and Marilyn ate her Michaelmas daisies.'

'What did Boxer eat?'

'Nothing. He just stared at her coal bunker. I think he was a little bit overwhelmed. Why are you laughing?'

'I'm not. Just clearing my throat.'

I stared at him suspiciously. 'You're a horse. You don't clear your throat.'

'Of course I do. I'm a horse. Have you seen the size of my throat? Takes a lot of clearing, I can tell you.'

'Can we get back to me leaving the gate open?'

'Certainly, since you seem so eager to dwell on it.'

Silence fell.

'Well, go on then.'

I felt rather stupid and said in a tiny voice, 'I left the gate open.'

I thought he stared at me for rather a long time.

'Well, say something.'

'Is this Joy? My goodness, hasn't she grown? What a pretty little girl.'

'Thomas!'

'You told me to say something so I did.'

'About the gate.'

'What about the gate?'

'I left it open.'

'No, you didn't.'

'Yes, I did.'

'No, you didn't.'

'Seriously? Are we starting this again?'

He sighed. *'I can see I won't get any sense out of you until you get all this out of your system. Go on then, tell*

*me what happened, why everything is your fault, and how
unworthy you are.'*

'I'm not unworthy.'

'Yes, you are.'

'Thomas!'

'Sorry – couldn't resist. Tell me about the gate.'

I did. I told him everything. I started with possibly
seeing Christopher outside Sharon's shop, all the way
through to Mrs Balasana's visit, which he greatly enjoyed,
asking me to repeat the bit about the Patagonian Attack
Chickens several times.

*'Good old Russell. He never fails to amaze and
entertain, does he? Sorry, go on.'*

I moved on to finding them in Mrs Balasana's garden,
getting them out, and then meeting her in the lane. He
listened carefully, and I had to repeat that, too.

At the end, he said nothing for a very long time.

I said, 'Well?'

He sighed. *'Jenny, you're an idiot.'*

I hadn't expected that. I never thought that Thomas, of
all people, would say … I stepped back, hurt beyond
words. 'Thomas, why did you say that?'

*'So that when Russell tells you the same thing you
won't burst into tears.'*

I hung my head. 'I … see.'

'No, you don't.'

I said angrily, 'This isn't a joke.'

'No, and it isn't a tragedy either, Jenny.'

'You said I was an idiot.'

*'Listen to what you told me, Jenny. Actually listen to
what you said.'*

'About what?'

'About the gate.'

'I told you. I left it open.'

'Not that gate. The other one. Mrs Balasana's gate.

101

Close your eyes and picture it. You've just seen them. You have to get them out of the garden before Mrs Balasana comes back. What do you do?'

I closed my eyes. 'I unlatched the gate.'

'That's not quite what you said before.'

'Oh. Sorry. I struggled with the latch on the gate. It's stiff and new and I couldn't get it open. I had to wiggle it a bit.'

'Yes?'

'Yes what?'

'Jenny, you've just told me. You struggled to open the gate. Which was closed. And latched. And the latch was stiff. Now picture Boxer and Marilyn. Which one of those two geniuses do you think unlatched the gate, marched into the garden, and closed and fastened it again after them?'

I stared at him. 'Well, neither of them, obviously. Oh.'

'Exactly.'

'But that doesn't mean I didn't leave *our* gate open.'

'Jenny, either I can hear a talking earthquake coming down the landing or Russell Checkland is on his way. I suspect the latter, although you never know at Frogmorton. You will tell him what you told me. You will listen very carefully to what he says and yes, he will tell you you're an idiot, my funny little Jenny, because that's exactly what you have been.'

He faded away, leaving me alone in the middle of the room and before I had chance even to draw breath, Russell bounced in.

'What are you doing in here in the dark?'

'Joy's got a bit of a … snuffle. I was just…'

'No, you weren't.' He seized my wrist and pulled me out of Joy's room, into ours and dropped me onto the bed.

'Now. What's the matter? Out with it.'

'There's nothing…'

'Yes, there is. Ever since yesterday you've been walking around looking as if you've been hit by a combine harvester. What's happened?'

I remembered Thomas saying, *'You will tell him everything you told me.'*

I took a very deep, very wobbly breath. 'Russell, there's … something I … must tell you.'

Restless as usual, he began to wander around our room, picking things up and putting them back in the wrong place. I hastened to rescue my precious bottle of perfume. After Joy was born, Russell bought me a bottle of Joy, the perfume. I thought it was a lovely gift, until he told me he could have bought Frogmorton twice over with what it cost. Now, I only wore it on special occasions because it was obviously going to have to last me the rest of my life.

Finally, having disarranged everything to his satisfaction, he plumped himself down beside me. 'Go on then.'

Start with the bad news. With luck, he'd be so furious I wouldn't get the chance to say anything else. I turned to face him.

'I left the … gate open.'

'No, you didn't.'

Oh for God's sake! Not again!

'I did.'

'You didn't. You can't have.'

'Russell, I'm … telling you that I did. I know you always … try to shield me, but…'

'You didn't leave the gate open. No one ever leaves the gate open.'

'Well, I … managed it,' I said angrily, because I was confessing here and he just wasn't taking me seriously.

'No, you didn't.'

I refused to be dragged into pantomime mode again.

'Why can't I have?'

'Seriously? How long have you lived here?'

I stared at him. 'What has that ... to do with anything?'

'Come with me.'

He grabbed my wrist again and the next moment I was being towed from the room. We both of us nearly fell down the three little steps outside the bedroom. He did slow down for the stairs, but only marginally, because this was Russell, and he doesn't do slow. We raced through the darkened sitting room, through the kitchen and out into the mudroom, where he grabbed two wellingtons, apparently at random, stuffed me into them, and draped a smelly old coat around my shoulders. Seizing a torch, he whirled us out into the rain.

There was a hiss and a curse as Russell and the cat encountered each other in the dark, and then all the outdoor lights clicked on as we hurtled across the yard. I could see the rain sleeting down. I pulled the coat around me and shivered.

We halted at the gate to Boxer's field.

'Right,' he said, switching on the torch. 'Open the gate.'

'Russell...'

'Quickly, Jenny, before Mrs Crisp comes out to find out what's going on and accuses me of trying to give you pneumonia.'

Too cold, wet and crushed to argue, I unlatched the gate and pushed it open.

'Right open.'

Sighing, I pushed hard and it swung fully open.

He shone the torch and we both stared at the gate and the rain. For two or three seconds, nothing happened. I could hear the rain pattering into the hedgerow and then, slowly, the gate began to swing back again. I watched in amazement because, not only did it swing closed, but the weight caused the latch to engage as well.

'Do it again.'

The rain forgotten, I did it again, my head spinning with relief as, once again, the heavy gate thunked into place and the latch caught.

'Don't you see, Jenny, you couldn't have left the gate open. It's not possible. It shuts itself. It has those special hinges that do it automatically. Andrew and I fixed them years ago. When I first got Boxer. Andrew said if he ever got out we'd have a catastrophe on our hands. And given how dim he is – Boxer, I mean, not Andrew – it made sense to have a gate that's smarter than he is. And so I have.'

I still couldn't believe it. I think I must have been light-headed or something because I couldn't stop. I couldn't help it. I unlatched the gate, pushed it open, and watched in delighted disbelief as it swung shut. I did it again. And again, laughing my silly head off. Russell laughed and applauded as well, and then we spent a few minutes jumping up and down in the puddles until the back door opened and Mrs Crisp, brandishing a sweeping brush in one hand and a torch in the other shouted, 'Who's there? Be off with you. I've called the police.'

'It's me,' shouted Russell, as if that was any sort of reassurance. 'Don't panic.'

'Russell? What are you *doing*?'

'Teaching Jenny how to close a gate.'

'It's midnight.'

'I don't think that matters very much, Mrs Crisp. It's the same technique no matter what time of day or night.'

'It's pouring with rain.'

'Still doesn't matter.'

Further up the lane, one of Martin Braithwaite's dogs began to bark.

'We'd better go inside,' he said, 'or Mrs Balaclava will be complaining about us again, although frankly, as a respectable householder, I see no reason why I shouldn't open and close my own gates whenever I please. Come along, Jenny. Don't stand around or you'll get soaked.'

I was too delighted to care.

Back in our bedroom, I towelled my hair dry and tried to get into bed. Russell wasn't having any of it.

'Three years you've lived here, Jenny. How could you not have noticed how the gate works?'

I looked up in surprise. 'Are you ... saying I'm stupid?'

'Yes, I am.'

I stood, stricken. Yes, I know Thomas had warned me, but it's another matter to hear the words actually spoken.

He carried on. 'And before you get all bent out of shape, there's a big difference in accepting that you've never noticed how the gate works – which given that you're in and out every day is almost beyond belief – and automatically assuming everything is your fault because you're too stupid to do anything properly. Surely you can see that?' He picked up speed. 'Three years we've been together, Jenny, and you couldn't talk to me about it? We said – we agreed – that if something was wrong then you'd tell me. You wouldn't make me guess. And all this time I've been thinking all sorts of dreadful things. I half expected to find you were considering running off with Andrew.'

I couldn't help a choke of laughter.

'That's better,' he said. 'Jenny, you really are a nit-wit sometimes, and I'm saying that to your face so that once again, you can distinguish between me telling you when you've done something a bit daft and you going back to thinking you have no worth. Please tell me you can see the difference.'

I nodded. 'I...' and couldn't go on.

He grinned. 'It's always the same with you, isn't it? Always the promising start and then a complete failure to follow through. You ... what?'

Oddly enough, while kindness might have undone me completely, Russell's in your face technique of direct honesty, abuse, and humour was making me feel better with every passing second. Yes, he was calling me dumb – and I could see now that I had been – but being Russell, he would say it to my face. Dragging everything out of the self-esteem curdling dark in which I'd been living, and pitching it into the bright light of day. Well, the bright light of midnight actually, but I knew what I meant.

'It was ... guilt, Russell. You married ... me – yes, I know, for my money,' I added hastily before he thought I was becoming maudlin and sentimental, something he hated, 'but you ... kept me on after you discovered I didn't have any and you ... gave me a home and everything and ... look how I repaid you and...'

I never got any further. He started across the room towards me, stumbled over one of his stupid shoes, cursed, and kicked it under the wardrobe. I sighed, knowing who would have to fish it out with a coat hanger tomorrow morning.

'I thought we were over all this, Jenny. You must understand that you bring me more – much more – than just money. Why can't you see that?'

'But...'

'No. Be quiet,' he said, drawing himself up and pushing his hair out of his eyes. 'Listen to me. I am your husband and the head of this household. My word is law – or it certainly should be – and I'm telling you now: no more of this nonsense, or you'll find yourself incurring my extreme displeasure. As my wife, it is your duty to carry out my every command. I specifically remember

107

you promising to do so on our wedding day.'

I opened my mouth to tell him he was too drunk to remember anything of our wedding day, and then thought better of it.

Not that I would have had the chance anyway. He was rushing on. 'I thought I had made it quite clear at the time, Jenny – your main duty as my wife is to smile, nod, and agree with everything I say. Oh, and attend to my every need of course. *Not* to race around beating yourself up over something that didn't happen, and even if it had, which it didn't, then I wouldn't have blamed you for the consequences, because there weren't any for me to blame you for. Which I wouldn't have.'

He paused to run through his last paragraph and presumably found it wanting because he said softly, 'Jenny, you're an idiot.'

I nodded. 'I know. I'm sorry.'

'So you should be.' He regarded me with extreme severity. 'Whatever are you wearing?'

'They're pyjamas. I was just going to … bed when you dragged me out into the rain.'

'They're hideous. Take them off.'

'But…'

He sighed. 'Do I really have to go through the whole wifely obedience thing again? At this time of night?'

He undid the top two buttons and slid his hand inside. 'What did I say about arguing with me?' His hand was very warm and very gentle.

I shivered. 'I'm striking a … blow for wifely independence.'

He eased down my top, exposing my shoulder. He bent and kissed it. I shivered again.

'How's that working out for you?'

'I'm reasonably … optimistic,' I said, trying to ignore what his other hand was doing.

108

'Are you? Even when I do this?'

'Yes. Still hanging in … there.'

'Or this?'

'Meh.'

'All right. How about this?'

My knees sagged.

He laughed and after a moment, so did I.

'God, I'm good,' he said complacently.

I snorted. 'You are as soft as putty in … my hands.'

'Good grief, I hope not. Well, not for the next thirty minutes anyway. Turn out the light, will you.'

CHAPTER EIGHT

The next morning was lovely. And, in my case, guilt free. Everything was fresh and clean after the overnight rain. Little fluffy clouds bounced around a blue, rain-washed sky. Brilliant sunlight reflected off the droplets lying on the grass and caught in the hedges. The effect was dazzling. I felt my heart lift. The world was wonderful again. And Thomas was back.

Things were good downstairs as well. Russell had taken Boxer out for an early morning ride, so we had a peaceful, although still egg-free, breakfast. Joy's snuffles had disappeared. Well, to be honest, they hadn't been that serious in the first place.

When she'd finished eating, I stuffed Joy into her stroller and took her out into the walled garden. The air was warm and damp and still. We walked slowly along the paths, looking at the flowers lifting their heads after the rain. Everything was quiet and peaceful. Thomas was waiting for me by the fountain, staring down into the water. About a year ago, Russell had plonked in half a dozen tiny goldfish, warned them sternly of the consequences of misbehaviour, and left them to get on with it. They were repaying him by doubling in size every month or so and now swam slowly to and fro, fat and lazy. They were the quietest things at Frogmorton and I was grateful.

I parked Joy where she could see what was going on and opened my mouth to tell Thomas he had been right about everything, but he spoke first.

'Do you remember the day we discovered this?'

I did. The garden had been a wilderness and Kevin and I, both seeking a purpose in life and without the slightest idea of what we were doing, had armed ourselves with vicious gardening implements and the boundless enthusiasm of ignorance, and waded in. We'd pruned the climbing roses according to instructions downloaded from the internet and, miraculously, they'd thrived. Which was more than we had done on that first day, returning to the house dirty, scratched and bleeding. There had been a bit of a row about that. But, inch by inch, with frequent references to gardening books, we'd cleared the garden and, right in the centre, we'd discovered this old stone pool with a statue of one of those hussies whose clothes are always falling off. She stood on a mossy plinth in the centre of the basin, pouring a trickle of water into the pool. According to Russell, her bosom had formed an important part of his education, at least until he'd discovered real girls, after which, again according to Russell, he'd never looked back.

There were two hens scrabbling away under the ceanothus. They shouldn't be there, but I really couldn't be bothered to do anything about them. The morning was too lovely for the squawking complaints that would ensue should I try to remove them.

'Everything all right,' asked Thomas. *'Not that I don't know the answer to that one.'*

'Don't you ever get tired of being right?'

He considered that, head on one side, looking at his reflection in the water. *'No.'*

I laughed and so did Joy, waving her arms in excitement.

'Thomas, can she see you?'

'She's her mother's daughter. Of course she can see me. For a little while, anyway. Until the day her rational mind tells her that giant invisible golden horses are

112

impossible, and then I'll fade away to just a memory.'

'That's very ... sad.'

'But also very inevitable.' He shook himself. *'Now then, Jenny, how are you this morning?'*

I nodded. 'Relieved.'

'But still an idiot.'

'Oh, for heaven's sake. Now what am I missing?'

'Don't start getting agitated again – it's understandable that you're too relieved to have taken it all in yet, but you need to ask yourself some questions. If you didn't leave the gate open, then how did they get out?'

I hadn't given that a moment's thought. 'You mean someone deliberately ... but who would do that?'

'The same person who let them in, of course.'

'What? In where?'

'Into Mrs Balasana's, Jenny. You said yourself, you struggled with the latch. It was stiff. You had to work at it to open the gate. And while I strongly suspect that Marilyn is very bright, even for a donkey, she didn't lead Boxer up the lane to Mrs Balasana's, open the gate, usher him inside, close it and latch it behind them, now, did she?'

'You're saying that someone let them out, took them up the lane and shoved them into Pear Tree Cottage? Why? For a joke?'

'More than a joke, I think.'

He was watching me carefully, but I already knew the answer. I couldn't believe I'd been so dense.

'Christopher?'

'Of course it was, Jenny. He took them from their field. Well, he took Marilyn. Probably all he had to do was brandish something edible. She followed him, and Boxer followed her. You told me you'd seen him outside Sharon's shop.'

113

'Yes, but I'd convinced myself I'd imagined it. And I might have. I only saw him for a second. And surely they'd never go off with Christopher? Of all people?'

'This is Marilyn. She'd go anywhere for food. Even with Christopher.'

I nodded. Sad but true. Contrary to popular belief, animals have no discrimination. It's a myth that they instinctively know who's good and who's bad. Look at Bill Sikes and Bull's Eye. Anyone approaching Marilyn with a packet of Jammy Dodgers would find themselves wearing an affectionate donkey who would consider them best friends for life. Christopher had sussed out Mrs Balasana when he'd called on her, pretending to be looking for me. And then having lured them up the lane, he'd simply shunted them into her front garden, shut the gate and strolled away.

'But why?'

'I suspect nothing more than a desire to make trouble for you. And it worked, Jenny. Look at the state you got yourself into.'

'And to let me know he's here.'

'And that. You should talk to Russell.'

'Perhaps I should, but he has enough on at the moment. Especially with this exhibition. I will tell him, but I'll wait until I have something definite to tell him. Besides,' I said, with the memory of my unfounded panic over leaving the gate open still fresh in my mind – something I could surely have sorted out myself if I'd only taken a moment to stop beating myself up and think properly – 'I can't keep running to Russell with every little thing.'

Thomas looked at me through his forelock. I knew that look.

'I will talk to him, Thomas, I promise, but you yourself once told me that I was all grown up now. And I am. We

114

don't have anything concrete. We have no proof. Let's wait and see what happens next.'

'*Jenny, I don't know…*'

'Well that's just it, isn't it? We don't actually know anything. A few days ago, I saw someone whom I thought *might* be Christopher. Someone put Boxer and Marilyn into Mrs Balasana's garden, presumably in the hope of making trouble, and that someone *might* be Christopher, but that's all we do know.'

He might have said more, but at that moment I heard the clip-clop of Boxer's hooves in the yard and Marilyn trumpeting a welcome to the lost travellers in her usual enthusiastic manner. Boxer neighed a response. The ladies squawked in outrage and alarm. Joy squealed and clapped her hands.

'*Russell's back,*' said Thomas, unnecessarily.

Russell was turning Boxer out into his field. Marilyn bustled forwards, half of her attention on scolding Boxer for something or other, and the other half on Russell – the man who could always produce a carrot.

'Ah, there you are,' he said, fending her off. 'Will you pack it in? No, not you, Jenny. You've had one, now push off. No, not you, Jenny, I've got something to tell you. Give over, will you?'

Eventually tiring of a small donkey trying to shove her nose into his pockets – she's not fussy where she nibbles and it makes him nervous – he picked her up off the ground and carried her into the field. I closed the gate as he came out, giving it a little shake, just to check the latch had caught.

We leaned on the gate and watched Marilyn fussing around Boxer. Rather like a small tug trying to get an ocean-going liner into a small parking space.

'Another one,' said Russell, gloomily, turning away

towards the house. 'My heart goes out to him.'

I had no idea what he was talking about. 'Another … one what?'

He sighed deeply. A man in torment. 'Another one labouring under the yoke of female oppression, of course.'

I stared at him in disbelief. 'How can you say that?'

'Well,' he said, kicking off his boots in the mudroom and entering the kitchen. 'Look at the facts. There's you – female; Joy – female; Mrs Crisp – female; Sharon – female; six hens – all female; and me – not female. How is that not oppression?'

'You have…' I counted things on my fingers '…at least ten females all poised to cater to your every whim and you're complaining?'

'What whim? When does anyone around here ever pay any heed to my needs?' he said, accepting a cup of tea and slice of cake from Mrs Crisp.

'And you're not alone … Boxer's a boy. And the cat. Well, a former … boy.'

'You're not making your case for Team Boy here.'

'What did you want to … tell me?' I said, before he began to feel too sorry for himself.

'Ah, yes. Any chance of another slice of … Oh, thanks very much, Mrs Crisp. Yes. Good news, Jenny. I've got that exhibition space in London. I don't have the details yet, but they might take five, possibly six pieces.'

'Do you have so many?'

'Four definitely and another one nearly completed so, yes. Just for once I'm ahead of the game.'

'Russell, that's wonderful news. I'm so pleased for you. Mrs Crisp, did you hear?'

'I did,' she said, trying to take his plate off him. 'And it won't take you long to bang out the sixth, either. Especially if you get out of my kitchen and make a start now. Slosh a few paints on a bit of canvas and you could

116

be finished by lunchtime.'

'There's slightly more to it than that,' said the artist indignantly, struggling to reclaim his plate.

'That's as maybe,' she said, gaining possession at last, 'but it was the getting out of my kitchen part that I wanted you to pay particular attention to.'

'I have to go into Rushford to have a word at Swallows,' he said. Swallows was our local art gallery. 'It was Elliott Swallow who recommended me, and the London man is there today. It's a chance to meet him.' He picked up his car keys. 'Want to come too?'

'Love to,' I said.

'Especially after you've had a shower, changed your clothes, and combed your hair,' said Mrs Crisp to Russell, taking his car keys back off him.

'Can I refer both of you to my previous comments on female oppression?'

We clattered into Rushford. I was instructed to look for a parking space. It was market day and the place was heaving, so I wasn't optimistic. I looked left. Thomas was supposed to look right but soon became distracted by all the window displays. He's such a shopping victim sometimes.

'So tell me all about the exhibition.'

'It's not just me exhibiting,' said Russell. 'In fact, it wouldn't be me at all if someone hadn't had to drop out. I'm afraid it's going to take me a while to work my way up to a solo exhibition again.'

'That doesn't matter. Once they see your stuff, they'll be offering you wall space all over London.'

'Well, it doesn't work quite like that, but thank you anyway, Jenny.'

He swerved into an unexpected parking space. There was the usual amount of hooting. I found the parking disc under the seat and set the correct time.

'What are you doing?'

'Ensuring you don't get yet another ticket. What time is it?'

'Eleven thirty.'

He set it for twelve o'clock.

'Russell!'

'No one will ever know and it gets us another half hour. Come on.'

Slamming the door shut, he strode along the pavement. I trotted beside him. And no, he never bothers to lock his car. And no, no one ever bothers to steal it.

The first person we met was little Charlie Kessler. Charlie goes to the special school on the other side of Rushford. He and Marilyn had starred together in our Nativity play last Christmas. Obviously there had been a Baby Jesus and a Virgin Mary and all the other traditional players, but it was Marilyn the Donkey and Charlie, the Star of the East, who had stolen the show. With additional credit to an unscheduled appearance by a new-born lamb half way through the first act. It had been quite an afternoon.

I hadn't seen Charlie since, but there was no doubt he remembered us. We own a small, omnivorous donkey. Everyone remembers us.

'Hello Mr Checkland,' said Charlie, placing himself squarely in Russell's path and tugging at Russell's jeans, just in case he hadn't noticed him.

Russell screeched to a halt and I bumped into him.

'Hey, Charlie. How're you?'

'I've got a beetle.'

'That's fantastic. Can I see?'

Charlie began to rummage in his pockets. Quite a lengthy process. Russell is frequently oblivious to the passage of time and stood surprisingly patiently until

Charlie eventually found a matchbox in his shabby jacket.

I glanced over the road at Swallows. 'We'll be late,' I said to Thomas. 'And this is his big opportunity.'

'And this is Charlie's opportunity to show Russell his beetle,' said Thomas, gently.

He was right, of course, but I couldn't help worrying on Russell's behalf. I tried twice, saying, 'Russell…' and each time he grinned at me and said, 'Won't be a minute, Jenny. Charlie's showing me his beetle,' so I gave it up and thought about how much I loved him instead.

Charlie's mum appeared from the newsagent's, harassed and overburdened with shopping. Hers was a large family and she doesn't always have the time for all of Charlie's needs. I abandoned all thought of getting Russell to his appointment on time, and indicated I could keep an eye on the pair of them if she had more to do. She nodded, mouthed 'Two minutes,' and disappeared into Boots.

The two of them were examining Charlie's beetle, currently housed in the matchbox with a leaf and a small twig for company.

'An excellent beetle,' pronounced Russell, carefully closing the box. 'If I'm not mistaken, that's a rare specimen of the Rareificus Beetleicus species. Well done, Charlie.'

'His name's Jim.'

'An excellent name for an excellent beetle. Do you have a home for him?'

Charlie nodded. 'In my box.'

'That's good,' said Russell, 'but this is the Rareificus Beetleicus. Did you know they're famed for their guarding instincts?'

Oh God, this was going to be the Patagonian Attack Chickens all over again.

Russell was forging on. 'You should let him live in

your garden, Charlie, and then you'll never have any trouble with aliens, burglars and local government officials as long as you live.'

'Cool,' said Charlie. 'We've got a tree. He can live there.'

'Good idea. The Rareificus Beetleicus loves trees. Well, we have to…'

'Can I come and see Marilyn?'

'Of course, but only if your mum says it's OK.'

'But I want to come now.'

'Sorry, Charlie, I have to go somewhere today.'

Charlie's face fell with disappointment and you'd have to be a lot tougher than Russell is to walk away and leave him standing alone on the pavement.

He smiled. 'I tell you what I'll do – I'll draw you a picture of Marilyn which you can take away with you and put on your bedroom wall, and when I get home, I'll draw her a picture of you for her to look at. So she doesn't forget you.'

His face shone. 'OK.'

The two of them sat down on the pavement there and then. It was market day. Rushford was packed. The market is just behind the high street and I could hear the sounds of animals, men shouting and horseboxes reversing. People on their way to somewhere else streamed all around them. Russell pulled out his notebook and began a quick drawing of Marilyn. Charlie watched, entranced.

'I want to be a drawing man when I grow up.'

I looked up and down the high street. It was quite possible that Charlie was slightly the more responsible of the two of them, but people knew them both. They'd be fine on their own for a while.

'Go,' said Thomas, amused. *'I'll keep an eye on them.'*

I slipped into the newsagent's and bought a big

120

colouring book and a jumbo pack of colouring crayons.

They were exactly where I'd left them, Russell was putting the finishing touches to his sketch and Charlie was practically sitting on his lap, breathing heavily in excitement.

'Can I be a drawing man one day?'

'You can,' I said, handing him his book and crayons.

He was nearly speechless with delight.

'A new colouring book and a beetle,' said Thomas. *'It must be his lucky day.'* He paused and then said quietly, *'You have a good man there, Jenny.'*

'I know,' I said proudly. Because I did. He could keep ten million chickens in the bath if he wanted to, so long as he found time to sit on the pavement with Charlie Kessler and draw him a donkey.

We were nearly twenty minutes late arriving at the gallery. Elderly and silver-haired Elliott Swallow was waiting for us, together with a man who, at first glance, looked to be half the size of Yorkshire. This was the London gallery owner, Jeremy Law. I know no one should judge by appearances, but while Elliott was everyone's idea of what a gallery owner should look like, this man looked like a cross between Ben Nevis and an angry butcher.

Having begun badly by being late, we made things worse. Mr Law did not seem best pleased at being kept waiting. And we had no excuse. The gallery was directly opposite so neither of them could have failed to see their noon appointment sitting on the pavement drawing donkeys.

Jeremy Law looked pointedly at his watch. Russell looked pointedly at the ceiling. This wasn't going to go well.

'Shall we begin?' said Elliot. 'Because Jeremy can't

stay long. He has another appointment at one.'

'Well, I'm sure he can stay long enough to meet Jenny, my wife,' said Russell, smiling that special smile he always used to keep for Aunt Julia.

I turned to Mr Law, dark against the shop window and, conscious of how important this was, made a complete hash of it.

'How … do … you … do?'

He stared at me. 'Bloody 'ell. We could be here all day.'

Russell was there in an instant. 'Please address any and all offensive language to me, Mr Law.'

Things went very quiet. I could hear the sounds of everyday life on the other side of the window but in here things were very quiet indeed. Everyone stared at everyone else.

'Wow,' said Thomas. *'It's like the gunfight at the O.K. Corral, isn't it? I think this one's up to you to save, Jenny.'*

I was already taking a deep breath and focussing on the texture of Russell's jacket, but I didn't get the chance.

'As you can hear, my wife sometimes has a little difficulty,' said Russell, gently. 'Obviously we who know and love her don't have a problem with it at all. I'm sorry if dealing with it is an insurmountable hurdle for you, but since I've taken an instant dislike to you that's not going to be a problem for either of us, is it? Come on Jenny, what do you say we go and see if Charlie wants to come and visit Marilyn this afternoon?'

He was already heading towards the door and picking up speed. I couldn't let him throw away his big chance. I put out my hand and said, 'Goodbye … Mr … Law. I'm … sorry you …won't get a … chance to show Russell's … work. He … really is … rather … good, you know.'

He took my hand in his massive paw. His grip was surprisingly soft and gentle. I suspected he'd had to train himself not to break people's fingers accidentally.

'Now then, lass. No need to take the hump. Nor that touchy young fellow of yours neither.'

Russell turned reluctantly, hair falling over his forehead, jeans still dusty from the pavement and with a smudge of something on his collar.

Still holding my hand, Mr Law said, 'So tell me about this husband of yours then.'

'Well,' I said, 'his work is wonderful and...'

'No, not his bloody paintings. Tell me about him.'

'Um,' I said, wondering what on earth to say. 'Um ... well ... he um...'

Russell folded his arms. 'Well, go on then, Jenny, what am I like?'

I turned to Mr Law. 'He ... never picks up his ... shoes. He rescued our ... donkey and ... saved me from ... her owner. He can't ... be trusted in ... the pub by himself. He named one of ... our chickens after his ... ex-girlfriend. He saved our ... horses in a ... fire. He shouts ... all the time. He ... told our ... neighbour we had ... Patagonian ... Attack Chickens. He eats ... everything in ... sight. He hides ... pizza boxes in ... his studio. He keeps ... chickens in the ... bath. He's teaching ... our daughter her colours ... by showing her cans ... of lager. He...' I stopped, exhausted.

'Bloody hell, Jenny,' said Russell, stunned, although whether by my eloquence or this catalogue of his supposed attributes, I wasn't sure.

Mr Law shouted, 'Language!' and gave a great shout of laughter.

'Well done, Jenny. That was perfect. I'll leave you to it now,' said Thomas, wandering off to look at the artwork, because apart from fancying himself as a bit of a

connoisseur, he's very nosey. On the night of our engagement, Russell took me to a restaurant and Thomas spent the entire evening inspecting the wallpaper and commenting on everyone else's meal choices. If you take him to one of those big out-of-town stores, you've lost him for an hour or so.

Anyway, Swallows gallery specialised in colourful abstracts, very like the stuff Russell was producing at the moment. In fact, I spotted two of Russell's on display.

Thomas inspected every one closely, his head tilted to one side and his tail swishing gently. Always a sign of deep thought in a horse, he says. The occasional phrase drifted over.

'I like the brushwork on this one – lots of energy.' And a moment later, *'Good grief – I'm surprised this one doesn't leap off the wall and try to eat us all. And look at this one. What was the artist thinking?'*

I tried to close my ears and concentrate on what was going on.

Jeremy Law didn't hang around. 'I've seen the images you sent. I'd like five pieces – perhaps six. Call it six. How soon could you meet me in London?'

'Whenever you like,' said Russell, matching him in briskness, pulling out his phone and checking his calendar. 'Is tomorrow OK for you?'

Elliott rolled his eyes. I wondered if perhaps there was some sort of ritual to be observed first. The artist should play hard to get. Or argue about the number of pieces required. Or the terms of payment. Whatever. Russell doesn't do that. It's not that he can't negotiate – you should have seen him sort out my Aunt Julia when we broke the news of our engagement – he just doesn't see the point. Jeremy Law apparently wanted Russell's stuff. Russell wanted to give it to him. Where was the problem?

'I'd like to check out the space and sort out hanging

details while I'm there.'

'Aye, I'll introduce you to my manager.' He stared challengingly at Russell. 'Don't suppose you have your bio written?'

Russell tapped at his phone. 'I've just emailed it to Elliott.'

'Arriving morning or afternoon?'

'I'll come up on the train so late morning.'

'We'll talk money then. Anything else?'

'No,' said Russell, not to be outdone on brusqueness. 'I'll see you tomorrow. Ready Jenny? I'll buy you lunch on the strength of my future sales.'

'In that case, I'll order the … most expensive thing on the … menu.

'We're going to McDonald's.'

'Oh good,' said Thomas, who loves McDonald's.

'Well,' said Russell briskly, once we were on the pavement outside. 'That didn't go quite according to plan, but we got there in the end.' He looked down at me. 'You did really well, Jenny.'

'And your show… will go equally well. You'll be a huge … success.'

'You don't know that. I might not sell anything.'

'You will. I … know it.'

He smiled sadly. 'Don't you sometimes think your boundless faith in me is a little blind?'

I gave serious consideration to the question and shook my head. 'No, I don't think so.'

He turned suddenly to stare at a row of wheelie bins.

I was just about to ask what was wrong now, when he spun back again, caught me in a bone-crushing hug and buried his face in my hair.

'Jenny, you're a good person. When I'm with you, I'm a good person too. Never leave me.'

'I … never will,' I said, somewhat muffled because my

125

face was being crushed into his jacket, but he seemed happy with the response. He dropped a brief kiss into my hair, cleared his throat, and said, 'Really Jenny, can you tidy yourself up a little bit, please. You look like a bird's nest. Not a good look for the wife of a famous painter.'

I smiled up at him.

He grinned back. 'Come on. Let's have lunch.'

That night, Thomas said, *'You should tell him, Jenny.'*

I nodded. 'Yes, I should. But if I say something now then he might not go to London tomorrow. You know what he's like. He'll insist on staying here and this exhibition is so important to him. I'm perfectly capable of looking after myself for a day or so.'

He made a snorting noise.

'Language,' I said, channelling Russell. 'There are young children in this house and as a responsible parent…'

'Jenny…'

'I have you, Thomas. And Kevin. And Mrs Crisp. I could probably even have Bill the Insurance Man if I asked politely. It's not like before. When I was on my own.'

'Jenny…'

'And then I'll tell him when he gets back. When he has time to listen properly.'

'And when Francesca's not on the phone to him every five minutes.'

'That too.'

Russell made a real effort. We all did, and when he left the house the next morning, his hair was under control, his tie was straight, and his shirt was clean. I knew that by the time he arrived in London his hair would be flopping over his eyes again and his tie would be in his pocket but, as I said to him, at least he left the house looking beautiful.

He laughed, kissed me, kissed Joy, had a tea towel flapped at him by Mrs Crisp, and roared out of the yard.

The usual sudden silence fell and I was, once again, conscious of the absence of Russell Checkland.

Mrs Crisp began to clear the breakfast table and I took Joy into the garden to play. There wouldn't be many more days like this, this year. There would be a big storm one night – the wind would whip the leaves from the trees and the rain would beat down the remaining flowers – and suddenly we'd be into autumn.

I sat on the bench by the pool, listening to the trickling water. Joy rolled on a blanket at my feet, alternately talking to her feet or trying to put everything within reach into her mouth. The sun was warm and everything was peaceful.

But not for long. I opened my eyes to find Mrs Crisp standing in front of me.

'Mrs Balasana is here.'

I groaned. 'Has she brought the bill for the damage to her garden?'

'I don't think so. I think this might be a social call.'

Oh my God – I'd issued the usual vague sort of invitation and obviously she'd decided to take me up on it.

'Come along Jenny. Be polite.'

'I don't see why I should. Russell never is and he gets away with it every time.'

'You're not Russell.'

'No,' I said drearily. 'I'm not, am I?'

'Shall I show her into the sitting room?' said Mrs Crisp.

'Yes,' said Thomas.

'Why?'

'Well, I haven't met her yet. She sounds interesting.'

127

'She's not interesting. She's bossy and she complains a lot and she never seems to get dirty and...'

'*And?*'

'And I don't think she's very happy.'

'Mrs Checkland?'

'Oh, sorry Mrs Crisp. I was miles away. No, don't let's ... make her too comfortable. Keep her in the kitchen. She'll either scorn us or take ... pity on us, but either way, she won't want to linger.'

Believe it or not, it was Russell who was responsible for breaking the ice with Mrs Balasana. And he wasn't even here. In fact, I did wonder if she'd deliberately taken advantage of his absence. Anyway, whatever the reason, she was here and I had to deal with her.

Shooing away two or three opportunistic chickens, I edged my way in through the back door and we sat at the kitchen table. Mrs Crisp served tea and then, despite all my frantic gesturing, made herself scarce. I glared at her as she went.

I poured the tea – we did the sugar and milk thing – and then we sat in silence. I kept waiting for her to produce her bill – surely the reason for her being here – but she sat quietly at the table, sipping her tea. Mrs Crisp, who likes to observe the social niceties, had used the good cups, thank heavens. I really couldn't picture Mrs Balasana drinking from Russell's 'This is what AWESOMENESS looks like' mug. Mrs Crisp's social obligations had not, however, extended to offering her cake. The biscuit tin sat between us. I know we hadn't long had breakfast, but to break the silence and to give myself something to do, I whipped off the lid and offered it to her.

'Please help yourself.'

The silence went on for far too long.

Thomas craned over her shoulder, uttered an enormous

snort, said, *'Jenny, I'm sorry, but you're really on your own for this one,'* and disappeared to the far end of the kitchen.

'Thomas?'

'Only at Frogmorton...'

What was going on?

I've never visited a taxidermist, but now I know how someone would look if they were stuffed. Rigid and with those funny glassy eyes that never look real. I wondered if she was having some kind of fit.

'Mrs Balasana, are you all … right? Are you ill?'

I got to my feet, scraping my chair across the tiles.

Mrs Crisp stuck her head around the door. 'Everything all right, Mrs Checkland?'

Thomas was still at the other end of the room, laughing his head off and being absolutely no use whatsoever.

'I don't know,' I said. 'Mrs Balasana…?'

Mrs Crisp bustled forwards, picked up the biscuit tin – presumably to remove it – glanced inside and herself went rigid.

Oh, great. Another one.

Silently, she handed me the biscuit tin. It was full of mealworms. Fat, wriggly, happy mealworms. Hundreds of them. Wriggly things don't particularly bother me, but you don't expect to find them in your biscuit tin on the kitchen table. I couldn't even guess at the effect they'd had on Mrs Balasana at eleven o'clock in the morning.

'Is there a good time to discover mealworms in your biscuit tin?' enquired Thomas, thoroughly enjoying himself.

I slapped the lid back on again and shoved the tin under the table.

Mrs Crisp exploded. 'Russell! That boy! I tell you now, Mrs Checkland, I…' Words failed her. She drew a deep breath and began to scrabble in her apron.

'What are you … doing?'

'My phone.' She pulled it out. 'I'm going to telephone him now and tell him…'

I took it from her. 'Leave this to me.' I found his number. Surprisingly, he picked up. *'Maybe he thinks you're Francesca,'* said a wicked voice from the other end of the kitchen. With whom I would be having words later on.

I didn't give him a chance to speak. 'Russell. It's me.' I thought of the seething mass of mealworms currently under the kitchen table and said chattily, 'We've just offered Mrs Balasana a biscuit. I don't think I need say any more. You should run. Run for your life. Mrs Crisp wants a word with you. Mrs Balasana wants a word with you. And when they've finished, I want far more than a word with you. So run. Run to the end of the world. And then keep going. And hope we never ever find you.'

I snapped the phone shut, feeling rather pleased with myself.

'Well done,' said Mrs Crisp.

I smirked. 'You noticed?'

'I did indeed,' she said. 'Not a stammer in sight.'

I looked down at the tin. Maybe we could market mealworms as the latest thing in speech aids.

A faint sound recalled us to our visitor.

'Oh, Mrs Balasana, I'm so … sorry. Please believe we had … no idea…'

She had her hands over her face and was rocking backwards and forwards, which I thought was a little excessive. They were mealworms, not giant scorpions.

'I know,' said Thomas. *'And it's not as if they leaped from the tin to eat her eyes or crawl up her nose or anything.'*

'You,' I said, 'are not helping. Go and stand by the window again while I try to think of an unconvincing

130

explanation.'

'Jenny, I'm always telling you. You shouldn't panic until you actually have something to panic about. Look.'

I did look. It was a miracle. She was laughing.

'Well,' said Mrs Crisp to me. 'I'll go to the foot of our stairs.'

'And you can go with her,' I said to Thomas, who was laughing himself.

No, Jenny, really, this is a blessing. She's laughing. Who'd have thought? And all thanks to Russell.'

'Do not tell him that.'

'Wouldn't dream of it.'

We settled down. Mrs Crisp poured herself a cup of tea. I sat back and tentatively smiled at our guest.

'It's nice to see you again, Mrs Balasana. Sorry about the … biscuits. I think we might have some Hobnobs somewhere …

She shook her head. 'Not for me, thank you.' She paused delicately. 'May I enquire…?'

'Russell,' I said bitterly, and she nodded her complete comprehension.

'He's breeding mealworms. They're very good for chickens. I think, somehow, he's got his biscuit tins muddled up.'

This was the polite explanation. It was all too likely that Russell wouldn't have any problems at all with keeping mealworms in the pantry. I could hear him explaining that it was all food anyway and demanding to know what the problem was.

She sipped her tea. 'I quite understand, Mrs Checkland. Now that I've made your husband's acquaintance, believe me, you need say no more.'

'Well, thank you for … taking it so well.'

'Actually, it was quite funny.' She looked suddenly sad. 'I've just realised I haven't laughed for quite a long time.'

Mrs Crisp put down her cup. 'I remember you,' she said suddenly. 'You were two years behind me at school. Annie ... Trott. You were Annie Trott. Well, presumably you still are,' she said, hurriedly. 'I mean ... You know what I mean.'

'I thought I knew you. Elizabeth...' she paused '... Morris. You were on the netball team.'

'That's right. Goal attack. Fancy you remembering that. We were runners-up in the County Cup.'

There was a silence. The words, 'whatever happened to you?' hung in the air.

I sat quietly, temporarily forgotten and quite happy to be so.

Mrs Crisp, master tactician after years of living with Russell, busied herself with pouring more tea, thus neatly tossing the conversational ball back to Mrs Balasana.

Thomas and I waited quietly, hardly daring to breathe.

'After I left Rushford ... I got a job in an advertising agency. I worked my way up. To the top. And then I bought them out. I'd had to borrow heavily, of course, and I had to work every hour God sent to keep my head above water. But we survived. After a while, we flourished.'

She accepted her cup from Mrs Crisp. 'I thought it was all I ever wanted. The status, the money, the lifestyle.' She looked around our shabby kitchen in such a way as to imply that however disillusioned she might have become over her own lifestyle, she was never going to want to emulate ours. 'It was a long time before I saw what was right under my nose.'

She stopped again and stared at the table.

'What?' said Thomas. *'What was right under her nose?'*

'Shhh.'

Fortunately, Mrs Crisp asked, so I didn't have to.

'Gerald. My accountant. He was with me right from the beginning, you know. It was on his advice that I bought the agency. We worked side by side. There were long hours, weekends, no holidays, but we were determined to make the agency successful. And we were. Very successful.'

She laughed suddenly. 'It took him two years to ask me out. And then another two years to propose. And do you know, as soon as the words left his mouth, I realised that was what I wanted to do. More than anything in the world, even more than running an advertising agency, I wanted to be Mrs Gerald Balasana.

'He wasn't handsome. He was shorter than me, and not fashionable. Not in any way. Nor glossy. No, he definitely wasn't glossy. But he was such a dear man. It was always his dream to live in the country.

'We had a quiet wedding – just us and a few friends – and then, almost immediately afterwards, he … he had a stroke. Not a big one. He seemed to recover. But it was a wake-up call for both of us. I sold the agency. We planned to buy a cottage in the country and live … well … happily ever after. We spent hours online, looking at properties, trying to decide where to live. We got so much enjoyment from planning our new home, choosing furniture, even arguing over which plants to put in a garden we didn't have yet. I always remember that winter. The wind and rain outside and the two of us warm and snug inside, planning our future together. Then we saw Pear Tree Cottage – not that it was called that then, of course – and it was just what we wanted. We put in an offer. I went to see the bank. And then, when I came back, clutching all the paperwork and babbling with excitement, he was dead. He'd had another stroke and I hadn't been there. Bundle was sitting on his lap, crying and licking his face, but he was quite dead.'

'Oh, my dear,' said Mrs Crisp, her face soft with sympathy. 'I'm so sorry. What a dreadful shock for you.'

'Well, it was,' she said, sitting up and squaring her shoulders. 'But I've put all that behind me now. I went ahead and purchased the cottage anyway. I wanted to … Well, I suppose I wanted to create the home we'd planned together. To make everything perfect for him. A perfect world in his memory. Sometimes I think he's standing at my shoulder. And all the time I just keep thinking that if only I'd been in time, even by a few minutes – even if was only to say goodbye … Anyway, here we are, Bundle and me.'

'This is so sad,' said Thomas. *'She's trying to create the perfect world she thought they would have. That explains a lot I suppose.'*

There was a short silence and then, obviously in an effort to lighten the mood, Mrs Crisp got up, disappeared into the pantry and returned bearing a bottle and three glasses.

Mrs Balasana stared suspiciously and I don't think either of us blamed her.

'What's that?' I asked.

My special fruit cordial, said Mrs Crisp. I make a bottle or two every year. She poured a little into each glass. 'Tell me what you think.'

We sipped cautiously. I don't know what was in it, but it managed to be both fruity and fiery at the same time.

Mrs Crisp smacked her lips. 'Better than last year, but not as good as the year before that. What do you think?'

'Extremely pleasant,' said Mrs Balasana.

'Very nice,' I said.

Mrs Crisp topped us up.

Mrs Balasana said, 'Did that man ever contact you – the one who called at my house?'

I said, 'No,' belatedly realised I'd sounded too abrupt

134

and added, 'No, he didn't.'

I looked at her, wondering how much say. The … thing is, Mrs Balasana…'

'Ananda…'

'Ananda … if he … calls again, I wouldn't answer the … door, if I were you. Telephone here and Russell will … come and…' I was going to say 'sort him out', but amended that to the slightly less sinister, 'deal with the situation'.

'What situation?' she said, all her old fears about living next door to a bunch of unstable lunatics rearing their heads again. 'Is he dangerous?'

'He's my cousin,' I said.

'Not quite the reassurance you intended, Jenny,' said Thomas from his end of the kitchen. *'For all she knows your relatives are a bonkers as you are. How can you tell if this cat is dead or not?'*

'Does it smell?'

'It certainly does.'

'It's not dead then.'

Mrs Balasana was still peering at me.

'A family dispute,' I said, possibly inspired by Mrs Crisp's cordial.

'Oh, well done, Jenny,' said Thomas. *'Both accurate and completely misleading at the same time.'*

She nodded. Everyone knows about family disputes. Many people still bear the scars. 'Should I be concerned?'

'Oh no. I have Russell and Kevin and…'

'I meant should *I* be concerned?'

Thomas coughed back a snort.

'I shouldn't think so,' I said, knocking back the remainder of my drink. 'You have … Bundle after all.'

'Yes, I do,' she said. 'I'm very lucky.'

'Have some more cordial,' said Mrs Crisp recklessly.

'Thank you. It is quite delicious.'

'That will be the fruit,' said Mrs Crisp, who was never going to go to heaven.

'It is nice, isn't it?' I said, holding out my own glass for a refill and ignoring the snort from the other end of the kitchen.

She stayed for another hour. There wasn't a lot of cordial left when she got up to go. We walked her to the gate, which was just as well because, for some reason, we couldn't seem to manage the latch and it took all three of us to get the gate open. For some reason, Thomas found this quite funny.

All in all, though, quite a pleasant morning, and I like to think that when she left, incidentally looking quite cheerful, we liked each other a little better. Although Russell was still a subject best avoided.

CHAPTER NINE

On Thomas's advice, I took myself upstairs for a bit of a lie-down. The fruit cordial had made me sleepy. Mid-way through the afternoon, however, another visitor turned up. Someone I hadn't seen for a long time and, frankly, I'd never expected to see again.

I was standing at an upstairs window. The yard was empty apart from our chickens who were grouped around the back door, waiting for someone to open it for them and then, presumably, not notice half a dozen chickens streaming past on their way back to the family bathroom.

I didn't realise who it was until she got out of the car. The last time I'd seen her, she'd been driving a top-end model, and this shabby, drab little economy hire car wasn't her style at all.

She stood in the yard, looking about her. Not wanting to draw attention to myself, I stayed absolutely still, watching from behind the curtain. I don't know why. I think I hoped that if no one went out to her she would get back into her car and drive away again.

'*Not likely,*' said Thomas. '*I suspect she's driven a long way to see you today. Is that a suitcase in the back of the car?*'

'Could be,' I said.

'*And no sign of Uncle Richard.*'

'No.'

She still stood, staring around her, holding her handbag in front of her like a shield. Her face was slightly turned away from me and I couldn't read her expression.

'*Shock, I expect,*' said Thomas. '*She probably has no*

idea people live like this.'

'So – not admiration and envy, then?'

'Probably not,' he said gravely. *'But why don't we go and find out?'*

'Or why don't we stay quietly up here until she goes away?'

'She's driven a long way to see you today, Jenny. She's not going to go away.'

I sighed. 'No, she's not, is she.'

'Just a thought, Jenny, but do you think it's possible she's come to warn you about Christopher?'

'Why would she do that? He's her darling boy.'

'She doesn't want your death on their conscience.'

'It never bothered her before.'

'Perhaps she's afraid she and Richard will be implicated in some way. You have to admit, when it comes to self-interest, you'd have to go a long way to beat the Kingdoms.'

'They are implicated, whether they like it or not.'

'Or perhaps she regrets her past actions and has come to make amends.'

'I don't think it's any of that, Thomas. I think she wants money. Look at that car. Normally she'd drop down dead rather than drive around in a little tin box like that. I suspect there's no money left and she's come for some more. To give to Christopher, probably.' I stopped, overwhelmed by righteous indignation. 'I must be the only person on the planet expected to fund her own murder.'

'That's a little dramatic, Jenny.'

'Well, I'm feeling dramatic.'

'I suspect she wants the money for herself.'

'What makes you say that?'

'Suitcases in the car and no Uncle Richard.'

'You think she's running away? Why?'

'To avoid being involved in whatever is being planned. But we're not going to find out anything skulking up here. Let's go and see, shall we?'

'Well, whatever her reason, she's doomed to disappointment. I wouldn't help her even if we had some money to spare which, thanks to her and Uncle Richard, we don't.'

'And, she's come to you rather than Francesca. Why do you suppose that is?'

'I've no idea,' I said.

'I suspect Francesca was her first choice and either Francesca's own self-interest kicked in, or Daniel put his foot down and showed her the door. Could be either. Or even both. Doesn't really matter.'

'She's going to be equally unlucky today. Good job Russell's not here.'

Thomas said nothing.

'Do you think she deliberately waited until he wasn't here?

'I can understand her not wanting to encounter Russell, because...'

'Because?'

'Because she thinks you'll be easier to deal with.'

Suddenly, I stopped being slightly annoyed and became really annoyed. 'Oh? Really? Well, she's got that wrong. Come on.'

'Jenny, I have to say you're developing a very aggressive streak these days.'

'You ain't seen nuthin' yet.'

'Actually, I don't think that makes sense. I think "You haven't seen anything yet," is more grammatically correct.'

'Are you going to stand there all day warbling on about grammar?'

'Well, given the mood you're in, I'm not sure that

139

wouldn't be the wisest course of action. Where are you going? Wait for me.'

I was half way through the door.

'I don't know,' he grumbled, catching me up on the landing. *'I can remember the days when I had to push you to stand up for yourself. Now I'm not sure I shouldn't be holding you back.'*

I stopped dead and he all but bumped into me.

'You're right, Thomas. After all, I'm only little Jenny Dove who's far too stupid to be out by herself.'

He eyed me doubtfully. Doubting Thomas.

I shouldn't have done it. I don't know why I did. Whether it was because I was fed up with being little Jenny Dove – always the weak link – or the sheer nerve of her turning up here after what she and her family had done in the past … I don't know. I do know I should have sat quietly and gathered as much information from her as I could. I should have held my feelings in check and remembered that she really wasn't a nice person at all. I shouldn't have been so keen to get rid of her. Above all, I should have seen that she was very frightened and wondered why.

Mrs Crisp met us on the landing in a bit of a fluster.

'It's Mrs Kingdom…'

'Yes, I know, I saw. Where have you … stashed her?'

'She's still in the yard.'

'Well, with a … bit of luck, Marilyn has eaten her.'

'Sadly – no.'

'I'll see her in the … sitting room. Don't bother offering her any refreshment. That … never ends well.'

I gave her a few minutes to usher her in and then made a grand entrance, sweeping down the stairs.

She'd made herself comfortable on one of our saggy sofas. I took a moment to regret the cat hadn't found the time to join us. We'd had some Jehovah's Witnesses around once, and I think it must have been their shortest ever recorded visit. Russell, bored, had invited them in for a good argument. You couldn't fault their diligence but I think even they found that while the cat's unnerving one-eyed glare and unpleasant smell was bad enough, it was the still-twitching remains of the unfortunate rodent laid mischievously at their feet that were the final straw. A grudgingly grateful Russell opened a tin of salmon for him afterwards. Anyway, the cat was out doing whatever it is disreputable old cats with no social conscience do every afternoon and, like all the men in my household, was absolutely no help at all in a crisis.

Close up, she was much less smartly dressed than I'd thought. She certainly wasn't dirty or scruffy, but if you'd known Aunt Julia in her heyday, expensively dressed and immaculately turned out, you could see it.

She surged across the room towards me, affection written all across her face. For one moment, I thought she was going to kiss me. 'Jenny, my dear. How are you?'

I said in a faint, wispy voice, 'I'm …very … well … thank… you.'

'And you have a little baby now. How delightful. You must let me see her before I go.'

I said nothing, and if she wanted to interpret that as a sign of weakness or fear then I wasn't going to stand in her way. Although she'd see Joy over her own dead body.

'Jenny,' said Thomas from the corner. 'What are you going to do?'

'I'm going to show her I'm not the person I used to be.'

'How?'

'Not sure yet.'

Aunt Julia seated herself and gripped her handbag. I could see her knuckles were quite white. 'Jenny, you must

141

wonder why I've popped in today.'

'She lives three hundred miles away,' murmured Thomas. *'That's not a pop, that's an explosion.'*

'Well, obviously, dear, we've missed you. Your uncle and I often speak of you.'

'I bet they do,' muttered Thomas

'We wonder how you're doing. Here. In this ... lovely farmhouse.'

She glanced around. As did we all. Possibly waiting for the words to choke her.

Again, sadly – no.

'I have to say, Jenny, it's lovely to see you doing so well here. In your lovely home. With your lovely little baby.'

'Lovely!' murmured Thomas.

I said nothing. What did she want?

She fidgeted with the catch on her handbag, snapping it open and closed. I don't think she realised she was doing it.

'Anyway, I was wondering ... Well, I ... I've had a bit of bad luck recently and ... and I was wondering whether you could see your way to lending me a small sum of money. Just to tide me over for a while. I find myself having to undertake a small journey and, well, as you know, I just don't have the funds these days.'

She paused so I could understand that her current lack of funds was all my fault for having been unreasonable enough to catch them helping themselves to my money.

'Anyway, your uncle's money is paid quarterly and, as you know, there's another three weeks at least to quarter day, when I would, of course, not only be delighted to pay you back, but include a small amount of interest as well.'

I said nothing. The silence took on a sharper quality – as did her voice.

'Jenny?'

142

I still said nothing.

Licking her lips and assuming such a forced expression of affection that for a moment I thought the effort might see her off altogether, she said, 'What do you say, Jenny? Are you able to help out your old aunt?'

She paused for a moment. The words, 'Especially after I took you into my family, put a roof over your head, and brought you up,' were not spoken, but they might as well have been.

For my part, the words, 'Shut me away, told people there was something wrong with me, and stole from me,' were also not spoken.

I took a deep breath, my usual prelude to painful utterances. Familiar with the signs, she waited. I made her wait a little longer.

'Where's ... Uncle Richard?'

If possible, she went even paler. 'I'm sorry he's not here today, Jenny. Obviously he was very keen to see you, but he's not ... He couldn't...' She tailed away.

'Jenny, I don't like this,' said Thomas, suddenly.

Neither did I.

I thought of Joy upstairs. Of Russell, possibly on his way home and finding her here. Of just getting her out of my house as quickly as possible. But I should have taken a moment to think.

'I'm ... sorry... Aunt ... Julia...' I paused, ostensibly to gather a little strength before plunging valiantly on, 'I ... can't.'

'Won't, you mean,' she cried angrily. 'You ungrateful little...'

I thought I heard a faint sound from the other side of the door and I knew, just knew, that Mrs Crisp was standing, Le Creuset frying pan in hand – a weapon that had already more than proved its worth at Frogmorton – awaiting the bugle call to battle. Hopefully Kevin was there, too.

She made a huge effort, licking her lips again and pinning on a quite dreadful smile. 'I don't think you quite understand,' she said gently. 'I'm sure that if you did – if I could just explain – you'd be only too happy to help, wouldn't you, Jenny?'

'Oh yes,' I said earnestly. 'I ... would. I ... would. As ... much ...as y ... y ... you want.'

'Over-egging the pudding,' said Thomas, warningly.

Her face collapsed with relief. 'Really? Well, that's very generous of you, my dear. I always said you were a good little girl.'

She smiled kindly at me and I felt sick. Did she really think their last words to me, 'Who were you compared with us? You're nothing. That's how we always think of you. The nothing girl,' didn't still reverberate around my head? And always would.

'Thank ... you, Aunt Julia,' I said. I watched the hope grow in her eyes. 'How much ... do ... you think ... you will ... need?'

She snapped her handbag open and shut again. Perhaps she hadn't thought it would be this easy. I wondered if she was mentally adding noughts to the original sum. I found I rather hoped she was, tried to feel ashamed of leading her on, and failed.

'Well, I was thinking, because nothing is cheap these days, is it, around seven thousand pounds, but it's probably easier for everyone if we round it up to an easy ten. Let's call it ten thousand, shall we? Not that it matters. You'll be getting it all back – plus a little extra, of course – as soon as the next quarter day rolls around.' She smiled that bright, desperate smile again. That bright, desperate, *greedy* smile.

Well, that made everything simple. We didn't have ten thousand pounds. Nor anything like ten thousand pounds.

And if we did have ten thousand pounds then I'd be spending it on the roof and not my really rather unpleasant relatives. If she'd been a little more moderate in her demands then I might have found say, five hundred pounds, but ten thousand was so beyond the realms of possibility that I could turn her down with a clear conscience.

I nodded and smiled back again.

'Well, Jenny, I have to say you gave me a bit of a scare there, saying you wouldn't do it, but I knew that once you had thought about it...'

'Oh no,' I said, 'I really can't do it.'

'But you just said you would.'

'No, I didn't.'

I watched her ransack her memory and realise that no, I hadn't.

'Why not?'

I took another deep breath and lied through my teeth. 'Well, after ... we ... parted a couple of years ago – you'll remember that, I'm sure.' And I too flashed a bright smile as false as her own. 'Russell ... told me that all this ... silly financial stuff would be ... much too difficult for me to understand, and so I should leave it all to him. And he ... was right ... because I really can't comprehend this sort of thing at all. I mean, it's all so ... complicated, isn't it, and I ... get upset when people try to tell me difficult things, so he said *he'd* look after all that ... side of things and I ... wasn't to ... worry about anything.'

I watched her struggle with the implication that Russell had beaten her at her own game.

'But you ... needn't worry. I'll tell Russell you've ... been here and when he hears ... what you ... wanted, I'm sure he'll ... know exactly what to ... do.'

She stared at me, mouth and eyes wide open. The

silence went on and on. I didn't know what else to do to get rid of her. There was always the possibility she knew that, according to Russell, paying bills was something that only ever happened as a last resort, and that he was more than happy to leave everything to me, but I doubted it. In her household, Uncle Richard handled all that sort of thing. In her world, men paid the bills. That was what they were here for. And we both knew she would never, in a million years, approach Russell. She really had no choice now but to leave.

I rose to my feet and waited for her to sweep from the room. Something she always did really well, but she didn't. She just sat, staring, empty-eyed into the distance. The silence lengthened.

'Thomas, something's not right.'

'No,' he said. *'It's not, is it?'*

I sat next to her and took her ice-cold hand. She was trembling all over.

I called, 'Mrs Crisp.'

The door opened immediately. I knew she'd been waiting for my call.

'Could you bring some tea, please?'

Without even a pause, she said, 'Of course, madam,' and left the room. She only ever called me madam when Aunt Julia was around. As far as I know, she never called Russell madam at all.

I said softly, 'Aunt Julia? Please … tell me what's wrong.'

She tried to speak but no sound came out. I began to be afraid she was having some sort of seizure.

'Perhaps it's better if you don't try to speak. Just sit back for a moment.'

I pushed her gently back against the cushions and reached for the old throw to put across her knees.

Thomas had moved back out of the way as I fussed

146

around, lifting her feet up and tucking the throw around her. She was a dreadful colour and I seriously considered telephoning for an ambulance.

Kevin opened the door and Mrs Crisp came in with the tea trolley. Closing it behind her, he said, 'Is everything all right, madam?'

Bless him. 'I'm not sure, Kevin. Could you wait around, just in case I need you?'

'Of course.'

Mrs Crisp busied herself pouring tea. She put a cup and saucer on the coffee table in front of Aunt Julia, who was in such a state that a mug would probably have been safer, although I don't think Aunt Julia is actually aware of the existence of mugs, far less their function.

I became aware of the comforting smell of ginger biscuits. Thomas was doing his bit in our current crisis. I don't know if Aunt Julia was aware of it or not, but her breathing became more regular, some colour returned, she sat a little straighter.

I handed her the cup and saucer. She sipped slowly, not looking at me.

I let her finish and then began again.

'Aunt Julia, please. Won't you tell me what this is all about? What's happening?'

She shook her head. I took a chance.

'This is about Christopher, isn't it?'

She burst into tears.

The door opened again and Mrs Crisp came in again with a box of tissues and we did our best to mop her up. We weren't particularly successful, and I remember thinking it must have been a measure of her agitation that she wasn't giving any thought to her personal appearance. I needed to get to the bottom of this.

'Gently,' advised Thomas, and I nodded.

I took her hand and tried my best to sound stern and

147

authoritative. 'Now, Aunt Julia. Tell me. Let me … see if I can help.'

She twisted her hand so that now she clutched mine. Her grip was very strong. 'Just give me the money, Jenny. You must give me the money.'

'I can't. I don't have it.'

'You must. You don't understand. I can't go away without it.'

I sat back. Suddenly, some things began to fall into place.

'Did Christopher send you?'

She jumped, looked terrified and then shook her head. So who was the money for?

'Thomas – the suitcase.'

'I beg your pardon?'

'The suitcase in her car. The money's not for Christopher. The money is for her and Uncle Richard. They're running away.'

'And she's too afraid to go back and tell him she hasn't been able to persuade you to part with the money.'

I said slowly, 'No, wait. There was only one suitcase in the car.'

And then the truth hit us both simultaneously.

'She's running away from both of them. Christopher and Uncle Richard. Whatever they've got planned, she doesn't want to be any part of it.'

'Jenny, this is quite serious.'

'I know. But if she genuinely wants to get away … Look how terrified she is.'

And indeed she was. The cup and saucer rattled in her hands as she leaned forwards to put it on the table.

I came to a decision.

'Aunt Julia, do you need the money to get away from Christopher and Uncle Richard?

She looked over her shoulder as if either of them could

hear her. 'You don't know what he's like.'

'Who? Christopher?'

Her lips never moved. It was as if she was afraid to utter his name. 'Richard.'

I patted her hand. 'If you can wait two or three days, then I could probably let you have two thousand pounds. If you want money now then I can write you a cheque for, say, four hundred.'

She clutched my arm. 'Could you?'

'Yes, I can. Forget … what I said earlier. I'll help you get away. If that's … what you really want to do.'

It was as if she suddenly saw light at the end of the tunnel. All right, four hundred pounds wasn't ten thousand, but if you're desperate, it's enough to get you quite a long way away. And I would say she was desperate.

'Just promise me you won't go back, Julia. Promise me you'll just drive off to somewhere and never look back.'

'I will. Oh God, I will. I'll never come back, I promise. I'll never see either of them again. Just help me get away, Jenny, I beg you.'

There could be no doubt her fear was genuine and that was when I made my mistake. I disengaged her clutching hands and rummaged through the pile of stuff on the table for my cheque book. I wrote her a personal cheque, tore it from the book and handed it to her.

Her hands shook as she folded it and slipped it into her handbag.

'Aunt Julia, what's … going on?'

She looked around again and said in a whisper, 'I don't know. They wouldn't tell me, but do be careful, Jenny. Promise me you'll be careful.'

'I will,' I said. 'But … I'm well protected.'

She looked around, her glance passing over Kevin and

Mrs Crisp as if they weren't there. 'You're here alone. You shouldn't be alone.'

I sighed. She hadn't changed that much. I had Mrs Crisp and Kevin, but they weren't Real People, according to Aunt Julia. I remembered I'd never liked her. And sometimes I'd hated her. The brief sympathy I had felt for her was beginning to evaporate. Her terror wasn't for me – it was for herself. Her self-interest was boundless. I should have followed my original intentions and made her leave with nothing, but seeing her huddled against the cushions, a sad remnant of her former self, what else could I have done?

I said, 'Are you all right to drive?' and she nodded.

Clutching her bag, she struggled to her feet.

I tried again. I said quietly, 'Aunt Julia, is there anything else … you want to … tell me.'

I hoped she had more to say, but she had what she'd come for. Her old dislike of me was returning, and I hadn't had the sense to withhold the cheque until she'd told me what I wanted to know. Not that I thought she knew much. Now that she had the money, however, she couldn't get away quickly enough. If only she had just said, 'Actually, Jenny, yes,' and sat back down again and talked to me – actually talked to me – but she remained Aunt Julia right to the very end.

She drew herself up and in something like her old manner, said, 'You probably wouldn't understand and I can't spare the time.'

Once, I might have been hurt, but those days were long gone. I nodded at Kevin, who held the door open for her, saying, 'Your car is waiting, Mrs Kingdom.'

She took the hint, sweeping from the room without saying another word.

I followed her out and waited by the back door. Two chickens – I couldn't see which from here – were sitting

150

on the warm bonnet. They took one look at Aunt Julia, however, and wisely flapped away.

'Look at her face,' said Thomas.

I was looking. Once there had been Aunt Julia – member of the Townswomen's Guild, former chair of the WI, member of the Conservative Association, fundraiser and social climber. Now there was Aunt Julia, tight-faced and anxious. So anxious she never realised that she'd trapped a fold of her coat in the car door.

'Yes,' I said. 'Thomas, I think I might have made a big mistake.'

She drove jerkily out of the yard, crashing the gears as she turned into the lane, and disappeared. Slowly, the sound of her engine died away and we were left in peace. And I was right. I'd just made a big mistake.

CHAPTER TEN

'Now what?' said Thomas, after a couple of restorative cups of tea.

I'd been thinking.

'I think,' I said, slowly and with great reluctance, 'that I have to talk to Francesca. Perhaps she knows something.'

'Unlikely, but I agree we should try.' Thomas lowered his head towards me. *'Are you all right, Jenny?'*

I smiled bitterly. 'I've been living in a bubble, Thomas. A golden bubble. I've been blind and stupid, while all around me, bad things are gathering.'

He didn't deny it, saying only, *'You will talk to Russell, won't you?'*

'Oh yes. As soon as he gets back. But first, I need to see Franny.'

Francesca, in case everyone has forgotten, is my other cousin: Christopher's sister. She's tall and wonderfully beautiful. She doesn't have hair – she has HAIR – a great red-gold cloud of it framing her face and setting off her brilliant green eyes. In addition to being breathtakingly beautiful, Francesca is also breathtakingly stupid. Stupid enough to dump Russell, anyway.

I absolve her of deliberate cruelty – she's too dim for the mental effort required – but she's staggeringly self-centred. She is, she thinks, not only the centre of her own universe, but everyone else's as well. I don't think she ever considered the effect on Russell when she so casually dumped him in favour of Daniel Palmer. Being with

Russell Checkland, that up and coming young artist, had taken her so far, but Daniel was a TV producer who could take her career in the direction she wanted to go. I still get angry just thinking about it.

Russell fell apart. She was his life and – worse – she was his inspiration. He stopped painting, put down his brushes and picked up a bottle instead, destroying all his work in one drunken, heart-breaking afternoon.

He pulled himself together eventually. Before the damage to his career was irreparable anyway, but it's been a long road back for him.

Francesca now lived with Daniel and they had a very pretty house on the other side of Rushford. Despite his appalling taste in girlfriends, I quite liked Daniel. He was a kind man and, best of all, he took no nonsense from Francesca. I wasn't sure whether to hope he was in or not. He had no time at all for my aunt and uncle and had frequently expressed a commendable desire to punch Christopher's lights out. Although he'd have to wait behind Russell for that particular pleasure. If he was at home today he might be able to offer a helpful perspective. On the other hand, he might just order Franny to go abroad out of the way and pick up the phone for the police. Despite his TV background, Daniel is a very respectable man. You'd never catch him stealing a donkey or banging on about Patagonian Attack Chickens.

Kevin drove me over, declining to get out when we arrived. He pulled out a battered exercise book.

'I'll just wait out here, if you don't mind, Mrs Checkland. I'm working on a layout for Mrs Crosby's herb garden.'

I'd spent the short journey turning over various approaches in my mind and rejecting them all.

'What are you going to say?' asked Thomas, as we climbed the shallow steps to the front door.

'Not sure.'

Daniel's house basked in the afternoon sunshine. His gardens were much neater than ours, but then he had staff. And the money to pay them.

Francesca opened the door to us herself.

'Oh. Jenny. I thought it was Russell at last.'

'No,' I said gravely, 'it's me.'

She threw a look over my shoulder, just in case I'd failed to recognise my own husband materialising behind me, and stood back to let us in.

Thomas paused in the hall, looking around him. Daniel had a wonderful art collection and Thomas loved his art.

'Go,' I said to him. 'I'll be all right. I'm only going to talk to her for a moment. She's not likely to do me any harm in her own house, is she?'

'Actually, it was her safety I was thinking of. I'd better come with you.'

'Come into my private sitting room,' she said.

Who has a private sitting room? At Frogmorton we had only one sitting room and, far from being private, it was frequently overrun with cats, babies, erratic husbands, Andrew, and the occasional chicken still seeking to return to the land of her golden youth.

It was certainly a lovely room. Daniel had decorated it especially for her and it was done out in shades of cream and gold. Without asking me to sit down, she sprawled on a sofa and picked up a glossy magazine. It seemed she'd been passing the time looking at pictures of herself. She looked relaxed and comfortable. Time to put a stop to that.

There's no point in being subtle with Francesca. I stood in the doorway, and announced dramatically, 'Francesca – I know everything.'

She dropped her magazine and shot bolt upright, her eyes big with alarm.

'Oh my God. Russell told you. But he swore he wouldn't.'

The shock jolted me from head to toe. I'd only said it to wind her up but now … Was it possible I'd completely misjudged the situation? I know I'm not balanced about Francesca, but now my world stopped turning. What had Russell sworn he wouldn't tell me? Christopher, Aunt Julia, everything went straight out of my head. All I could think was – all those telephone calls. The ones where I heard the hello and goodbye, and never the bit in between. The important bit.

Sometimes – not often, but sometimes – a stutter is a huge advantage. I was too shocked and surprised to say anything and, judging from his silence, so was Thomas, and that was the upside. People don't like silence. Especially people with a guilty conscience. People always like to get their story in first. Presumably mistaking my silence not for the paralysing shock it was, but as silent denunciation, she raced to get her story out.

'Believe it or not, Jenny, I'm the innocent party here. I've been wanting to tell you for ages but Russell kept saying no, not just yet, and now you've found out and I can see it's come as a shock, but blame Russell. If he wasn't so protective of you, we could have sorted everything out long ago.'

'Breathe,' said Thomas, who had obviously pulled himself together much more quickly than I had. *'Don't try to speak. Just wait for her to tell you what's going on, but do bear in mind that it's Francesca talking. There's a chair here. Sit down.'*

I walked slowly to the armchair, sat, smoothed my jeans, clasped my hands and waited for whatever bombshell she was about to drop on me.

'Right,' she said, 'where to begin?'

She turned her head and stared out of the window. I

wasn't sure whether she was seeking inspiration or offering me the chance to admire her profile, because it is admirable. Naturally since she's a model. She's not a top model, but since Daniel began advising her she's been prepared to take a wider range of jobs and has won herself more publicity. In her defence, she's not a completely worthless human being – she does a lot of work raising funds for the local donkey sanctuary. She's always being snapped with hugely photogenic baby donkeys and the public loves her. She's also very big in Spain and jets over regularly to pout on a Spanish beach, wearing the latest swimwear, huge sunglasses, and a bronzed young man.

A magazine once ran an article on her, extolling her Renaissance colouring and beauty and now she's famous for only ever wearing black, white or green. Colours which set off her red – sorry, deep auburn – hair and milky white skin.

Today was obviously an inside day because she was wearing white: a top which draped beautifully, form-fitting white jeans, and her bare toes were painted blood red. Her long hair was pulled back in a casual plait that on lesser women would just look scruffy but which on her was effortlessly elegant.

I began to wish I had at least stopped to wash my face and brush my hair. I told myself that the faint aroma of farmyard belonged to Thomas and was in no way connected with me.

'You wish,' said Thomas, amused.

Either deciding I'd had enough of a good thing profile-wise or, more likely, having thought of two or three simple sentences to string together, she turned to face me and began.

'About six months ago...'

I bounced in my seat. Joy was eight months old so I'd just given birth at the time. How could he? I remembered

157

what I thought of at the time as his obsessive care of me. He'd insisted I rest for two hours every afternoon and – oh my God – he'd walked me upstairs, settled me on the bed, covered me with a blanket and calmly left the house – to visit Francesca. Love in the afternoon…

And then, thank goodness, common sense kicked in.

'And about time, too. Really, Jenny, have a little faith.'

She was hurrying on. '…Anyway, he wasn't keen at first. I have to say I did keep on and on at him, and eventually he said yes. I'm a little annoyed with him because he kept insisting we wait a while, at least until Joy was older, but time is ticking on and now he's putting me off with tales of being worried about you and, frankly, I'm rather annoyed with him. He keeps promising, but somehow the moment is never quite right.' She looked at me hopefully. 'I'm a little annoyed with you, too, Jenny. You look perfectly healthy to me. Perhaps if you could have a word with him. Tell him there's no problem and you're happy to take him.'

'I should be … delighted,' I said, finding a voice at last, 'if I had any idea … what you're … talking about.'

She sighed in exasperation. She's a lot nicer than she used to be, but sometimes the old Francesca bubbles to the surface like one of those lethal gas pockets that sinks ships in the Bermuda Triangle.

'Oh Jenny, do try to concentrate. I can't make things much simpler for you. Jack, of course.'

'Jack?'

'Jack?'

'Jack.'

Bearing in mind my audience, I kept things simple. 'Who's Jack?'

'Jack the donkey, of course.'

I turned to Thomas, thus giving her the chance to admire my profile and check out my effortlessly scruffy ponytail.

'No. Sorry. Not a clue here, either.'

I said carefully, 'I think, Franny, that it would be best to assume I know nothing. Perhaps you could start at the beginning.'

'You didn't ask her to keep things simple for you.'

'I shall rely on you to translate when she becomes un-understandable, so concentrate.'

'Well,' she said, settling herself, 'about a year ago, the donkey sanctuary took in a stray. You know, like they do. Because they're a sanc-tu-ary.' She enunciated the last word carefully for my benefit.

I once collaborated with her husband on a TV programme that was nominated for an award – it didn't win, but that's not the point – and still she treats me like a refugee from a remedial class.

'Don't kill her now. It'll interrupt her flow and you know how difficult it is to keep her to the point. She'll start on the latest reality show or nail polish or something and we'll never find out about Jack.'

'Or Christopher.'

'Or Christopher.'

'Anyway, he didn't settle. He pined and he wouldn't eat. They said he'd been someone's pet and that person had died and he needed lots of attention and it would be better if he could be a pet again and who did I know, and I said Russell. Because that's what he does, isn't it? Collects waifs and strays and gives them a home.'

'Am I permitted to slap her?'

'Of course – but not yet. Our purpose today is to extract information – not gratify your primitive urges.'

'So I asked Russell and he said don't talk to me now my wife's pregnant. So I said what about afterwards, and he said after what, and I said after the baby's born, of course, and he said maybe. And then you had the baby,

159

and I said what about now, and he said – well, he was quite rude, actually, but I don't think his picture was going well – so I waited nearly a whole week and then mentioned it again, and he said for God's sake, all right, I'll go and look at him, and he did, and I think he felt sorry for him, all alone and sad, and he said yes but not now because of Jenny – that's you – and I agreed, although I think he coddles you a little sometimes, Jenny. You mustn't be selfish, you know. And then, just as he was going to mention it to you, something else apparently came up, and I said, oh Russell, and he was actually quite rude again. So I said *I'd* mention it to you if he was too busy, and he said no for God's sake don't do that, so I didn't.'

She beamed at me.

Thomas had retired to the other end of the room and was examining the view from the window. The occasional snort drifted my way. Sometimes, he's not a lot of help.

'And while Russell's messing about, time is slipping by and I'm off to Spain next month, so if we don't get the photo shoot organised soon then we'll be into winter and I particularly wanted an outdoor shoot, with grass and trees and…' She paused for more outdoor words to catch up.

I was bewildered. 'What outdoor shoot?'

She sighed heavily. 'For the publicity, of course. They want to do a short film of me saving the donkey.'

I couldn't help myself. 'From what?'

'Well, from … you know…' She stopped to collect her thoughts.

'Wolves,' said a voice, helpfully. *'Pirates. Earthquakes. Dinosaurs.'*

'Forgive me,' I said, 'but how are *you* saving the donkey?'

She waved that aside as irrelevant. I gathered that while the time and effort and expense would be Russell's, the credit would be hers.

Amongst the many, many instructions heaped upon me as a child was the exhortation always to be a Good Girl. Never to cause a fuss. To be quiet and well behaved and unobtrusive. Always. And I'd done as I was told. In fact, I'd been so unobtrusive that I'd very nearly disappeared from the world altogether.

I'd been the very epitome of a Good Girl. Although it would be fair to say I've never really had the opportunity to be anything else. If there is a living, shining example of a Good Girl, then it's me. I dislike conflict and confrontation. She who fights and runs away may well live to fight another day, but she who never fights in the first place leads a quiet life. I'm not Russell, happily flinging the most provocative remarks into any conversation in which he's involved. I like peace and quiet, with everyone getting on with everyone else. So I really don't know what made me say it.

'Well, really, Franny, that's so … typical of Russell. Here you are, selflessly wearing yourself out … trying to help others, and he's just … being no help at all. It's too bad of him.'

She said automatically, 'Don't call me Franny.'

'Sorry. Your problem, *Francesca*, is that you're just … too nice.'

'But you're exactly right, Jenny. How clever of you to work that out.'

'Well, I think you've been much … too … soft with him. You … know what he's like; you have to … keep … telling him things. Incessantly.'

She looked a little confused.

'Too many syllables,' said Thomas from the far end of the room.

'I mean, you have to tell him over and over again, otherwise he doesn't remember things.'

'You've noticed that, too?'

'I have indeed and I always ... find the best way to ... deal with him is to stand in his face and just repeat the same thing ... over and over again, until it goes in. He's always ... grateful afterwards.'

She nodded. 'That's such a good idea. Thank you, Jenny. That's exactly what I'll do.'

Thomas was still snorting in the corner. *'Jenny, you ... devil!'*

'And we'll be ... delighted to take Jack. Tell him he ... must sort it out as soon as ... possible. Keep on at him until he does it. You know what he's like, Franny ... cesca. He ... doesn't remember a thing from one moment to the next unless you ... keep reminding him.'

She nodded and stood up. Being Franny, of course, now that she'd achieved her goal, the interview was over. I stayed put, because as far as I was concerned, it was only just beginning.

'Just one thing, Franny...'

'Don't call me Franny.'

'Get a move on. I think she's nearly exhausted her daily quota of rational thought.'

I took a deep breath. 'Your ... mother came to see me.'

That got her attention. *'My* mother?'

I don't know why she put the emphasis on the word 'my'. My mother was dead so whose mother did she think I was referring to?

She stared at me, bewildered. 'Why you? Why not me? What could she possibly want with you?'

I hesitated. What should I say? How much should I tell her? Especially since it was obvious Aunt Julia hadn't been here.

'She's not involved,' said Thomas. *'And she has Daniel to look after her. Don't tell her anything at all.*

162

Safer that way.'

I didn't answer directly. 'Are you in … contact with Christopher at all?'

She shook her head vigorously. 'No. Daniel made it very clear I wasn't to have anything more to do with him.'

'So you haven't seen him recently?'

She moved towards the door, clearly uncomfortable. 'I haven't seen him at all and I think it's very unkind of you to bring him up. You must remember what he did to me.'

My kindly thoughts towards her fled. Christopher's financial incompetence had led Uncle Richard to rob me blind for years. Christopher had endangered our lives. We suspected he'd set fire to our feed store. But, most seriously of all, he'd embarrassed Francesca. It was a miracle she'd allowed him to live. I shook my head. She really was the centre of the universe.

'Let it go,' said Thomas. *'We've got what we came for. She's not involved. Even Christopher's not that stupid.'*

I stood up. 'Don't forget to … tell Russell. Several times, just to be on the safe side. In fact, ring him now. He's in London at the … moment, so keep on … trying.'

'I will,' she said, already pulling out her phone.

Much though I would have loved to hang around and listen, it was time to go. 'I'll see myself out.'

Thomas was chuckling as we went back to Kevin and the car. *'Wouldn't you love to be a fly on the wall for that particular conversation?'*

163

CHAPTER ELEVEN

Thomas kept urging me to talk to Russell. *'All right, you've not seen Christopher recently, and Francesca clearly knows nothing, but your aunt calling is something he should know about, Jenny. Tell Russell.'*

'I will when he gets back. Well, after I've asked him how things went.'

'Remember how you felt when Francesca let slip he'd been keeping Jack secret from you. And that was just a donkey. Tell him.'

'If it *was* Christopher I saw.'

'If it was then Russell has a serious problem and he needs to know.'

'But suppose it wasn't.'

'Then his wife is going mad and he has a serious problem and he needs to know.'

I meant to. I really, really did. I thought I'd wait for him to tell me how it all went, have a drink or two, play with Joy, have something to eat, and then when he was nicely mellow – or at least less excitable than usual – tell him about Christopher.

Unfortunately, the best-laid plans...

Some of it was my fault. Francesca had obviously availed herself of every opportunity to telephone him. His train had been delayed. He was cold and tired and hungry. The wall space was not what he had imagined and they'd been very clear he'd only got the spot because someone else had pulled out.

'The space is too big,' he said, prowling around the room, drink in hand, 'and they want another two works on

165

top of the original six. I have something almost completed, which I think might do and I've an idea for another. Which is good, but I have to get cracking. And as if that wasn't enough, I've got Francesca yammering at me twenty times a day.'

'Oh yes,' I said tightly, 'about Jack.'

'Oh, she told you about that, did she? Why did she do that? I said I'd handle things.'

I didn't know whether he was genuinely missing the point or just avoiding it. He raced on. 'God, I wish I'd never said I'd think about it. They say no good deed goes unpunished. Well, I certainly won't do that again.'

'He doesn't have a clue, does he?' said Thomas, and I thought he might be right.

It wasn't having the additional donkey that was the problem – I was happy to have him – it was not having been told we were having him that was annoying me. Much as I was touched by his consideration, I don't need to be sheltered from the world any longer. I endeavoured to convey this to Russell who was standing at the table, rifling through the mound of papers, and generally not listening. Normally, I wouldn't have wasted my breath. I'd have held my peace and waited until he was back in the real world again, but today was one of those scratchy days when nothing had gone right for either of us. He'd had a difficult time in London – I'd had Aunt Julia – and we'd both had Francesca.

Not only did we manage to have a row, but it wasn't even about any of the quite major problems we were having at the moment.

We don't row often. As I said, I'm a Good Girl and I dislike confrontation and shouting. It doesn't take much to render me speechless and Russell knows it, but he's not a bully and never takes advantage, so we generally muddle along quite happily. He always says that the recipe for a

166

happy marriage is for me to nod, smile and agree to everything he says, and in general I do. In return, he makes sure that everything he says is noddable, smileable and agreeable to. It usually works well for both of us.

Not today, however.

He was scattering papers in all directions looking for the feed bill when he pulled something out, saying, 'What the hell is this?'

He was looking down at my chequebook, left open on the table.

I opened my mouth to explain but by the time I'd assembled the words he was off again. 'You gave Julia Kingdom four hundred pounds?'

To be fair – it wasn't the money. I can spend whatever I like whenever I like – he doesn't care. It was the fact I'd given the money to Aunt Julia that was bending him out of shape.

I tried again. 'I...'

He poured himself another drink and I guessed he'd had a few on the train, as well. Tossing it back, he said, 'Why would you do that?'

'Because...'

He wasn't listening. He wasn't listening to anyone. I should have recognised that he was tired and that a great deal of stress and frustration was fighting its way to the surface. I should have just sat back and let him get it all off his chest, left him to sleep it off on the sofa, handed him a coffee the next morning, listened to his apologies, kissed him better and then told him about everything.

None of that happened. A tiny spurt of unaccustomed anger ran through me. Everything was always about everyone else, wasn't it? I had problems too and no one ever took a blind bit of notice. I was being stalked by a deeply unattractive pyromaniac psychopath who, I was convinced, meant to do me harm. The woman who had robbed me of more than money had turned up, insulted me and my home, demanded yet more money and then made off without telling me what the hell was going on. Then I'd had to travel fifteen miles to be talked down to by my husband's ex-girlfriend who planned to foist another donkey upon us. And I was married to the most selfish man on earth who – yes all right, wasn't having too good a time at the moment either, but that wasn't the point –who had yet to tell me about said donkey. Oh, and the bloody roof still bloody leaked. And no one – no one at all was taking any notice. Was I always destined to be overlooked? Even by those who said they loved me?

He was still ranting on. 'And what was she doing here in the first place? Did you invite her? Is this a regular thing? Dear God, no wonder I can't afford to get the roof done. What were you thinking? Is it not enough that they robbed you of nearly everything you had? Now you're voluntarily giving them money? What's going on with you, Jenny? I thought we said no secrets.'

The sheer injustice of this slammed the words into my head.

'So … tell me about Jack,' I said. Oh no, sorry, you can't. He's a … secret, isn't he?'

'That's different. I was waiting for the right moment.'

'Like you did with the chickens? You'd have told me just as he was coming through the gate?'

'You like our chickens.'

'That's not the … point.'

'I don't know what is your point. I don't know anything.'

'Of course you … don't. You're the … great Russell Checkland, who is so wrapped up in himself and his own … concerns that … that he never even … notices anyone else's problems, far less … does anything about them, does he?'

168

Russell is not the only one who can overstate an issue.

He tossed back his drink. 'Oh, come on. What problems could you possibly have?'

'Well, I'm … married to the … most selfish, unobservant … man in the world. We could start with that and work up.'

He slammed down the glass and strode into the kitchen. I stamped up the stairs, even more furious because I didn't have the luxury of slamming the bedroom door in case I woke Joy.

Thomas was waiting for me, standing in the corner as he always did, swishing his tail. *'How did it go?'*

I looked at him.

'Well, never mind. Tomorrow would probably be better anyway. When everyone's a little calmer.'

I blew my nose on a handful of toilet roll and said defiantly, 'It doesn't matter. I don't need Russell. I shall sort this out for myself.'

He regarded me gravely.

'You don't think I can?'

'Of course you can. You can do anything you want to, Jenny. But you don't have to do it alone.'

I blew my nose again. 'I can't see Russell being any sort of asset. He needs to paint. I shall handle this myself.'

It was time to show people what I was capable of.

From outside, I heard the clatter of Russell's Land Rover as he roared off into the night. I had no idea where he was going. Andrew's probably. No – he'd had too much to drink. He'd be roaring up the lane to the Braithwaites. They'd take him in and let him sleep on the sofa. He'd wake in the morning with a monumental headache, crushed underneath the weight of their two enormously fat cats and with Fiona offering to showing him her gerbils.

It was hard to feel any sympathy.

169

CHAPTER TWELVE

Russell disappeared into his studio for two days. Under normal circumstances – that is, if we were speaking to each other – I'd wander in around mid-morning, hand him a coffee, and we'd have a chat about whatever he was working on. He would scribble ideas on old bits of paper, chattering half to himself and half to me, and then I would leave him to get on with it, carefully removing the old pizza boxes he thought Mrs Crisp didn't know anything about.

As things stood at the moment, I couldn't care less what he was up to, and he could smother in pizza boxes for all I cared.

'Jenny,' said Thomas, uncertainly.

I said brightly, 'Let's go for a walk.'

When we came back, I said, 'Let's play with Joy.'

When she fell asleep, I said, 'Let's help Mrs Crisp.'

When I was driven from the kitchen, I said, 'Let's feed the chickens.'

When even they were stuffed, I said, 'Let's ring Tanya and go to lunch tomorrow.'

When we returned from an afternoon's shopping, I said, 'Let's have an early night.'

When we got up the next morning, I said, 'Lets…'

'Jenny. Enough.'

'All right, let's pop into his studio and rip his head off.'

'I sometimes think you've made a little too much progress these last few years.'

'You can wait outside if you like.'

He sighed and we trailed along the landing.

Russell was painting like a madman. I was familiar with the signs. He would stab at the canvas, roughly scrubbing the colour into the tooth and then use his fingers to mix and blend. He had a huge smudge of green paint across one cheek. In fact, he was covered in paint. Half his hair was standing on end and the other half flopping across his forehead. Even as I watched, he brushed it impatiently aside and adding a smear of ultramarine to the green. A good amount appeared to have gone up the wall as well. Even his bare feet were flecked with paint. In the corner, the Rolling Stones were singing 'Paint It Black' at window-rattling volume. I used all this frantic activity as an excuse not to venture in. I thought he said something as I closed the door, but I didn't go back.

'You should talk to him. Explain about Julia. And Christopher. You need to work together on this.'

'Not now. He's busy. He won't hear a word I say.'

'Jenny, when you speak, he listens. You must have noticed.'

'Well, that makes it even worse, doesn't it? He would immediately stop painting and start racing around the countryside looking for Christopher. And we both know what would happen if he found him. I'm pretty sure they won't let him paint in prison.'

'I think that might be a little extreme.'

'I don't think Russell is the type to let him off with a friendly warning. It's not for long, Thomas. Just let him get this exhibition out of the way and then I'll talk to him, I promise. If we're speaking to each other by then, of course.'

'Jenny...'

'No, Thomas. Enough.'

And I walked away.

I walked out of the house. Without a word to anyone, I

172

walked out of the house. Up the lane. Past Mrs Balasana's cottage. As usual, everything was immaculate. The grass was cut. All the flowers were perfect. Even all the leaves seemed to point in the same direction.

'It's like something from The Twilight Zone,*'* said Thomas, in awe. *'The horticultural equivalent of* The Midwich Cuckoos.*'*

I walked on past the Braithwaites' farm, through the gate at the top of the lane, and up onto the moor. I stood for a moment, enjoying the silence and then strolled slowly to the stream and sat on my favourite flat rock, watching the brown water as it swirled past.

The day was hot and still and the only sound was the gurgling water. There were no sheep in sight, no birds, no nothing. Just me. I thought how nice it would be to spend the rest of my life here, sitting on this warm rock like a landlocked mermaid, watching the stream splashing and falling, and never have to worry about anything again.

I looked up and Christopher was watching me.

He was some way off, but I knew it was him. I had no idea what he could be doing all the way up here, and then a nasty little voice in my head said, 'He followed you.'

My first instinct was to run. Run far and run fast. My second was to stay put. Because I always ran. In times of trouble I always ran away. But now, now that my heart was thumping with fear and my blood was up, my second instinct was to stand my ground.

I was in no immediate danger. He was on the other side of the stream. He could wade across if he wanted but here, just at this point, it was fast and deep and rocky. By the time he struggled over to my side, I could be as far away as Rushford. And I remembered again, this was Christopher. Bully and coward. Face to face confrontation was not for him. He was all about arranging accidents, or setting fires and then making himself scarce. He really didn't do up close and personal. Neither did I, but he didn't know that. I hoped.

I stood slowly, so I could run if I had to, and faced him.

We stood looking at each other for a very long time. I forced down my panic and made myself look at him properly. To note details.

My first thought was that he had lost some hair. Yes, he was wearing his dark hair shorter, which didn't suit him in the least, but his hairline was definitely moving towards the back of his head. He looked older, too, with heavy pouches under his eyes that I didn't remember from the last time we met. And he'd thickened around the middle. He wasn't tall – not much taller than me, and I'm not tall – and the extra weight made him look as if he had a football under his shirt. I was fairly confident that if I had to run for my life, he wouldn't be able to catch me.

Unless, of course, he had a gun.

'*Where on earth would he get a gun?*' said Thomas, comfortingly close.

'No idea. Where does anyone get a gun? The gun shop?'

My heart was beginning to slow to its normal rhythm. I was remembering to breathe. I was quite safe. Thomas was here.

'Don't take your eyes off him.'

'*Why?*'

'I want to see where he goes.'

I didn't know what his purpose was today. Whether he wanted to frighten me, or make me run away, or just have a bit of fun from a safe distance. The stream gurgled on and somewhere, high overhead, a bird trilled. Then, without any warning, he turned and jogged back uphill. He paused for a moment on the crest, silhouetted against the sky, and then he disappeared.

'Why has he gone?'

'Because Russell's coming,' said Thomas, looking around. *'Talk to him.'* And then he too disappeared.

Russell flung himself onto my rock and pulled me down beside him, retaining his hold on my hand. His hair was even more disarranged than usual. He still had green and blue paint on his face and he was breathing hard as if he'd been running.

'Jenny, I need to speak to you.'

And I needed to speak to him. I made up my mind. No more stupid messing about. He would just have to drag his mind away from his exhibition, because he needed to hear this. I thought I might begin with a quick sanity test.

'Did you see that man?'

'The hiker? The one who just walked back over the hill?'

Well, that was a relief. I was scared, unhappy and still resentful but not actually insane.

I took a deep breath, focussed on the swirling water, took another, and said, 'It was Christopher.'

The silence went on for a very long time, giving me an excellent opportunity to wish I'd never said anything, before he said, 'Jenny, I think that may be connected with what I wanted to talk to you about. I'm sorry, love, but I have something to tell you.'

Something in his voice made me turn to face him, stupid quarrel forgotten.

'What? What's happened? Is it … Joy?'

'No, no she's fine. But there's been an accident.'

Panic gripped me. Christopher had been here. What had he done?

'Who? Not Andrew? Or Kevin?'

'No, no.'

'Then who?'

'Julia.'

175

Whatever I'd been expecting – it wasn't that. I felt my stomach slide away from me.

'Julia? What … happened?'

'Her car went off the road.'

'Is she badly hurt?'

'No.'

'How do you … know?'

'Francesca just rang to tell me.'

Oh really? Something resentful stirred inside me. 'Why did she … think you, of all people, would be interested?'

'She told me you went to see her and you asked her about Christopher. So, now I'm asking you. What's going on, Jenny?'

'I was going to … tell you and then…'

'And then we were too busy not talking to each other to talk to each other.' He shifted impatiently. 'Jenny … we weren't going to do this. We agreed. No stupid sulking.'

'I know,' I said. 'I know.'

'So, what's happening? Talk to me.'

'Julia was here.'

'Yes, I'd gathered that. And that she wanted money?'

'Yes – and a … lot of it.'

'So I saw. Four hundred pounds.'

'She wanted … ten thousand.'

I had the unaccustomed pleasure of seeing my husband speechless. Just for once.

'Did she say why?'

'She said she … wanted to go away.'

'Ten thousand pounds? Where was she going? The outer rings of Saturn?' 'Wherever it was, she … was going immediately. Her … case was ready … packed and in the car.'

'Did she say why?'

176

'No, but I assumed it was … something to do with … Christopher coming back.'

'When did you first see him?'

'I thought I saw him that … day we were at Half Baked.'

'When you dropped the cup?'

'Well, it was a bit of a shock … but before you start shouting again,' because he'd taken a deep breath, 'I honestly wasn't sure. I … mean, he was the last person I ever expected to see again and I … talked myself into believing I'd made a mistake and it was just someone who looked like him … because when I looked again, he was gone. The light was behind him and I only saw him for a second or two.'

Although it had seemed much longer at the time.

'Have you seen him since then?'

'Not until today, but I think he was the one who let … Boxer and Marilyn out. And shoved them in Mrs Balasana's garden.'

'To make trouble.'

'Well, that's what he … does, isn't it?'

'I think he's making more than trouble, Jenny.'

'You think he – that he was responsible … for Julia's accident?'

'She came here. And paid the price.'

I clutched his arm. 'Russell.'

'She's not badly hurt, Jenny.'

'That means nothing. He might have intended something serious and she was lucky. Why is he doing this? And where is Uncle Richard in all this?'

Because he was the one we should really be worrying about.

'I don't know, Jenny. He might be behind Christopher. He might not. Or,' he paused, 'he might be trying to rein him in and tie up any loose ends.'

A couple of years ago, after a dinner party that was memorable even by Frogmorton standards, Russell had thrown Richard and Julia out of our lives. And Christopher along with them. And then our feed store had caught fire. We were almost certain it was Christopher's parting shot – partly revenge and partly to destroy any evidence he thought we might have against him. We had no proof it was him, as we'd been careful to say when giving our statements, but since, less than three hours later, Julia and Richard had got him out of the country, everyone had drawn their own conclusions. The insurance company had refused to pay the claim – something else for Russell to hold against my horrible family – and we had thought that was the end of the matter.

'Are we … loose ends?'

He said very gently, 'We might be.'

'Russell – what about Joy? We have a baby.'

'Don't worry, Jenny – I've asked Kevin to come back and stay with us for a while. And Andrew will call in every day. We'll be fine.'

'What is Julia saying?'

'Wisely, she says she doesn't remember a thing.'

I nodded. He put his arm around me. I leaned against him and, for a moment, we sat in peace as the brown water swirled past us.

It didn't last, of course. His phone rang, strident and demanding. I was so glad I didn't have one of those things.

He glanced at the display and I saw his shoulders droop.

'Everything all right?' said Thomas, appearing like the Cheshire Cat. Minus grin, of course.

Russell sighed 'It's Francesca. Again.' He opened his phone. I couldn't make out her words but he was obviously enduring some sort of verbal onslaught. I sat back in the sun and, despite everything, enjoyed his struggle.

'No … Because I'm not at home … No, honestly, I'm not … Up on the moors … It's a lovely day – why wouldn't I be? Anyway, no. Not today, because … When? … What? … Why didn't you let me know? … I *do* answer my phone.'

I nodded. He did. The bloody thing never stopped ringing.

'Well, no, not when I'm painting, obviously … Because I'm concentrating and it gets covered in paint … Franny, look I … I've always called you Franny. Get over it … Well, if you want me to take this bloody donkey then you'll just have to put up with it, won't you? … No, I've always been rude. You know that … And heartless … And selfish, yes … Yes, and stupid as well, but not stupid enough to be abusing the person I want a favour from … Tell me again what you want me to do and try not to use the words useless, egotistical, self-centred, unkind or offensive … Yes, I thought so. You just can't do it, can you?… What? … What time? … Well, why didn't you say so?' He snapped his phone shut. 'We need to get back, Jenny. We're having a donkey delivered.'

'Do you still want to do that? With everything that's happening?'

'Well, I thought it would take your mind off things.'

'Off what? Our … non-laying chickens. Our possibly litigious … next-door neighbour? Your … painting deadlines? The fact we're living in a … state of … siege because my maniac relatives are running around somewhere?' I had a sudden thought. 'Russell, should we … call the police?'

'And say what? That a man who looked like Christopher might have stared at you in a threatening manner a couple of times?'

I nodded. True.

We walked back down the lane together, comfortably close. Russell put his arm loosely around my shoulders and talked. His latest picture, Boadicea and Desdemona's predilection for sleeping under the chicken house, Mrs Crisp's incessant demands for eggs, and a doom-laden prophecy about how the roof would fare this coming winter, all competed for my attention as we headed home. I think he thought his traumatic tale of buckets, tarpaulins, rising damp, falling damp and death by black mould spores would take my mind off our current problems.

'Such a thoughtful husband.'

And then Christopher went out of our heads altogether.

CHAPTER THIRTEEN

We arrived to find a single horsebox slowly backing into the yard.

'Perfect timing,' said Russell. 'Now then, Jilly.'

The driver, a young woman with lots of curly hair, freckles and a wide grin, jumped down. 'How do, Russell?'

She began to let down the back. 'He's a one and no mistake. I hope you can do something with him. We've done everything we can, but we just can't get through to him. We're hoping being a special pet again will help.'

She disappeared into the horsebox, emerging a minute later with Jack.

Accustomed as I was to tiny Marilyn, my first thought was – he's so big. My second was – he's so sad.

He stood at the top of the ramp. Over in their field, Boxer and Marilyn were nearly bursting with curiosity. If Marilyn stretched out her neck much further she could qualify as a giraffe. The chickens, with the exception of Francesca, up on the roof as usual, were huddled near their house, making nosey chicken noises.

Jack, on the other hand, showed no sign of interest in anything. He consented to be led down the ramp with Jilly's gentle encouragement and stood politely at the bottom.

I remembered when Russell had brought my horse, the other Thomas, to me. My birthday present. How he'd stood, bright-eyed, looking around him with interest, ears flicking back and forth as he took in the sights and sounds of Frogmorton.

Jack wasn't beaten or starved. Some of the cases at the donkey sanctuary were dreadful, but Jack looked perfectly normal.

And then I looked again.

Unlike Marilyn, Jack was black, except where the sun shone on his coat and then he was auburn. Again, unlike Marilyn, he had neat little feet. His mane and forelock lay tidily and were nowhere near as exuberant as Marilyn's. But he was so sad. So very sad.

He stood motionless, his ears drooping, staring at the ground.

'Hello, Jack,' said Russell, gently stroking his neck.

There was no reaction. I had the impression that if Russell had beaten him with a stick the result would have been the same.

I said to Thomas, 'What's the matter with him. Is he afraid of us? Can you do anything?'

'He's grieving,' said Thomas, very quietly.

'Oh, my goodness,' said Mrs Crisp, peering from the back door. 'He looks like Eeyore.'

'He is Eeyore,' I said. 'He's … more Eeyore than Eeyore himself.'

Russell went to help Jilly raise the ramp, signed something, and we watched her drive away in a cloud of dust.

Jack never even gave her a glance.

Marilyn was nearly killing herself trying to see through the gate. Five pairs of beady eyes watched from underneath their hen house. Rooster Cogburn asserted his independence on the water trough.

'All right, everyone. Standard procedure for a new arrival,' said Russell. 'I'll take him into his box. He can have a look around, and then we'll leave him in peace until I bring the other two in for their bedtime. He may as well get used to us as soon as possible.'

'He looks so sad,' I said.

'Give him a fortnight,' said Russell, 'and then…'

'He'll … look even sadder,' I said.

'Very possibly,' said Russell.

I went in a couple of hours later, taking a carrot or two with me. He was standing neatly in the middle of his box, staring at the wall. It dawned on me that his box looked immaculate, unlike Marilyn's whose bedding is kicked around and water spilled,. If we took him out now there would be nothing to show he had ever been there. He did look up as I approached and I thought I saw a flash of something in his eyes, then he saw who it was, and returned his stare to the wall. It was heart-breaking.

'He does that all time,' said Russell, coming in quietly for once. 'He's waiting for his owner to come back.'

'I thought she died.'

'She did. She's never going to come back.'

'Will he ever accept that?'

'I don't know. Andrew says donkeys do grieve. Sometimes they have to see a body to accept a friend is dead.'

I closed my eyes. 'Russell…'

'Don't panic – we're not going to dig her up.'

I relaxed.

'Unless we absolutely have to.'

I said, 'Hello, Jack,' and held out a carrot. He looked over, sniffed it carefully, and then turned his head away. Accustomed as I was to Marilyn enthusiastically consuming everything within reach, and then making every effort to get to things that weren't, I found this disconcerting, and mentioned it to Russell as we left the stables and he prepared to embark on his evening ordeal of chicken and donkey gathering.

'Give him a while,' he said. 'I expect we take a bit of

getting used to. Are you busy?' he added hopefully, but I, foreseeing the possibility of being roped into the daily circus, was already heading for the stairs and Joy.

We tried. We tried very hard. He did eat and drink, but not very much. Certainly not by Marilyn's standards. His coat was dull. His eyes were blank and incurious. He was surrounded by nosey chickens, a neurotic racehorse, an omnivorous donkey, and the cat from hell, and he ignored all of them. And us, too. Russell, not used to being ignored, was initially quite put out and then quite worried. If we turned him into the field with the others, he would stand for a while then begin to graze, neatly and quietly.

Most heart-breaking of all was the hopeful expression on his face whenever anyone approached him. His subsequent realisation that it wasn't whom he was waiting for brought tears to my eyes.

Russell sighed. 'He reminds me of you when you first came here.'

'What do you … mean?'

'Doing everything as quickly and quietly as possible. Doing the minimum. Hoping not to be noticed. Wrapped in misery.'

'He's waiting,' said Thomas

'For what?'

'For his owner to return.'

'But she's dead.'

'I know.'

It made me want to cry. He would look up every time the gate opened. Hoping for someone who would never come. And then the light in his eyes would fade and his ears would droop again.

Russell spent a lot of time with him that he couldn't really afford. He was painting furiously, trying to get everything ready for the forthcoming exhibition, and

184

although he said nothing to me, I knew he was worried about what Christopher might be up to. Aunt Julia was discharged from hospital. Francesca said she had gone north, to visit relatives. Whether that was true or whether it was something Julia had told her to throw anyone off the scent, we had no way of knowing.

Marilyn didn't help. Oblivious to the fact she herself was a donkey, she took one look at our new arrival and hid behind Boxer. Who took one look himself, decided he wanted nothing to do with any of it, and went to stand down at the very end of his field. Which meant that, to stand behind him, Marilyn was practically in the hedge.

'Boxer's actually showing some faint signs of intelligence not wanting to be involved with this little lot,' said Russell, panting past with a chicken under one arm. 'Who'd have thought? Look, can I leave this with you? Time's ticking on and if I don't set paint to canvas sometime today then I'm going to be in trouble.'

'Of course,' I said, relieving him of Agatha. 'I'll bring you a coffee later.'

I did take him a coffee. And one for myself as well. I didn't speak to him – he wouldn't have heard me anyway – but made myself comfortable on his scruffy sofa and watched him work. Today's music was a little more restful. The quartet from *Rigoletto* filled the room with beauty.

The place was a tip, which was a good sign. Sketches in charcoal and pencil were pinned to the walls, all liberally covered in painty fingerprints. Canvases in various stages of completion were propped against the walls and a mound of pizza boxes in the corner spoke of a period of creative productivity.

I'd remembered to leave his coffee some distance away from him. Russell's not big on concentration at the best of times, and the number of times he's dipped his brushes in his coffee and tried to drink solvent is beyond counting. In addition to everything else, I probably save his life about three times a week.

Eventually he became aware of the smell of coffee and peered around his easel.

'Hello Jenny, is that you?'

'Actually, it's your … morning coffee, but your … wife is attached if you want her to stay for a while.'

'Wife welcome,' he said, squinting at his painting.

'How's it going?'

He made a 'meh' sound. 'It's all right, but it's not…'

'Not what?'

'I'm not sure. Something's missing.'

'This sofa's really uncomfortable,' I said, to take his mind off things. He loves it and steadfastly refuses to get it replaced. Or re-upholstered. Or even re-covered.

He patted the arm affectionately. 'This old thing could tell a tale or two.'

I sighed in mock exasperation. 'Did you … sleep with all your models?'

'Of course not,' he said, shocked. 'Only one. And even she abandoned me in the end.'

He spoke lightly and I thought what a long way we'd both come. Not so long ago he'd been incapable of talking about Francesca leaving him. Not without a great deal of alcohol and anguish. In an effort to sort him out, his father had packed him off into the army. He meant well and I think Russell understood that now, but it hadn't ended positively. Relations between the two of them had deteriorated and then his father had died. Convinced that without Francesca he could never paint again, Russell had taken to drink as both his house and his world crumbled around him. Now, though, not only could he talk about it, but with humour, too. I put my arms around him.

186

'Steady on,' he said, grinning. 'Just because I'm covered in Payne's Grey doesn't mean you should be too.'

'So tell me about these models then,' I said, sipping my coffee. 'Tell me about all these naked women you had to force yourself to look at.'

'What an ordeal, Jenny. Day in and day out. No respite. None at all. Every time I looked up there was another piece of female anatomy dangling in front of me. People have no idea how we artists suffer. It was exhausting.'

'Well, if you … slept with all of them, I'm not surprised.'

He was shocked. 'What do you take me for? No, never mind,' he added, as I opened my mouth to tell him. 'Apart from anything else, there were thirty other people in the life class with me. I know Andrew always says I'm a bit of an exhibitionist, but even I draw the line at performing in front of thirty other people. Not that most of them would have noticed. They'd have just told me to hold it right there and picked up another brush. A big brush, of course.' He grinned at me.

'Would that have been the one for your head?'

'The one I do remember, though … Christa. She had all this red hair. Really, really red. The most gorgeous vibrant crimson red. And the collar and cuffs matched, if you get my drift.'

'Russell…'

He wasn't listening. He was lost in his past. 'I remember her stretched out on an acid green silk sheet and the way the shaft of sunlight just caught her hair…' He stared into space, mug in one hand and brush in the other. 'I think I might still have it somewhere.'

'Christa?'

'No, idiot. The sheet.' He put down his mug and brush, crossed the room, and wrenched open a cupboard door. A

187

pile of different materials lay folded on the bottom shelf. 'Yes, here it is. Oh, wait – look at this, Jenny. I'd forgotten I still had this.' He yanked something free. 'Stand back.'

With a dramatic gesture, he threw a great length of glorious blue velvet in the air, to settle over the couch. But it wasn't just one colour. Depending on which way the nap lay, it was purple, or it was turquoise, or it was nearly every shade of blue in between. Sumptuous and opulent, it lay across the couch, reflecting the light and capturing the shadows.

I experienced a stab of jealousy, imagining myself stretched out on blue velvet while Russell painted … I pulled myself together. 'Who lay on this one?'

He didn't answer, staring at it, deep in thought. I'd lost him again. I smiled, shook my head and moved towards the door.

'Where are you going?'

'I was leaving you to your lascivious thoughts.'

He crossed to the door and locked it. 'Jenny, you are my lascivious thoughts.'

We looked at each other for a long time.

'Take off your clothes.'

'What? Now?'

'Yes, I mean it. Take off your clothes.'

Well, the door was locked. Joy was with Mrs Crisp. Thomas had disappeared, doing the things that invisible golden horses do at eleven o'clock in the morning. It was just me and Russell. And *Rigoletto*, of course.

He heaved the canvas off his easel and stood it carefully against the wall. Selecting another, he set it up and looked around impatiently. 'Do you want a hand?'

'Russell, it's half past eleven in the morning. I can't just…'

He grinned wickedly, his hair flopping down over one

188

eye. 'Can't you?'

And suddenly, I felt wicked too. I pulled off my T-shirt, kicked off my sandals, slipped out of my jeans and stood awkwardly, wondering what to do next.

'And the rest,' he said, pulling out a new palette. 'All of it, Jenny.'

I did as I was told, pulling a fold of the blue velvet around me for warmth and modesty.

He glanced up and frowned. 'Not quite.'

He came to stand in front of me. 'Don't be afraid, I'm not going to eat you. Now, let's get this hair down.' He arranged it gently on my bare shoulders. I shivered under his touch. 'Now, give your head a good shake and let it fall over one eye.'

'What?'

'Think Jessica Rabbit. Now, I need you to trust me for this next bit.'

'What next bit?'

He picked up the velvet and swirled it loosely around me. 'Look at me Jenny. The couch is just behind you. I want you to fall backwards. You won't hurt yourself. Just trust me. Close your eyes if it helps.'

I closed my eyes.

His lips were very close to my ear. I could feel his hot breath as he whispered, 'Just … let go.'

I let go and the next moment I was sprawled across the couch, entangled in folds of heavy velvet.

'Perfect,' he said. 'Just what I wanted.' He twitched the material aside. 'Where's your leg? Ah, got it.'

He gently lifted my leg clear and laid it back on the velvet. 'Is that comfortable? Could you stay like that for a while?'

'Russell, you're not … painting me nude.'

'You're not nude. You're wearing three acres of blue velvet. And very nice you look too. Everyone will think so.'

I struggled to sit up. 'They ... bloody won't.'

'No, don't move, Jenny. I mean it.'

'But people will recognise me.'

He picked up a piece of charcoal and began to sketch. 'No, they won't.'

'They'll see my ... face.'

'It's not your face I'm painting.'

'Somehow that doesn't help.'

He made no reply. I'd lost him again.

Time passed. I was actually quite warm and comfortable, if a trifle unconventionally posed, but the door was locked.

Russell worked at a tremendous rate, rubbing charcoal into the canvas, muttering to himself, pushing his hair off his face, staring from me to the canvas and back again. Transferring energy from himself to the canvas in front of him.

Eventually he stood back. 'I haven't finished. Don't move.'

He rummaged in a drawer and pulled out an old polaroid camera. Moving around, he snapped me from every angle, paying particular attention to the folds of velvet and the way they fell to the floor. That done, he seized a palette and began to squeeze paint. Blue, purple, magenta, green, white – huge blobs of colour dotted the surface and, it has to be said, a great deal of Russell as well. Seizing a couple of brushes, he began to lay in the colour – wild sweeps of it if his arm movements were anything to go by.

He worked steadily for about forty-five minutes, talking to himself, humming odd snatches of music and occasionally bursting into song. Once he said, 'You still OK, Jenny?'

'I'm fine,' I said, because I was. The pose wasn't

difficult. I could listen to the music or close my eyes and daydream a little.

'Not much longer. I just want to make sure I've got the colours right and the light is perfect at the moment. Your hair glowing but your face is in shadow. I really think, Jenny, that this might be quite good.'

He worked furiously for about another half hour, scrubbing in the paint, working as much with his fingers as with his brushes.

Finally, he had what he wanted. He laid down his palette and stared hard at what he'd done so far. I was dying to see it myself, but I lay still as instructed. Because I'm a Good Girl.

That done, he stepped away from his easel and stared first at me, then at his work, then at me again. Comparing, measuring.

I lay back and watched him through my eyelashes.

He came closer, crouched, and inspected the way the material was falling, making a minute adjustment.

My bare leg looked very long and pale against the dark material. He reached out and touched it very gently, running his fingertips up the inside of my thigh, and I felt it with every cell of my body.

Russell has two ways of making love. The first is cheerful and chatty and makes me laugh and is full of joy and fun. The second is more dangerous. His eyes grow dark and intense. His focus is complete. He doesn't talk at all and usually, by the time he's finished, neither can I. It's a wild ride, sometimes.

This was one of those times.

CHAPTER FOURTEEN

He worked solidly for two days and nights. I barely saw
him. But he seemed happy enough and if the loud singing
all over the house was anything to go by, this new
painting was going well. If it turned out as well as he
hoped, it would be included in the exhibition. I was torn
between panic at people knowing it was me and a huge
satisfaction knowing that Francesca would no longer be
the only person who'd had a stunning Checkland portrait
forming the centrepiece of a London exhibition. I felt a
moment's guilt at such an unworthy thought. But only a
moment's.

Emerging on the third day, mostly paint free, he
announced it was time for another driving lesson. Not that
I was very enthusiastic. Not with everything else going on
at the moment.

'*Oh go on,*' urged Thomas. '*I'd love to see you
driving, Jenny. How clever you are.*'

I shot him a look, which he blandly ignored.

Even Russell was unexpectedly firm.

'You mustn't give up just because you've had some
setbacks,' he said, handing me the keys. 'Do you
remember what happened when you were learning to
ride? When you kept falling off.'

'I do,' I said, bitterly, handing them back. 'You pulled
me to my feet with one hand, dusted me down with the
other, and made me get straight back on again. Whether I
wanted to or not.'

'I did, didn't I?' he said, proudly.

'My nose was bleeding!'

'I remember it well.'

'And then Mrs Crisp came out and shouted at you.'

'I don't remember that at all. I'm sure you've got that wrong. Anyway, what I'm saying is – a driving lesson is just what you need. There's nothing like crushing a few oil drums under your front wheels – much easier than pedestrians by the way. They tend to try to run away and can be quite hard to catch sometimes – and – I've lost the gist. Where was I?'

'Crushing pedestrians beneath his front wheels,' said Thomas, amused. *'I can't believe you're letting Russell Checkland teach you to drive.'*

'He's very good,' I said, doggedly placing wifely loyalty over accuracy once more.

It didn't go too badly, although oil drums f and p would never be the same again, and the next day was the opening of Sharon's cupcake shop. Really, with everything going on at the moment, I hardly had time to think about Christopher at all.

We all went, all wearing something green or purple, or both. Joy was a sensation in her green and purple babysuit, specially made out of the same material as Sharon's tablecloths. Russell offered to hire her out on an hourly basis.

He took it upon himself to greet people at the door but, not feeling this was enough to stretch his talents sufficiently, left his post to roam up and down the street outside, as if the possession of a plate of cupcakes was an excellent reason for accosting ladies of all ages. I have to say his hit rate was impressive, so he may have been right.

Tanya and Andrew turned up. Russell ignored Andrew and flirted madly with Tanya who regarded him with Teutonic calm. Andrew and I sat down outside the kitchen on the back step with a quiet cup of tea while I told him about Christopher. And about Julia. He sat for a while staring at his tea, and then offered to come and stay at Frogmorton for a while. And Tanya too.

'It's not as if you don't have the room, Jenny. And we'd be happy to do that.'

'It's very kind of you, but we haven't seen hide nor hair of him for nearly a week now.'

'Typical Christopher,' said Andrew, grinning,' you just can't get a decent class of stalker these days.'

I grinned back and we were interrupted by Russell demanding to know what we were doing.

'Deploring declining standards in today's modern stalker,' said Andrew.

'Well, if you're talking about Christopher,' said Russell, 'then I'm in complete agreement. I, however, am talking about the fact that every time I turn around you're smiling at my wife. Go and smile at someone else's wife.'

'You do it beautifully,' I said to Andrew.

'Thank you,' he said, radiating Checkland charm.

It was a lovely afternoon, spending time with friends, helping out where required, and enjoying Sharon's success. Everything was light and happy and wonderful.

And then – all of a sudden – it wasn't.

We stayed until the very end. When even Russell had to admit he couldn't force down another cupcake. Although that didn't stop him accepting a boxful from Sharon – for later, she said. When he would be hungry again.

'In about thirty minutes, then,' said Thomas.

We said goodbye to Sharon and Kevin in the kitchen, while Mrs Crisp waited for Bill to come to take her away and do … whatever it was they did together.

'Hello,' said Thomas, as Bill edged his way through the door. *'Who's this?'*

'Bill the Insurance Man.'

'That's an odd choice of surname. Isn't it lucky he went into insurance. Imagine being a doctor with a name like that. Doctor Bill the Insurance Man will see you now,' he said, thoughtfully. 'It doesn't trip off the tongue, does it?'

'Well, it's not his real name, obviously.'

'What is his real name?'

'Good question. Waite. Wayman? Russell probably knows.'

'Are you sure about that? What do you know about him?'

'We know he's Mrs Crisp's boyfriend.'

'And?'

'Um...'

'Good grief.'

'Well, I expect Mrs Crisp knows all about him,' I said desperately, trying to make out we'd done our due diligence.

'Good afternoon, everyone,' said not Doctor Bill the Insurance Man.

We murmured politely.

'Can we give you a lift anywhere?' said Russell, fishing.

'No, thank you,' said Bill. 'It's not far.'

'Are you sure?' demanded Russell, adding another worm to the hook. 'It's no trouble, and Mrs Crisp has that thing with her leg.'

'What thing with my leg?' demanded Mrs Crisp, breaking off her conversation with Sharon.

'You know – you mentioned it the other day when I wanted you to help me worm Agatha.'

'It comes and goes,' she said, straight-faced.

'Really – and what causes that do you think?'

'I'm not sure. It usually comes on when I hear your Land Rover pulling into the yard.'

'Would you like me to get Andrew to check you out?'

'He's a vet.'

'I know that, but the principle's the same, isn't it? A leg is a leg.'

'There is nothing wrong with my leg,' she said dangerously.

'You don't have to be brave for me. Let's face it, the sooner poor Bill here is aware of your – well, other people might say "shortcomings", but we who love you prefer to think of them as your little quirks. For instance, Bill, did you know that on the nights of the full moon…'

I removed him before he experienced a quirky tea towel around his ear.

Andrew and Tanya followed us in their car. We were all having a takeaway and DVD evening back at Frogmorton.

Russell was in a happy mood, singing 'What shall we do with the drunken sailor?' loudly all the way back home and tooting the horn in time to the chorus. Joy squealed and waved her fists.

'More like her father every day,' said Thomas. *'Do you have plans for any more children?'*

'The only plan I have is for crispy fried beef and the new *Star Trek* movie.'

The afternoon had passed as we pulled into the yard. The place looked strangely empty without half a dozen challenged chickens running around, and Marilyn skittering all over the place, peering beguilingly through her fringe in the hopes of being given something to eat.

'I'll go and let them all out,' said Russell in resignation. 'Although by the time I've done that it'll be time to get them all back in again. Do you ever remember the days when we didn't spend all our time hauling livestock around?'

'Fondly,' I said, climbing out of the car with Joy before I could get roped into imminent livestock hauling. 'I'm off for a nice bath but I'll try to remember to spare you a thought.'

Andrew and Tanya had gone for the takeaway. I suspected they were deliberately dawdling, waiting until the dust settled and all our animals were in their rightful place.

The house had been shut up for the afternoon and smelled of dry sunshine and dust. I popped sleepy a Joy in her cot and went downstairs to open the French windows.

I didn't see him at first. I pushed open the doors and pulled the curtains well back to let in the fresh air.

And there he was.

He wasn't doing anything. Just standing in the garden, looking up at the bedroom windows. About twenty feet away. And suddenly, he was looking at me.

I froze, one hand still on the door handle.

Long, long seconds went by and nothing happened. All sound fled from the world. It was just him and me. Staring at each other. I realised that there was no barrier of any kind between us.

He moved first. Holding my gaze, he walked two steps to the fountain, unzipped his jeans and relieved himself into the pool. I could see the stream of urine in the sunlight and hear it splashing into the water.

I couldn't move. I was paralysed with fear. I don't know for how long I stood there while Christopher urinated into our pool, never taking his eyes off me, his face frighteningly expressionless.

Jenny. I'm here.

I was suddenly enveloped in the comforting smell of warm ginger biscuits. In one swift instinctive movement, I slammed the door shut and pulled the curtains across the window. A fraction of a second later, I thought No! Idiot!

That's how he got away last time, and fumbled the curtains open again.

Too late. He'd vanished. If he'd ever been there. Was I mad after all?

Another fraction of a second later, I thought Joy! I was half way up the stairs before I had time to think about it. I raced along the landing to Joy's room, crashing through the door. I don't know what I thought I might see, but there she was, on her back, legs in the air, talking to her feet. She turned her head towards me and smiled.

The sudden surge of relief completed what the shock of seeing Christopher had started, and my legs gave way. If I hadn't grabbed the back of a chair, I'd have been on the floor.

I can't remember crossing the room to her cot. I rested my arms on the rail and took a few minutes to get my breath back.

And then I had another thought.

Russell.

'Go,' said Thomas. *'I'll stay with Joy. She'll be quite safe. Go and find Russell.'*

I made sure her window was securely fastened and shot out of the room, colliding heavily with Russell, who was just on his way in.

He caught my arms. 'Steady on, Jenny. Where's the fire?'

I clutched at his jacket, praying the words would come. If ever there was an occasion in my life when it was vital – vital – to convey a warning, it was now.

I took a deep shuddering breath and struggled to assemble some words.

'Jenny, what's wrong?' He looked past me. 'Is it Joy? Is she ill?'

He pushed past me to see her lying in her cot, gurgling and happy as always, and turned back to me in puzzlement.

I tried. Oh God, how I tried. I could feel my stomach muscles clenching … my throat closing…

'Ru … Ru … Ru…'

There are those who take Russell Checkland at face value. The feckless artist racing around town in his clapped out Land Rover, shouting at the world. But, buried beneath all that – quite deeply buried, sometimes – is a clever man who sees far more than some people could ever imagine.

I've heard people say 'Oh, so and so is a rock,' and I can agree with that because Russell is my rock. And yes, I know he's also the jagged reef in Mrs Balasana's Sea of Tranquillity, and that if anyone could justifiably be described as an erratic boulder then it's Russell Checkland, but I also know that whenever I really, really need him – he's always there.

He was there now.

'All right, Jenny. No. Don't try to speak yet. Just breathe. And again. That's it.'

He held my face between his warm hands.

'Close your eyes. Take your time. That's very good. Lean on me and breathe.'

I was so busy gasping for breath, I didn't notice at first, but here it came again. I could smell the spicy tang of warm ginger biscuits again. Thomas was working his magic and the world was a different place.

I stopped gulping and breathed gently, concentrating on the pattern of his shirt, following first one colour and then another until, finally…

'Chris … topher … Saw him … Garden … here. Looking at me.'

I closed my eyes again, waiting for him to say, 'Are you sure?' Or 'You're imagining it, Jenny,' and he didn't. He never hesitated. Not for one moment. I knew there was a good reason I loved him. Turning his head, he shouted, 'Andrew!'

He believed me. I felt such a rush of gratitude. Tears sprang to my eyes.

'Jenny, stay here with Joy. Don't leave her. I'll come back in a minute, but you stay here.'

He clattered off down the stairs, still shouting for Andrew.

Braver now that I knew Russell and Andrew were around, I went to the window, opened it wide, and hung out, trying to see as much as I could.

Below me, the walled garden slept in the early evening sunshine. It was so quiet that I could hear the bees over the sound of the tinkling fountain. There was nothing there. No one in sight. The gate was open but the garden was empty. I closed the window and turned back into the room.

In the distance, I could hear Andrew and Russell calling to each other. There was no sign of Christopher anywhere. I tried to decide which was the greater catastrophe – me going mad or Christopher actually being here, and decided that if someone could assure me that Christopher was safely on the other side of the world, I could probably deal with madness. Because every time I saw him, he seemed that little bit closer. That little bit more threatening.

Someone tapped at the door. I jumped a mile before realising that Christopher was hardly likely to knock, was he? Instinctively I moved between the cot and the door. 'Yes?'

Tanya entered with a tray. 'I have brought tea.'

The adrenaline was draining from my system, leaving me cold and with a nasty taste in my mouth. I was aware that I was very thirsty and I would very much like a cup of tea. I managed a wobbly smile and nodded.

She set down the tray and prepared to bring order out of chaos. 'Jenny – you will sit down and drink this at once. You will feel much better afterwards.'

'And that's a command,' murmured Thomas.

'Andrew and Russell are outside now, locking everything up. I have closed all the windows downstairs. Christopher cannot get in. You and the little one will be safe. Now – you will drink your tea before it gets cold. And here is juice for Joy as well.'

I smiled and nodded my thanks, sat by Joy and didn't take my eyes off her until Russell came back.

Andrew and Tanya both offered to stay, but they had work the next day and, as Russell said, what could they do? Only lend a hand in beating Christopher to a pulp and he could do that all by himself, thank you very much. In fact he was looking forward to it.

We ate, and then they left, driving away into the night. Russell left all the lights turned on. I checked the upstairs windows and Russell the downstairs ones. He locked and bolted every door and, finally, we went to bed.

Russell sat thoughtfully on the bed and wound his battered alarm clock. 'Why would Christopher be doing this, Jenny? What do you think?'

I still felt cold and shaky. 'To frighten and upset me?' It's not nice to be reminded there was someone out there who actively meant me harm.

'Well yes, not a nice thing to do but why risk returning to Rushford for such a trivial purpose?'

'I'm not a … trivial purpose,' I said indignantly.

He grinned. 'We're really going to have to do something about this ego of yours, Jenny. To those of us who love you, you are, of course, quite delightful. Even with all your odd little quirks. You must try to accept the fact, however, that although I can't live without you,

202

you're hardly the most important person on the planet to everyone else. You used to be such a shy little thing. And so modest, too. Where did all this me, me, me come from?'

I slapped his arm and he grinned at me. 'That's better. But you're right, Jenny. What does he want? And why is he here? For all he knows he's top of every wanted list in the area.'

'Obviously he doesn't care. Is he?

He seemed miles away. 'Sorry, is he what?'

'Is he top of every wanted list?'

'No idea. We gave our statements after the fire and, as far as I know, that was it. I wonder…'

'What?'

'Well, I wonder if Bill knows anything.'

'Bill? Mrs Crisp's Bill?'

'How many other Bills do you think there are around the place? I know there's another of your deranged relatives out there and you're terrified for your life, but do try and buck up, Jenny.'

'Sorry,' I said meekly, feeling better every moment.

'I wonder if that's why he's here.'

'Christopher?'

'No, Bill. Concentrate, Jenny.'

'But why would Bill look for Christopher here. Surely this is the last place…'

'But that's what good hunters do. They work out where their prey will be and simply go there and wait.'

And now I'd forgotten Christopher completely. 'Do you mean it's Christopher he's after and not Mrs Crisp after all?'

'I'm beginning to wonder.'

'Or…' I said, and stopped.

'Or?' he prompted.

'Or he's in it with him.'

'Or he's in it with him,' he repeated, so calmly that I knew he must have thought of that himself.

I stared at him in horror. 'Oh Russell. No. Poor Mrs Crisp. What can we do?'

'I'm not sure at the moment, but if Bill does turn out to be not who we think he is – or who he wants us to think he is – then I shall definitely be taking him around the back of the barn and having a quick word with him.'

'Russell.'

He patted my arm reassuring, in much the same way he does for Boxer. 'Oh don't worry. They'll only be little words and they won't take long.'

'I still don't understand what Christopher hopes to get from this. Is he hoping I'll go insane? Or that we'll split up? What could possibly justify the risk he's taking?'

'No idea,' he said cheerfully. 'But I expect we'll find out soon.'

CHAPTER FIFTEEN

I hardly slept that night, lifting my head off the pillow for every sound. And believe me, there are a lot of sounds in the country at night. Several times I got up to lean out of the window, checking to see if the garden was still empty. Russell had left all the outside lights on and the whole place was bathed in a harsh, white light. I was betting we'd have Mrs Balasana around in the morning to complain.

We'd moved Joy's cot in with us. I could hear her deep, regular breathing in the dark. The third time I tried to get out of bed Russell tightened his arm around me and said, 'It's like sleeping with a revolving door. Go to sleep.'

'I can't sleep.'

'Then allow me to make a suggestion as to how to pass the time until morning. Give me your hand.'

'Your daughter is in the room. What sort of pervert are you?'

'I'm not any sort of pervert at all. I was going to suggest counting sheep on your fingers. What did you think I meant?'

'Nothing,' I said hastily.

I was up early the next morning. Up even before Russell, which doesn't often happen. I changed Joy, took her to him, and left the two of them playing Duvet Dinosaurs together while I went downstairs.

Just for the record, I had Boxer in his field, the chickens out of their henhouse, and Jack and Marilyn installed in the yard in under one sixteenth of the time it takes for Russell to achieve the same thing.

Mrs Crisp brought me a mug of tea and I took a moment to sit on the bench by the back door, enjoying the unfamiliar peace. It was yet another beautiful morning, and sitting here in the sunshine, with all the normal everyday noises of Frogmorton around me, it was hard to believe that Christopher had ever been here.

Jack walked slowly across the yard and took up his usual position by the wall, staring at the ground.

'He's not getting any better, is he?' said Thomas.

I shook my head.

'I'm beginning to wonder if drastic measures might be called for.'

I twisted to look up at him. 'How drastic?'

'Oh,' he said vaguely. *'I don't know. Don't worry about it, Jenny.'*

'Don't tell me you're considering digging up his owner, as well?'

'As well as who?'

'As well as Russell.'

'Why would I need to dig up Russell?'

I closed my eyes.

We had a late breakfast together. All of us – and it was rather pleasant. The only thing missing – as Mrs Crisp pointed out – were our breakfast eggs.

Russell demanded to know what this obsession over eggs was all about anyway, and she said she didn't know – it was so long since she'd seen one she'd practically forgotten what they looked like. Russell replied that eggs weren't the only things on the breakfast menu these days and he personally would be quite happy with a kipper. She responded by saying that he had a much better chance of getting a kipper from those feathered nitwits than he ever would of seeing an egg, and just as they were preparing to get down to it properly, there was a tap at the door and Bill walked in.

I'd completely forgotten it was Thursday.

Russell muttered something and pretended to be interested in a leaflet giving details of the Harvest Festival – something which he'd refused to attend on the grounds that the last religious ceremony we'd attended had been famous for real-life parturition and he wasn't doing that again.

Mrs Crisp slapped down the teapot and pointed out that:

a) He hadn't been at the Nativity play.
b) The only things giving birth had been a small sheep and his wife.
c) If he wanted kippers he'd have to go and get them. Or dig a hole, fill it with water, and raise his own. And that we could just as easily do without kippers as we could without eggs. And that if Russell was involved then we would probably have to.

He lifted Joy from her chair, tucked her under one arm in much the same way as one of his chickens, snatched up two pieces of toast, informed us, with dignity, that he would be in his studio, and left the room.

I smiled at Bill.

'Hello. Would you like some coffee?'

'Thank you, no. I'm just passing through.' He smiled. He had a nice smile. His crinkly grey hair was neatly trimmed and he dressed well but I couldn't get the image of Bill the Hunter out of my mind.

Thomas stared hard at him.

'What are you doing?'

'Looking for signs he's using Mrs Crisp for his own unscrupulous ends.'

'How exactly would you recognise these signs?'

'I'm a horse. I have wisdom and insight.'

'And what exactly is your wisdom and insight telling you right at this very moment?'

'That he seems like a very nice man.'

'Exactly the same conclusion the rest of us have come to.'

'Yes, but my conclusion was reached through wisdom and insight, Jenny. You only guessed at it.'

I was conscious that Russell would expect me to take advantage of this opportunity to glean information from Bill. By any and all means available.

'Are you going to water-board him?' asked Thomas.

'If necessary.' I turned to the really not very sinister at all figure standing patiently by the door.

'So, what's happening today?'

'Mrs Crisp and I are going into Rushford later today,' he said gravely.

'That's nice. Anything special?'

'Not today.'

'That implies there might be something special on other days,' said Thomas, quickly. *'Probe further.'*

Since I had no idea how to do any such thing, it was fortunate that Bill pulled out a thick brown envelope and handed it to her. 'This came this morning. I thought you might like to see.'

'Interesting,' said Thomas. *'Quick – ask what it is.'*

I'm not Russell, however, and I was still struggling for some way to phrase things tactfully, when Russell himself re-entered the kitchen. He eyed Bill with disfavour, 'Still here?' turned to Mrs Crisp, spotted the envelope and opened his mouth to probe further.

Mrs Crisp, however, had lived with Russell for most of

his life.

'Oh, silly me,' she said brightly. 'Russell, I'd completely forgotten to tell you that Mrs Balasana telephoned earlier. She wants a word about our lights being on all night. Apparently she didn't get a wink of sleep and she wants to talk to you about it and … Where are you going?'

Russell was half way across the yard before I could stop him. We heard his Land Rover clatter into life and roar out of the yard.

Mrs Crisp patted her hair complacently, and smiled at Bill. 'I'll see you this afternoon, then.'

I thought Mrs Crisp had been joking about Mrs Balasana and the lights, but no such luck.

I was looking out of the window at the time and for one moment could hardly believe my eyes. We had both Marilyn and Jack out so the gate was closed, but she was in such a hurry that she climbed over, rather than fiddle with the latch.

Jack, standing quietly by the water trough, looked up at her, pricking his long dark ears. I waited for his inevitable disappointment but, this time, something was different. He took two or three paces towards her and I just had time to think, hello, what's going on there? before Marilyn tip-tupped over and started giving her the once over for food.

Mrs Balasana ignored both of them, almost running to our back door. I said to Mrs Crisp, 'Something's wrong,' and went to let her in.

She looked dreadful. If I thought she was capable of such a thing I would say she had been crying. Her expensive jacket was unfastened, her scarf flung around her neck any old how, and her expensive jeans were dusty around the bottoms. She looked hot and distraught.

209

I flung open the door. 'Mrs Balasana, come in. Is ... something wrong? Can we help?'

I had to spend the next minute or so persuading the chickens that an open door was not necessarily an invitation to join us inside, and when eventually I got back into the kitchen, hot and bothered, Mrs Crisp had persuaded her to sit down.

'Whatever is the ... matter, Mrs Balasana? Are you...?'

I was struggling for the word 'ill' which wouldn't come out, but just for once, she didn't leap in ahead of me.

Mrs Crisp had the tea things ready on the kitchen table, including the biscuit tin. She surreptitiously whipped off the lid and Marilyn herself could not have subjected the contents to closer inspection than she did, but apparently all was well because she set it down again.

'Actually Jenny, I don't think she's come for a biscuit,' said Thomas.

He was right. I never thought I would use the word dishevelled to describe Mrs Balasana but her cheeks were flushed and she had a selection of small leaves and twigs in her hair.

'Please,' she said, grasping my hand across the table. 'You must help me.'

'Of course, we will,' I said. 'What's the ... matter?'

'Bundle's gone. I can't find her anywhere. She never goes out by herself and she won't know how to find her way back home. What shall I do?'

She didn't bother waiting for my answer. 'I must find her. I must. Please can you help me. I don't have anyone else. She's so small and she'll be carried off by a fox, or caught in a trap, or run over, or taken by vivisectionists...'

I caught her flying hands. 'Mrs Balasana. Ananda, please ... please try to calm down.'

210

I looked over to Mrs Crisp who was already pouring the tea. She nodded.

I turned back to Mrs Balasana. 'Of course we'll help. We'll be happy to. Just give us some details. Is she wearing one of her little coats?'

'No.' She shook her head. 'She doesn't wear them in the house.'

That was a shame. A dog wearing a bright red Royal Stewart tartan would be easy to spot. A thought struck me.

'How did she get out?'

'I don't know. All the doors were closed. But the windows were open. Perhaps she climbed out.'

I was dubious. On the other hand, she might, for some reason, have jumped onto a chair, from there to a windowsill and from there to freedom.

'Is she tagged?'

'Yes. Yes, she is.'

'Is Andrew your vet?'

'Mr Checkland? Yes. Yes, he's very good isn't he? Bundle loves him. Oh, where could she be?' And off she went again.

Mrs Crisp put a cup of tea in front of her and I handed her a piece of kitchen roll. She gulped and blew her nose, her hands shaking in distress.

'Well, Mrs Balasana, I … think you should drink your tea and when you … feel better, I think you should go home and…'

She jumped to her feet, chair scraping on the tiles. 'Oh no, I must look for her. She's never been out alone before. She'll be so frightened.'

'…because as you say, she's not used to … being outside and she's … probably had a quick … sniff around, decided it's not for her, and is sitting on the … doorstep, waiting for you to let her back in again.'

Her face lit up with hope. 'Oh, do you think so?'

'I do, yes. And I'm going to … telephone Andrew and see if he knows anything and he'll … put the word out. And then I'll … go and have a good look around all our … buildings, to see if she's managed to get herself shut in somewhere. That does happen, you know. And I'll telephone the … Braithwaites and they'll do the same.'

She reached out a hand. 'Thank you. Thank you, Mrs Checkland. You're so kind.'

'Not at all. I'm happy to help. I'll call Russell too – he can keep his eyes open on his way home. Please, drink your tea … before you go.'

She drained her cup in one unladylike gulp and set it back in the saucer. 'Thank you, Mrs Crisp. That was very welcome.'

Mrs Crisp blinked in surprise, and then smiled. 'You're very welcome. Mrs Checkland will be on the telephone for a while – would you like me to walk you up the lane?'

'No. Oh, no. I shall be perfectly all right. I'm sure Mrs Che – Jenny is right, and she'll be sitting by the gate waiting for me. I just … I can't … I can't lose her, you know.' She looked at Mrs Crisp. 'We lose everyone in the end, don't we?'

Mrs Crisp nodded. 'But sometimes, others find *us*.'

Mrs Balasana sat very still for a moment and then, with a flurry of Hermès scarf and Chanel No 5, she was gone.

Mrs Crisp picked up her cup and I picked up the telephone.

I wasn't going to sit quietly and wait for Russell to come back. 'I'll go and look around the stables and barn,' I said. 'In case she's shut in somewhere.'

Mrs Crisp nodded.

'Russell will be on his way back. He should be here in

212

about thirty minutes. I'll be finished by then and we can search the fields together.'

She was loading the dishwasher. 'Don't go too far, Mrs Checkland. Not without Russell.'

I promised I wouldn't and slipped out into the yard where Thomas was waiting. The afternoon sun was still strong. Sometimes it seemed as if this summer would never end. I led Marilyn into her field. Jack followed quietly behind as he always did. She bustled off to be reunited with Boxer. Jack remained by the gate, head low. I stroked his ears. He stood patiently, showing no signs of enjoyment. Nor of regret when I stopped. Nothing we did made any difference to him in any way. Marilyn and Boxer stood together under the trees and their quiet friendship only served to emphasise poor Jack's loneliness. Was there nothing that could reach him?

'Nothing seems to get through to him, Thomas.'

'Give him time,' said Thomas. *'You never know. Anyway, at the moment, we have yet another animal to worry about.'*

That was true. This afternoon we were searching for a small dog, out on her own for the first time. I genuinely believed she had already found her way home. At any moment I expected to hear Mrs Crisp call that Mrs Balasana had found her, sitting on the step, hungry and tired. But while I was out here I should have a good look. I don't know why I started in the barn. The door was open so she could have got out at any time. I looked behind odd bits of machinery and under old tarpaulins covering heaven knows what. I called her name. From there, I looked in the stables. I even went up the rickety stair to Kevin's old bedroom. She wasn't there, but I never thought she would be. I rummaged around in all our sheds and outbuildings. We had a ton of old rubbish in there, none of which could be disposed of because, said Russell, it might come in handy one day.

I even searched the hen house.

'Seriously, Jenny? It's not as if six by now quite buxom but still eggless chickens would be holding her against her will. Can you imagine them?' He assumed a gangster's voice. *'Give us more mealworms or the little dog gets it.'*

'I like to be thorough.'

I searched the area behind the barn where we have our bonfires and Russell parks his Land Rover, and she wasn't there, either. I hadn't really thought she would be. I knew she wasn't anywhere near Boxer's field, because Marilyn was calmly grazing. Something she would never do if there was a dog anywhere near her. Even a tiny dog like Bundle would have her climbing the nearest tree.

That just left the garden. I hadn't been in there since Christopher peed in the pool.

'Yes,' said Thomas. *'We ought to check whether the goldfish have survived their urinary encounter.'*

As always, it was several degrees warmer in the walled garden. I walked quietly down the path, calling Bundle's name, and stopping occasionally to listen for barks or whimpers. The hot, heavy afternoon silence was complete.

The fish seemed fine. Christopher's urine was obviously as ineffective as the rest of him. I made a mental note to ask Kevin to help change the water. The fish didn't seem that bothered, but I wasn't putting my hand in there until then.

I let myself back into the yard, looking around. There wasn't anywhere left to search.

Further up the lane, I heard a car start up. That was a thought. I should check out the hedgerows in the lane, just in case she'd got her collar caught on a low twig. I climbed over the gate as Mrs Balasana had done, and set

214

off downhill. I'd go to the end, checking out the right-hand hedge, and then turn and walk up the lane, checking out the other side.

I wouldn't have found her if it hadn't been for the car coming down the lane. I stepped up onto the verge to get out of the way – our lane is only one car wide and barely that at this time of year when the hedges have grown. Fortunately for Russell, he's not bothered about the paintwork on his Land Rover.

As I squeezed into the hedge, I thought I saw something. Not at ground level, which was where I had been looking, but about two feet in the air. Something … swayed. Curious, I crouched down to look.

'Jenny, be careful.'

It was Bundle. Swinging gently. Someone had tied a piece of rag around her neck and hanged her. She was dead.

I couldn't believe it. This was no accident. Someone had deliberately done this. Why would anyone do such a thing?

I had my answer immediately. I was vaguely aware of the car approaching and then equally vaguely aware it had stopped. I think I thought someone had stopped to help. I was about to turn around when someone grabbed my arms. I tried to struggle, saying, 'What …?' and then someone dropped something over my head and everything became very dark and very hot.

CHAPTER SIXTEEN

I don't know why I can't have relatives like everyone else. Kind, loving relatives who nag at you for your own good, or criticise your clothes and hair, or throw you surprise birthday parties, or open a bottle of wine when your boyfriend ditches you and tell you he was never good enough. You know, normal relatives. Great aunts who get drunk on sherry at family events. Uncles who tell dreadful jokes. Younger brothers who vie for the title 'Most Irritating Person on the Planet'. Sisters who borrow your clothes and look better in them than you do. The sort of relatives everyone has.

Except me.

I have the sort of relatives who robbed me blind for years, made me live in the attic – well, all right, quite a luxurious attic, but that's not the point – and told everyone I wasn't quite right in the head. Most importantly, I had the sort of relatives who would smother you with an evil-smelling blanket and throw you in the back of a car after having hanged your neighbour's dog just to get your attention. Rather late in the day, it dawned on me that Christopher might be out of control.

I don't know why he'd bothered with the blanket. I knew who he was. I tried to struggle but he'd thrown me on the floor between the front and back seats and there wasn't a lot of room. I was well and truly wedged and a heavy weight on my back didn't help at all.

I panicked. I'd fallen on my arms which were now trapped underneath me. The blanket had wrapped itself tightly around my face and I could barely breathe. My whole world had contracted to this tiny space – this tiny dark space. In which I couldn't breathe. I tried turning my head and only managed to make things worse. I tried to cry out but as I took a deep breath my nose and mouth filled with fluff and dust and made me sneeze. I panicked some more, shaking my head from side to side, trying to gain some purchase with my feet, desperately trying to loosen the blanket and make myself a little breathing space. The weight on my back increased. He had his feet on my back. I tried to push myself up on my elbows and the weight increased further. The oily fumes from the blanket were making me feel sick and if I vomited now I really would choke.

I struggled again and again only succeeded in making things worse.

'Lie still. Try to breathe slowly. Find which one of your arms moves most easily and try to pull the blanket away from your face.'

'Thomas? Thomas, I…'

'Yes, I know, Jenny, but first things first. Do as I say, now.'

I found that if I flexed my fingers then I could pull on a fold of blanket which in turn eased the tightness across my face. Not by much, but enough. I could breathe a little more easily.

'That's very good. Well done. Now concentrate on my voice. Try to remain as calm as you can.'

'I'm being kidnapped!'

'Yes, but it could be worse.'

'How? How could it possibly be worse?'

'You could be dead. Like Bundle.'

'He'd have *hanged* me?'

'No, of course not. That would be ridiculous. He would have needed a full-sized tree for that.'

'Thank you, Thomas.'

218

'I mean, it would have been a lot easier to have shot you, or run you over, or stabbed you, or...'

'Yes, thank you, Thomas.'

The journey seemed endless. If it hadn't been for Thomas, talking to me, soothing me, keeping me calm, I might not have made it. I very nearly didn't. I was as calm as I could keep myself, but I couldn't do anything about the smell of oil and petrol which was making me feel very ill indeed. The car braked sharply, turned hard, and began to crunch across an uneven surface. Only for a few minutes, but those minutes seemed endless, and they weren't good news, either. A bad surface meant we were away from civilisation. And travelling along a bad surface for some minutes meant we were a long way away from civilisation. Where no one could hear me scream.

'That's space,' said Thomas, not very comfortingly. *'Don't you remember? "In space, no one can hear you scream."'*

Before I could frame any sort of response to that, the car stopped. I wasn't sure whether this was a good or a bad thing.

I heard a door open and then someone grabbed my ankles and I was pulled out. It was surprisingly painful. I did my best to free my arms, but he was too strong for me. I was practically lifted off the ground and there wasn't a thing I could do about it. It's difficult to struggle when you can't get a purchase. A door opened. I heard the sound of feet on bare boards. We stumbled up some stairs. He was grunting with the effort by now, and there must have been a bend or something, because he staggered, and for a moment I thought we were going to fall backwards. He recovered however. Another door opened and I was flung forwards.

I hit a hard floor. Hard. If I hadn't had my arms in front of me anyway, it wouldn't have done my face any

219

good at all.

Without waiting to find out whether I was alone or not, I rolled over, and scrabbled at the blanket, pulling it away to suck in some welcome fresh air. Not that the stale air in this little room was very fresh.

I twisted around just in time to see the door close. A key turned in the lock and footsteps clattered off down the stairs. I lay on my back, staring up at a sagging, stained ceiling, and waited for my heartbeat to slow. Gradually, my breathing steadied. The sweat dried on my face and the feeling of nausea receded. Everything was very, very quiet. I was alone.

No, I wasn't. Of course I wasn't.

'Good afternoon,' said Thomas. *'Everything all right?'*

I opened my eyes. 'Well, as you pointed out – I'm not dead.'

'You could sound more grateful.'

I sat up slowly. I was bruised but mostly undamaged. 'I'm too busy trying to work out what's going on.'

'Me too. Let's recap.'

'Let's escape.'

'We can do both.'

I heaved myself up and began to prowl around the tiny room. The only piece of furniture was a very fragile-looking kitchen chair. If it was for me to sit on, then I was probably safer on the floor. I peered out of the grimy window. All I could see was a stand of trees in the near distance and a number of crows flapping about.

'What does he want?'

'I don't know. Can we just concentrate on…?'

'Yes, you do know what he wants. If you just stop and think for a moment.'

I stopped and thought for a moment. What could I possibly have that Christopher would want? And then I

220

had it. I don't know why I hadn't thought of it before.

'The bookshop. He wants his bookshop back. We'll be signing the contract to sell it any day now and once that's done it's too late. That's why he's here. That's why I'm here. He wants his bookshop back so he's the one who gets the cash when they develop the new pedestrianised area.'

'Very good, Jenny. You see, it only took a few minutes.'

'But why? Surely, all I have to do is say I signed under duress and the contract is null and void.'

Silence.

I said to Thomas, 'Go on, say it.'

'Jenny...'

'Say it.'

'You won't be able to say you signed under duress.'

'Because?'

'You...' He didn't seem able to go on so I finished it for him.

'I won't be able to say I signed under duress. I won't be able to say anything at all. He's going to kill me.'

'I don't think so,' he said, hastily

'I do.'

'I mean, I don't think Christopher himself would have the...' he tailed off again.

'Of course. How could I be so stupid? There's someone else here isn't there. There must be. Someone had to drive the car. He'll get them to do it.'

We were both silent, because we both knew that person was Uncle Richard.

I was about to have yet another silent rant about not having normal relatives, and then it occurred to me that I did. I had wonderful relatives. Kind, supportive, loving relatives. I had Russell – all right, he's impatient, noisy and erratic, but infinitely kind. And gentle Mrs Crisp, with her tea towel. And Andrew, quiet and confident. And Tanya, ferocious in her loyalty. And Kevin and Sharon. And Marilyn and Boxer and Thomas, the real horse. Even the cat. They were my family now – a little eccentric perhaps, but definitely a big improvement on the last lot. Sadly, none of them was here at this moment. I would have given a lot to see them galloping to my rescue but that wasn't going to happen. If I wanted to get out of here, then I was going to have to rescue myself.

Thomas was saying nothing, watching me work all this out for myself.

'But it's so stupid, Thomas. Even for Christopher it's a stupid idea. Does he think no one will be suspicious? I disappear and then he suddenly turns up claiming I signed the property back to him. It's ridiculous. And that's without Russell punching his lights out as soon as he claps eyes on him. And how will it look when I turn up shot to death. Or poisoned. Or stabbed. Or whatever.' I was gabbling because my legs had suddenly gone very weak and I was again feeling very sick.

Still Thomas said nothing.

And then I got it. Christopher didn't have to do anything. He would simply take the document and leave me here. To die of thirst. I'd be discovered eventually and people would assume that not very bright Jenny Dove had somehow got herself trapped in an old cottage somewhere and died before she could be found. A young mother, too. How sad. What a tragedy.

'Still won't explain away the contract though,' said Thomas, dubiously. *'There must be more to it.'*

'Well, I don't suppose Christopher will turn up in person. That would be asking for trouble. He'll be safely abroad with an alibi. He'll get a solicitor or…'

'Yes?' said Thomas, very gently.

Uncle Richard was a solicitor. Who better to present

the contract? Who better to broker a deal between two cousins than the father of one and the uncle of another?

'Don't tell me Russell wouldn't have something to say.'

'I'm sure he would say a very great deal, but how much of it would be listened to? How much could be proved?'

'All of it, surely. Why wouldn't it be? Russell is…'

'I'm sure he is, but you're missing the point, Jenny.'

'Which is?'

'Whatever the outcome of the legal battle is, you won't be here to see it. And how likely is it that Russell would take the law into his own hands, go after the seemingly blameless Christopher and end up, if not in prison himself, then certainly in no position to have people listen to any claims he might make.'

It was at this inauspicious moment that Christopher entered and suddenly, now that I was almost literally face to face with him, I didn't know why I'd ever allowed him to terrorise me like this. Now, close up, with him standing in front of me, I could see the lines around his mouth and eyes. His paunch. His seedy clothes. He'd been sweating. He smelled stale and unpleasant. Whatever he'd been doing during his enforced exile, he hadn't been a success at it. He was pathetic and ineffective. Unfortunately, he was also the one in control. And yes, he was weak – but weak men are often dangerous.

He dropped a closely typed document to the floor in front of me, and tossed a pen after it.

'Sign.'

I had forgotten his voice. Russell's voice was deep with a slight drawl, except when he was being enthusiastic about something – his art, usually – when he couldn't get the words out quickly enough. I think, years ago, Christopher must have tried for the same effect. And where the rest of us were happy with our Rushfordshire accents – even Aunt Julia – Christopher had abandoned his regional accent in favour of what used to be known as BBC English. I don't know whom he thought he was fooling. Loan companies and credulous old ladies, I suspect.

I kicked it back to him. 'I won't sign. I ... know what you want and I won't ... do it. And you can't ... kill ... me because then I'll never be able ... to sign, and you ... don't ... dare go anywhere near Russell ... because he'll just rip your head off.'

'Russell's not here,' said Christopher softly. 'You're on your own. Sign.'

I shook my head. I was negotiating from a position of strength. There wasn't anything he could do that would make me sign.

He said casually, 'You've got a baby, haven't you?'

Fear pounced. I took a step towards him. From the corner of my eye, I saw Thomas lay back his ears. Christopher couldn't see him, but he must have felt something. He stepped backwards, keeping a very careful distance between us.

I said, between clenched teeth, 'Never ... mind Russell. Touch Joy and *I* will tear you apart.'

He wasn't listening. He never listened to anyone, least of all me.

'I've been in her room, you know. Several times. Just watching her. Pretty room. Carefully baby proofed, but there'll be something I can use. You wear that nice perfume. Joy. Did Russell buy it for you? Nice thought. Bit pricey though. Although I wouldn't need much. A quick squirt in each eye. You won't miss it. I promise you I won't be wasteful.'

I didn't hesitate. Mrs Crisp would be there and I didn't want to speculate about what he would do to her to get her out of the way. It was just a bookshop. Money isn't everything. We would manage without. We always did. We had so far.

I knelt on the floor and dashed off a signature any old how. He bent to pick it up and as he did so, I swung at him with the chair. The chair fell apart and Christopher fell to the floor.

'Excellent work, Jenny,' said Thomas. *'Now – let's get out of here.'*

Resisting the impulse to put the boot in while he was down there, I made for the door, because getting out was more important than beating Christopher to a bloody pulp. I wrenched it open and Uncle Richard pushed me back into the room. I fell backwards over Christopher still on the floor, spraining a wrist and banging my elbow.

Thomas reared up, teeth bared, placing himself between me and the pair of them, but Uncle Richard was already dragging Christopher from the room.

I rolled to my feet, dusty and breathless, just in time to see the door slam behind them. Shrieking with fear and frustration, I hurled myself at it, kicking and beating my fists against the panels.

I was frantic. 'Thomas, he might still go after Joy. I have to get out.'

'Gently, Jenny. Deep breaths. Just take a minute to stop and think.'

He was right. He was always right. I pushed my hair behind my ears and examined the door, running my hands over it. I twisted the handle. I pushed. I pulled. Nothing happened. I tried to look through the keyhole. If the key was there, maybe I could push it out and somehow pull it back under the door.

The key was not in the lock.

'Never mind,' said Thomas. *'It was a good thought. Try and come up with some more.'*

I examined every inch of the walls. They were rough and solid. I wasn't getting out that way.

There was no fireplace. Not even a patch of new plaster where it had been bricked up.

The window, as I said, was tiny. And painted shut. Generations of thick paint covered the frame. Well, if I couldn't open it, perhaps I could knock out the whole thing, frame, glass, the lot, and squeeze out that way. Again, the frame was disappointingly solid.

I sighed in frustration.

What about …? I looked down. The floor was just bare boards. Perhaps I could prise one up and then another, kick my way through the ceiling below and get out that way.

No, the boards were solid and well-crafted and I had nothing to insert in the cracks. I broke several fingernails trying. I walked about, listening for squeaks or groans which might denote possibilities, but there were none.

I slithered down the wall, crouched in a heap, and put my hands over my face.

The smell of damp wood, old stone, and dust was replaced by that of warm ginger biscuits. Thomas said gently, *'Jenny…'*

'I know,' I said. 'Just give me a moment. I'm trying to think.'

And I was. Trying to think of all the ways in and out of a room. Through the door. Through the window. Through the walls. Through the floor. Through the … I looked up. Directly over my head was a tiny hatch. Through the ceiling. I could stand on the chair. If I could put it back together again and if it would bear my weight. The ceiling was low. I could reach. Pull myself through and … and think of something. Let's get out of this room first.

The chair had lost two of its legs, but they were unbroken. I picked them up and jammed them back into their sockets. The chair could barely hold itself together, let alone support me. It swayed and creaked as I very carefully placed it under the hatch.

'*Will you be able to pull yourself up?*' asked Thomas, anxiously.

'Yes,' I said firmly, at the same time thinking, probably not.

The chair swayed even more as I climbed aboard.

Standing up slowly and willing myself to be as light as possible, I pushed at the hatch, which came free quite easily

'*Close your eyes,*' advised Thomas. '*A ton of dirt and dust will drop on you when you try to move it.*'

I obeyed, carefully lifting the hatch and placing it to one side, but apart from a few tiny falls of dust, nothing dropped down onto my head.

'That was lucky,' I said.

'*Yes,*' said Thomas, thoughtfully.

I was even luckier. As I groped around the edge of the hatch for something to hang on to, I dislodged something, which fell, snakelike, past my head. I only just managed not to scream.

'*Look out,*' cried Thomas.

I covered my head as something black hung, swaying beside me.

A rope ladder.

'Thomas, it's a rope ladder.'

'*So I see. Is it safe? Give it a good yank before you trust your weight on it.*'

I gave it a good yank. It seemed firm enough.

'*Jenny, please take care.*'

'I will. See you in a minute.'

Climbing a rope ladder is not easy. Especially if you've never done it before, and I was rubbish. I swayed about all over the place, knocking the chair over with a clatter.

'Keep going,' said Thomas.

I did, because now I had no choice. Christopher must have heard the noise. He'd be up here like a flash. I couldn't afford to hang around.

I struggled up into the attic, expecting dark and dirt and dust and, yes, there was plenty of dirt and dust, but also plenty of light. Not only did a hundred tiny shafts of light filter through the broken tiles, but there was a big hole in one corner through which sunlight streamed, and I could see the sky.

Treading cautiously from joist to joist, I edged my way towards it, unable to believe no one had heard the noise I was making.

Reaching the hole, I crouched and stuck out my head. As holes went, it was the very king of holes – right at the very lowest part of the roof, and directly above an outhouse. I had only to step out, climb down, drop to the outhouse roof and from there, to the ground.

I began to scramble through.

'Wait,' said Thomas quietly. *'Then what?'*

'Run like hell for Frogmorton and Joy,' I said, impatient at the delay.

'In which direction? Which way is home?'

I stopped and looked about me. Apart from the small stand of trees with its incessantly cawing crows, there was no cover anywhere. Open countryside surrounded us on every side.

'Let's get away from here, first. Then we can decide what to do next.'

'Go slowly. If you twist an ankle, then we're not going anywhere.'

That was true. I clambered carefully out of the hole in the roof, and lowered myself carefully onto the outhouse. The roof was of some corrugated metal and I made a lot more noise than I would have liked. Especially when I went straight through it, landing heavily on a pile of old sacks. I don't know what was in them but they broke my fall beautifully.

I was worried the door might be locked and that I'd simply exchanged one prison for another, but it scraped open when I pulled and suddenly, I was free.

'Now what?'

'Well, there's the gate which leads to the lane, which will eventually lead to a main road, which will lead us back to civilisation and safety.'

'Yes, but my point is that we don't have the time to be running around the countryside. We need to get back to Frogmorton as quickly as possible.'

'Well, let's make a start.' He began to move away.

'No, stop and think.'

'There's no time. Any minute now, they're going to discover we're gone. In fact, I can't think what's taking them so long. Come on.'

Two cars were parked under the trees in the open space at the front of the cottage. One I recognised as Uncle Richard's. The other was a hire car. That one must be Christopher's.

'Rented under someone else's name, I suspect,' said Thomas quietly.

'It's from the same company as the one Aunt Julia was driving.'

'Interesting.'

I was staring at the cars. 'Wait. We'll never outrun them on foot. We should take one of these.'

'You can't drive.'

'Yes, I can.'

'In a field.'

'I've driven to Rushford several times. How is this any different?'

'You're a learner driver. Don't you have to have someone sitting next to you?.'

'You can do that.'

'Someone to instruct you.'

'You can do that.'

'With a licence.'

'Two out of three's not bad.'

'Jenny, what's got into you?'

'I have to do this. Think of Joy.'

'But...'

'Thomas, choose a car and get in.'

'All right! I used to think Russell Checkland was the irresponsible one, Jenny. What have you become?'

'Desperate.'

I chose the car facing the right way so that I wouldn't have to reverse. Now was definitely not the time to start disentangling my ovaries.

CHAPTER SEVENTEEN

I sat in this new car and surveyed the dashboard with dismay. This was definitely not Russell's Land Rover. I've seen fewer instruments and dials in an aircraft cockpit.

'You've never seen an aircraft cockpit,' said Thomas who seemed relatively resigned to a spot of 'Grand Theft Auto'. *'Stop panicking. You don't need any of this. You just need to switch it on.'*

I panicked again. 'I don't have the key. Do you have the key?'

'Of course not. I'm a horse. We don't have keys.'

'Well, I don't have the key either.'

I fumbled uselessly, looking for something I recognised. 'Do you know how to hot-rod it?'

'Hotwire, Jenny. Hot-rod is something else completely. Don't you know that?'

'Does it matter? There aren't any keys.' I was frantically pulling down the sun visors.

Thomas cleared his throat. *'Try looking in the ignition.'*

And there they were, dangling gently and catching the light.

I could feel panic eating away at me, but I still retained some last vestiges of common sense. Thomas snorted over that, but I ignored him. Switching on the engine was the very last thing I should do because they would hear the engine and come running. So I adjusted the mirror and seat. And then the mirror again. I checked we were in neutral. Putting off the moment...

'Jenny...'

'All right.'

Finally, when I couldn't put it off any longer, I turned the key. Instead of coughing like an old man who'd been on sixty cigarettes a day for sixty years, the engine purred smoothly into life.

'Wow,' said Thomas. *'Bet you didn't know cars could do that. This is a whole new world for us.'*

I engaged first gear, took off the handbrake, and we moved smoothly forwards.

'Well done, Jenny.'

'Thank you.'

'Why are we going so slowly?'

'Gate,' I said, between clenched teeth, clutching the steering wheel as if my life depended upon it.

'No, you should speed up.'

'What? Why?'

'It's padlocked. Do you have the key?'

'Don't start that again.'

'Well, unless you want our dramatic getaway to grind to a halt after the first twenty yards, Jenny, I suggest you speed up.'

'We'll hit the gate.'

'Exactly.'

'I'm not supposed to hit things.'

'Jenny, you're not trying to pass your driving test. You're trying to escape from two very unpleasant men who are going to do unpleasant things to you and your family. And only you can do something about it.'

True. I clenched my teeth and hit the accelerator. The car surged forwards.

'Wow. Pow-er,' said Thomas, sounding exactly like a TV car-show presenter.

We hit the gate head on. It shattered. Pieces of wood flew in all directions. Two or three bounced off the

232

bonnet. One clattered against the windscreen and then slid away.

'That's lucky,' said Thomas. *'No airbag.'*

'What's an airbag?'

He sighed. *'Perhaps you shouldn't worry about that now. Watch the road.'*

We bumped along some sort of track, listening to stones bouncing off the bottom of the car. 'This is not a road.'

'Just keep going.'

'We're doing it, Thomas. We're escaping.'

'We are indeed. Jolly well done, Jenny.'

'Are they coming after us yet?' I said, craning my neck to see in the rear view mirror. In my haste, I'd forgotten to adjust the wing mirrors so all I could see in them was me.

'You concentrate on the road ahead. I'll look behind.'

'What can you see?'

'Not a lot. It's getting dark. No signs of pursuit. Yet.'

'That was easy.'

'Yes,' he said quietly. *'It was, wasn't it?'*

We bumped down the last few yards and then I stopped. We'd run out of track. Ahead of us was a road. Which way should we go?

'I've no idea. Can you remember whether you turned left or right on to this track?'

'No. Sorry.'

'Well, don't beat yourself up about it.'

'I'm not going to,' I said indignantly.

'Well, I'm sure you would have got around to it sooner or later.'

'Left or right, Thomas?'

'I've no idea, and I don't want to rush you, but…'

I turned left. It seemed easier.

We picked up speed. I thought about fishing around for third gear.

233

'We need to speed up.'

'I can't see very well.'

'Well, switch on the lights then.'

I'd only ever driven in daylight. 'Um … How?'

'How should I know? There'll be a knob or a lever or a dial or something.'

I twisted something at random. The windscreen wipers flicked back and forth. Back and forth. Back and forth.

'That's quite mesmerising,' said Thomas. *'But try that one.'*

Two jets of water temporarily obscured the windscreen.

'Oh good. We're nice and clean now. Try another one.'

Familiar music flooded through the car. Dum de dum de dum de dum. Dum de dum de dum dum.

'That's very catchy. What is it?'

'The Archers.'

'What are The Archers?'

'It used to be billed as an everyday story of country folk, but now it's a contemporary drama in a rural setting.'

'Why?'

'Is that really important right now?'

'Can we go any faster?'

'I still can't see very much.'

And then, suddenly, I could. A car appeared behind us, and I noticed they'd managed to switch their lights on. The beams were dazzling, illuminating everything around us. Sadly, none of it looked particularly familiar.

'Isn't it nice to meet a driver familiar with the concept of headlights,' said Thomas.

'Good for him,' I muttered.

They were really close now. I had to squint to avoid being blinded by the dazzle of lights in the mirror. And

234

they were very, very, close. Too late, I remembered the second car. Wouldn't it have been a good idea to have disabled it in some way? I really was the world's most incompetent kidnap victim.

'Don't worry,' soothed Thomas. *'For a first attempt, you're really not doing too badly at all.'*

They were right behind us now, and their lights were blinding. I was driving by Braille.

'Jenny...'

'Yes, I know. I know.'

I pushed my foot down hard and the car leaped forwards. For a second we pulled away and then they were back behind us again. The inside of the car was flooded with light. I couldn't see a thing for the dazzle. 'They're very close. Why are they so close?'

'Jenny, hold tight.'

I heard a bang from somewhere behind us, the car lurched, and the wheel twisted in my hands. I screamed. We veered all over the road. My foot slipped off the accelerator. I groped around and stamped hard, missing the accelerator and hitting the brake by mistake. Tyres screeched. Ours and theirs. They dropped back and the light faded.

'Oh well done, Jenny. A very neat piece of driving.'

I was shaking so hard I could barely grip the wheel.

'Thomas, what's happening?'

'Well, I don't want to worry you but I think they're trying to run us into a ditch.'

Was this what they had done to Julia? No time to think about that now. They were behind us again. Crowding in close. I felt a pressure behind us and the car tried to move of its own accord. Were they trying to push us off the road?

I resisted the urge to brake and concentrated on trying to keep us on the road.

'Find the lights,' urged Thomas.

There was some sort of stalk on the other side of the steering wheel. I twisted. The entire road opened up before us. Just like The Yellow Brick Road.

'And then there was light,' said Thomas. *'Bravo Jenny. If I ever get kidnapped again you will definitely be my first choice for getaway driver.'*

'We didn't escape Thomas. It was all too easy. The loft hatch, the rope ladder, the keys. They let me go. I think this was the plan all along. They're going to run me off the road and make it look like an accident. What's the betting this car is in my name? They got Aunt Julia to hire it. That's why she was so afraid. That's why she was trying to get away.'

'It's still going to look extremely suspicious, though. Do you think they...?

'Can we discuss this later?'

'Good idea. Now, Jenny, you need to get us out of here.'

'I can barely drive,' I shouted as the lights closed in again.

'You've sat alongside Russell Checkland for three years now. Don't tell me you haven't learned anything at all.'

Actually, that was true. That was very true.

I took a deep breath, leaned back in the seat, tightened my grip on the wheel, channelled Russell Checkland, and put my foot down.

The engine roared. I'd like to think that was because of something I'd done, but I suspected I was still in second gear. I didn't dare look down to check. Besides, Russell's Land Rover frequently made similar noises even without murderous relatives chasing him across country.

Trees and hedges blurred past. And then the lights of a roadside cottage. And then a really sharp bend which we took far too quickly and I ended up on the wrong side of the road. Before I had time to feel the fear, we were out the other side and with a long, straight stretch of road ahead of us.

'Now,' said Thomas. 'Go, Jenny. You mustn't let them get past us. They'll block the road and then we'll really be in trouble because you can't do a three-point turn, can you?'

'Of course not,' I said crossly, watching the needle cross through 60mph. 'I can't even reverse.'

'Why ever not?'

'Because it twists my ovaries.'

For the first time I could ever remember, there was a stunned silence from the giant invisible golden horse next to me.

'I'm sorry Jenny. What?'

'Russell says...'

'Ah. Say no more. I need to have a word with that boy.'

I hunched forward over the wheel. I thought I knew where we were. There was another big bend coming up. I slowed and swung the wheel. Tyres squealed. Why didn't someone report my dangerous driving? Where's a speed trap when you need one? Yes, I thought so. We were on the outskirts of Rushford and I needed to slow down because just ahead there was a –

Before I had time even to realise we were airborne, we hit the ground with a crash. I bit my tongue and something fell off the back shelf.

'What happened? Were we fired from a gun?'

'Hump-back.'

'Whale?'

'Bridge. Sorry about that.'

'Well, on the plus side, still no airbag.'

'What airbag?'

'*Never mind.*'

We flew past the double-glazing manufacturers which meant that any minute now...

'Roundabout, Thomas. Which way?'

'*Right. No – you have to go left on a roundabout and take the third ... No, clockwise, Jenny! Too late. Oh well, I don't suppose it matters much. Nothing coming, fortunately.*'

'Sorry. Sorry.'

Suddenly, there were bright lights ahead of us. Rushford High Street. And it was crowded. Where had all these people come from?

'*Brake! Brake!*'

We surged forwards again. This was a very powerful car. 'I'm sorry. I got my feet muddled up and stamped on the wrong pedal.'

'*It's ABC. Accelerator, brake, clutch. How can you go wrong?*'

'Actually, its CBA.'

'*Doesn't matter – the important thing is that the brake is in the middle.*'

'I'll try to remember that. I can't believe I'm being taught to drive by a horse.'

'*It can't be any worse than Russell.*'

'How confident are you with that statement?'

The engine was making the most terrible noises. Red lights were appearing on the dashboard.'

'*Which gear are you in?*'

I had other things to think about. 'Gear?'

'*Never mind. It's not our car.*'

'Is he still behind us?'

'*Yes.*'

'What's he doing?'

He paused and then said, '*He's waiting for us to get through Rushford and head towards Frogmorton and then*

238

he'll have another go on the other side. Where that bad bend is. Where Russell's mother died.'

Where are the police when you need them? They were around quick enough when we were stealing donkeys and harbouring young runaways.

The darkness of country lanes had been replaced by brightly lit shop windows. People were going home from work. They were queued up outside the chippy. Talking by their parked cars. Loading their shopping. Lovely normal things. Not one of them was fleeing down the high street pursued by their own murderous relatives.

People turned to look at the noise our car was making. Those about to cross the road thought better of it and jumped back to the pavement for safety.

And bloody, bloody Christopher was still right behind us.

'There,' said Thomas. *'Over there. Look.'*

Sgt Bates and Mrs Balasana were standing on the steps of the police station. She must have been in to enquire about Bundle. I had forgotten about Bundle.

'Slow down,' said Thomas. *'Middle pedal. Now pull in and park neatly behind that police car,'*

I very carefully mirrored, signalled and manoeuvred and drove straight into the back of the police car. Which shunted forwards into a shop doorway. The shop alarm went off. The police car alarm went off. And our airbag deployed.

'Ah,' said Thomas, in tones of deep satisfaction. *'Finally.'*

CHAPTER EIGHTEEN

They took me to the hospital. I kept trying to tell them about Christopher and no one was taking any notice. I'd had a brief glimpse of him as he'd overtaken us at some speed and roared off down the high street.

'Making his getaway,' said Thomas.

Which was more than we were doing. I was unsure whether I'd been arrested or not.

Someone had called an ambulance which came flashing its way towards us and adding its own siren to that of the car and shop alarms.

A small crowd had gathered.

'Don't say anything,' said Thomas.

'Chance would be a fine thing.'

I confined myself to saying, 'I want my husband. I want my husband,' except it came out as 'I wad by hubbud. I wad by hubbud,' and then I shut up.

People milled around all over the place, exclaiming and taking photos of us on their phones.

Sgt Bates dealt with it all by shoving me into the ambulance and climbing in after me. Presumably someone else would sort out the chaos in our absence.

Thomas came along for the ride. He'd never been in an ambulance before and was fascinated, trying to see everything at once.

'What do you think this is for? What does that do? Oh, look at this, Jenny! Can we get them to put the siren on?'

I sat with some sort of ice-pack on my face, saying nothing. I needed to speak to Russell. I needed to tell him not to let Joy out of his sight.

241

*

Casualty seemed busy but reasonably quiet, although I was sure Russell's arrival would soon put a stop to that.

I was right. I'd barely been shown into a cubicle when there was a commotion at the reception desk. I could hear Russell's voice shouting 'Where's my wife? I want my wife. Jenny? Jenny?'

An unseen voice said, 'If you could just take a seat, sir.'

'Jenny?'

The tone changed. 'Look mate, sit down or I'll call security.'

Sgt Bates left the cubicle.

I looked at Thomas. 'I hope you're satisfied.'

I wouldn't have missed this for anything. Shall we take bets on how many of us are locked up for the night?'

'Jenny?'

I raised my voice. 'I'b id here, Ruddell.'

He was getting closer. 'Jenny?'

'Ruddell?'

'For heaven's sake, it's like one of those musicals where people call to each other from one mountain peak to the next.' He began to hum the Indian Love Call.

'Jenny, where are you?'

'Here.'

I heard the scrape of curtain rings and a scream from the next cubicle.

I heard Andrew say, 'I'm so sorry, madam. I'll remove him at once.' There were sounds of someone being ejected from a cubicle.

'Good grief.'

'Ruddell, I'b id here.'

'He's not coming in here,' said the doctor.

The curtain was flung aside.

'Jenny!'

242

'Oh, Ruddell.'

I was enveloped in a massive hug.

'Ow. Bide by dode.'

He held me at arm's length. 'What happened? What's wrong with your face? Where have you been? You've been gone for ages.'

'Ad by ribth.'

'For God's sake. Look at you. What have you been doing to yourself?'

'Airbag.'

'Oh. Yes. That would do it.' A belated thought took him. 'Whose airbag?'

'I dode doe.'

'What have I told you about getting into cars with strange men?'

'As if you haven't been getting into a car with a strange man every day of your married life,' muttered Thomas.

'I didun. Da car wad ebty.'

'So why did you get in?'

'I thtole it.'

'What did you do that for? You can't drive?'

'Yeth I cad,' I said, stung.

'Will you please get these people out of here,' said the doctor to Sgt Bates, who was standing quietly and listening to every word and probably eliciting far more information than from a formal interview. I made a note to be careful what I said. So far I'd admitted to stealing a car...

'TWOCing,' said Thomas, who watches too much television.

...driving without a licence, driving with reckless endangerment, having an accident in said stolen vehicle and God knows what else and I'd only said a few sentences. Talking is overrated.

'Whad beeble?' I said, looking around Russell who had effectively been blocking my view, to see, as well as Sgt Bates, Andrew, Tanya, Mrs Crisp, Sharon, and Kevin, all standing behind him.

'Just a minute,' said the sergeant, 'I want to hear what this lot have to say for themselves.'

'Not in here,' said the doctor sharply, and I could see his point. The tiny cubicle now held an unbelievable number of people, together with a bulky police sergeant and an invisible golden horse. Yet another instance of the NHS buckling under the strain.

I clutched Russell's arm. 'Whode … lookig after Joy?'

'The Braithwaites.'

Christopher was out there somewhere.

I tried to wiggle my eyebrows to indicate that Christopher was still out there, somewhere, but it hurt too much. I had to content myself with saying meaningfully, 'Will she … be all righd?'

He caught my flying hands. 'Jenny, there's Martin, Monica, their two enormous sons – including the one back from college for some as yet undisclosed but certainly disreputable reason – Fiona, four sheepdogs, two cats, three rabbits, a fluctuating number of gerbils, two horses, and countless sheep between her and any danger she might find herself in. She'll be fine. So tell me what happened. Why were you in someone's car? You weren't leaving me were you? You promised you'd never leave me.'

Those listening might have thought he was joking, but I could see his face.

'I'b dot … leebing you. Why would I leeb you?'

'Let me count the ways,' said Andrew.

'Shut up, Andrew. Why are you here?'

'You gibbered at me down the phone. I came to see what was going on. Tanya came along to keep everyone in line and make sure no one says anything incriminating.'

I persevered. 'Why would I ... leeb you?'

'Well, you just disappeared, Jenny. You don't do that sort of thing.'

I could hear another familiar voice drawing ever closer. Mrs Balasana had followed us here.

I clutched at Russell's sleeve, and whispered. 'Buddle dead.'

He looked down at me, his face giving nothing away and then nodded. 'Leave it to me.'

The same voice said, 'You can't go in there,' the curtain scraped back and Mrs Balasana stood in the entrance, dishevelled, distraught and in tears. She was obviously desperate to know about Bundle, and while I'm sure she was at least as single-minded as Russell, she had much better manners.

'Mrs Checkland, I saw it happen. Are you all right?'

I nodded.

'Did you find her?'

All right, not that much better manners.

I looked at Russell, who looked at Mrs Crisp. Some sort of unspoken communication passed between them and she said, 'Why don't you come with me, Mrs Balasana. Let's see if we can find you a coffee.'

They disappeared.

'That's better,' said Thomas, *'but do you realise there are still eight people in this cubicle. We should apply to the* Guinness Book of Records.*'*

'Thomas, are you even pretending to take this seriously?'

'No, of course I'm not. Who could? Oh, listen. Do you hear what I hear?'

On the other side of the curtain, I could hear Francesca demanding to know the whereabouts of Russell Checkland.

The same voice said again, 'You can't go in there,' but with much less conviction this time.

'No,' said the doctor firmly. 'Enough. Mrs Checkland may remain. Everyone else out. And you too, Sergeant, please.'

They all drifted slowly out into the corridor and stood outside the cubicle. Russell held the curtain back so he could talk to me and I could see what was going on.

Unfortunately, what was going on was that Daniel and Francesca were hurrying down the corridor towards us.

Francesca had brought the place to a standstill. She screamed when she saw my face. They had obviously been on their way out to an important event. She was wearing a white evening dress that sparkled under the harsh hospital lighting, together with the diamonds Daniel had bought for her last year. With her red hair piled high on her head she looked like a magnificent glittering candle. She was actually wearing a tiara. Like a duchess. Everything stopped dead. People just stared. Homeless people woke up. Some of the more confused may have mistaken her for an angel.

'What are you doing here?' demanded Russell, by no means pleased to see her. Daniel and I exchanged small smiles. We loved it when they argued.

'You were shouting at me down the phone. I couldn't understand you.

Sgt Bates, who surely by now deserved some sort of police medal, began again, perfectly calmly and pleasantly. I was not deceived. My face was so bruised she could easily start with the telephone directories and no one would ever know.

'Mrs Checkland, please tell me what has occurred. Why did you steal someone's car?' she asked.

I panicked. 'I'b doe … dorry. Ad I habunt even … god a licence for you do dake away. Plees don' let theb sed me do … priddun. I won' dow whad do do and I'b worried … subone will make me dare bij.'

There was a long silence.

'Bij?' said Sgt Bates.

'Bitch,' said Russell, enlightened.

She altered her stance slightly to face him.

'She's worried about becoming someone's bitch,' he added hastily. 'I wouldn't worry too much, Jenny. I honestly don't think anyone in prison would fancy you – you're really not bitch material, you know.'

There was another long silence. Even the doctor stared at him.

'He's an idiot,' said Andrew, at last. 'Ignore him, Jenny. You'd make a wonderful bitch.'

I tried to smile at him. 'Thag you, Andrew.'

'Stop that,' said Russell. 'Sorry, Jenny. What I meant to say was that I'm sure you could be any number of people's bitch if you really wanted to be.'

'Thag you,' I said.

'Mrs Checkland, could you just tell me what has occurred, please.'

'She just never gives up, does she?' said Thomas.

Sgt Bates had been the captain of the hockey team at Rushford St Winifred's and they'd never suffered a single defeat in the whole time. Apparently, they still talk of her in hushed tones of respect and she has her own special plaque in the gym.

I looked at Tanya. What could I say without revealing we'd covered up Christopher's arson? Which probably made us as guilty as he was.

'Mrs Checkland will not strain herself at this moment,' she said calmly. You will be aware that, for her, even normally the talking is very difficult. It is obvious she has incurred some minor facial injuries which make it painful for her to speak. She will speak tomorrow.'

247

Yes, tomorrow – when we'd all had a chance to get our stories straight.

'*And,*' said Thomas, '*when Christopher has had the chance to get his sorry arse out the country again.*'

'Language,' I said. 'Although you're right.' I remembered him roaring past us in Rushford High Street. 'If he has any sense he's just kept going. We won't see Christopher again.'

The voice said, 'You can't go in there, mate.'

The curtains scraped back again and there stood Christopher.

Francesca turned as white as her frock. Daniel put his arm around her waist and whispered something. My guess was that he was telling her to keep quiet.

I scrambled off the bed and looked for something to defend myself with.

'*I really wouldn't bother,*' said Thomas. '*I think Russell will have that more than covered.*'

We all gawped at Christopher. For several reasons.

Firstly – the state of him. He was bleeding from a number of facial wounds. Blood was running freely down his face.

Secondly – he was in handcuffs. Which I had no problem with at all.

Thirdly – he was accompanied by Bill the Insurance Man, who held him firmly by one arm. Whether to restrain or support him was unclear.

I wouldn't have believed it possible, but someone actually seemed to be having a worse evening than me.

Sgt Bates elbowed her way through the by now quite sizeable crowd around my cubicle. 'Mr Kingdom, I believe.'

He swayed. 'Keep them off. Keep them away.'

Everyone looked at Russell who said, 'Why are you all looking at me? I never touched him. I've been here the whole time. As Sgt Bates here can testify.'

We all looked at Sgt Bates who ignored us, correctly identified Bill the Insurance Man as the most intelligent among us, and said, 'Mr Wayland?'

'Wayland,' I said to Thomas. 'His name's Wayland.'

'I found him at Frogmorton.'

'William Wayland. That's a nice name.'

'What did you do to him?' said Russell in admiration. 'Can you show me?'

'I didn't do anything. He was like that when I found him.'

'So she'd be Lizzie Wayland.'

'Where did you find him?'

'Reeling around your yard with half a dozen chickens attached to his face. It was really very similar to that scene in *Alien*.'

'But why?'

'Patagodiad Attack Chicked,' I said before I could stop myself.

'Yes, I don't believe this is quite the right moment to bring that up, Jenny.'

Sgt Bates wheeled. 'You have *Patagonian Attack Chickens*?'

'Only id Ruddel'd head,' I said, trying to make amends. 'They're perfectly norbal chicked, really.'

We all looked at the severely beaked Christopher.

The voice said, 'Look, you really can't go in…' and Mrs Balasana told him not to be so silly.

She and Mrs Crisp were clutching enormous plastic cups of take-out coffee. I suspected this was a first for both of them.

'Bill,' cried Mrs Crisp, obviously delighted to see him. He smiled at her. 'Good evening, Lizzie.'

Russell bristled. 'Why exactly are you here?'

He stopped smiling at Mrs Crisp and turned back to

Russell. 'I've brought Mr Kingdom in for treatment.'

The doctor elbowed his way through the throng. 'Good heavens, what happened to him?'

'Patagonian Attack Chickens,' said Russell proudly. 'Extra rations tomorrow for the ladies.'

Mrs Balasana blinked at him. 'Are you seriously telling me that those ... your chickens...?'

'It would appear so,' said Russell. 'Believe me, no one is more surprised than me.'

I slipped down off the bed to make room for the latest casualty and went to stand in the shelter of Russell's arm. He kissed me very carefully and grinned. 'That's going to sting in the morning.'

'But why?' said Andrew.

'Always does,' said Russell. 'Always hurts more the next day.'

'No, stupid. Christopher.'

'Chickens can be very aggressive. You should know that. You're supposed to be a vet. I'm sure I remember you going off to college.'

'Not the chickens, cloth head. Why is Christopher in handcuffs?'

'Why not?' murmured Russell.

Bill sighed. 'I've been after him since the arson.'

'What arson?'

That boy has the memory span of a bucket.

'Your feed store? Remember?'

'Never mind all that,' said Russell, dismissing everything else as irrelevant in the scheme of things. He stared suspiciously at Bill. 'Are you a spy?'

'Of course not.'

'Then why do you own handcuffs?'

'They're not mine,' said Bill indignantly.

All eyes swivelled to Mrs Crisp who turned a stunning shade of scarlet. 'They're certainly not mine.'

'They belong to the company,' explained Bill.

'What company?.'

'The insurance company, of course.'

'What ins…?'

'*I take back everything I've ever said about insurance companies,*' murmured Thomas. '*They're obviously a lot more fun than anyone has ever given them credit for.*'

'The one investigating the fire at Frogmorton. The one I work for.'

'Really,' said Russell nastily, 'because I'd rather got the impression you'd been investigating Mrs Crisp.'

'No, I'm investigating the fire and I'm in love with Mrs Crisp.'

'What?' said Mrs Crisp, startled.

'So that's why you haven't paid the claim,' said Russell, getting his priorities wrong.

'Never mind that,' said Mrs Crisp, elbowing him aside. 'What did you say?'

'I said I was investigating the fire.'

Russell elbowed his way back again. 'By seducing Mrs Crisp?'

'What? No. Of course not.'

'No,' said Mrs Crisp, and I thought I detected a faint note of regret.

'So what's all this business with shooting off twice a week clutching big brown envelopes?'

They looked at each other.

'It's nothing,' said Mrs Crisp hastily.

'Lizzie…'

'No, I mean it, Bill. It's nothing. Let it go.'

Russell glared at Bill. 'What about you? Are you telling me it's nothing?'

'I'm not telling you anything at all,' said Bill, calmly. 'It's all up to Lizzie.'

Who shook her head and remained silent.

251

Sgt Bates cleared her throat, presumably to get us all back on track again.

'You can't prove anything,' said Christopher, wincing under the doctor's probing.

'Don't have to,' said Bill. 'The silly juggins was going to have another go. Car full of petrol cans, firelighters and matches.'

I thought of Marilyn, Jack and Boxer locked in the stables, unable to escape. The cat trapped in the house. Our home burning to the ground. Beside me, Russell tensed, but before he could take any action, the voice said, in the tones of one who has given up, 'Down the corridor and to the left, mate.' The crowd parted and Uncle Richard entered the cubicle.

I moved closer to Russell.

'Yes,' said Thomas. *'You might want to keep a tight grip on him.'*

Francesca obviously thought the same thing about Daniel.

Uncle Richard looked the epitome of respectability. Everyone's idea of the kindly, slightly shabby, country solicitor. He blinked in the bright lights and peered amiably over his spectacles. Even his voice was pleasant.

'Good evening, everyone. Sgt Bates, how nice to see you again. Mr Christopher Kingdom is my client. He will say nothing.'

His gaze swept over me without expression. You'd never believe he'd presided over my kidnapping and then tried to run me off the road. Actually, if I hadn't actually been there, I wouldn't have believed it, either.

'Nothing will be said. My son does not admit to the kidnapping. It's simply a joke that went too far. He is very sorry for the damage he has done tonight. I am confident that when the true story of the events emerges, it will be apparent that the whole thing is the result of poor judgement and high spirits.'

'Kidnapping?' said Sgt Bates. And everything went very quiet.

CHAPTER NINETEEN

Uncle Richard said, 'Jenny, I am instructing you to say nothing. You should leave this to me to sort out.' He turned to Sgt Bates. 'I'm sure you know that my niece is sometimes ... well, a little slow to grasp things, and I think it's apparent to all of us that somehow she's got hold of the wrong end of the stick. Obviously I acquit her of making malicious accusations – it's simply that she doesn't understand what's going on a lot of the time. I think perhaps the best thing to do would be to send her home – and her dangerously unstable husband as well, because heaven knows what he's taught her to say – while you and I sort this out between us.'

I tensed. If Russell thumped Uncle Richard now, then we'd all be in trouble. I think the same thought had occurred to Andrew. I was certain Uncle Richard was doing his best to provoke Russell into discrediting himself.

Russell, however, merely grinned at him and said, amiably, 'I'm so sorry, do please keep talking. I always yawn when I'm fascinated.'

Uncle Richard drew himself up. 'As I was saying, Sergeant, I think a brief, private conversation will be enough to straighten this out. My niece has simply been the victim of a prank that went too far. I'm sure you know how young people can be. My client apologises unreservedly for any inconvenience caused and will be happy to make restitution where appropriate. Looking at the state of Mr Kingdom, he's certainly appears more sinned against than sinning, don't you think? I'm sure you will agree that the simplest and most sensible solution will be for me to remove him – as soon as the good doctor here has finished with him, of course – and we'll all say no more about it.'

I was happy to see the good doctor cast him a very nasty look, but before he could say anything, Russell was off again.

'Do you know, Andrew and I could never decide whether you or your baboon-buggering son were the most unpleasant excrescences in the Kingdom family, but I think today you've finally settled that argument. So grateful.'

Christopher snarled. Russell regarded him with great interest. 'Go on then, Christopher. Surprise us all. Say something intelligent.'

'Hold your tongue,' snapped Uncle Richard, although to which of them he was speaking wasn't clear.

Russell sighed. 'I think we can all agree this has gone on long enough. As a responsible householder and council-tax payer,' his eyes misted slightly as he tried to remember whether he'd paid this year's demand, 'I advocate complete disclosure. So full steam ahead, Jenny, and damn the torpedoes.'

All eyes turned to me. Tanya nodded.

I took a very deep breath. 'Chidopher and Uncle Ridard kidnapped me ad thredeaned to spray perfume id by … baby'd eyed unled I signed a … contrack … gibbing dem back da bookshop.'

'Very succinctly put,' said Thomas. *'Well done, Jenny.'*

No one saw Russell move, but suddenly he was right up in Christopher's face, which went slack with fear.

I saw both Daniel and Andrew tense, ready to intervene. Sgt Bates placed a restraining hand on his arm.

Russell smiled, and it wasn't a nice smile. I hadn't

seen that look in a long time. He groped in his jeans pocket for an old business card.

'You'll need to apply for bail, Christopher. Here's my number. Ring me and I'll post as much as you need. And then, when you're back on the street, we can have a chat about people who threaten to blind little babies.'

I shivered. Thomas moved closer.

Sgt Bates increased the pressure on Russell's arm and after a very, very long pause, he stepped back. I breathed a sigh of relief.

'There is no question of bail,' said Uncle Richard, 'because he hasn't...'

'That is correct,' said Sgt Bates. 'There is absolutely no question of bail at this stage. Mrs Checkland, you will, health permitting, present yourself at the station tomorrow. I'm sure Miss Bauer will wish to accompany you. She usually does,' she added meaningfully.

'This is ridiculous,' said Uncle Richard. 'I cannot believe you are paying any heed to these preposterous allegations, Sergeant. I wonder if would be easier if I had a word with your Chief Constable about this.'

'As you wish, sir. You can do it from the station.'

'What? This is ridiculous. This stupid girl is simply parroting the lies her husband has taught her to say.'

No, she wasn't. I focussed on the yellow of her police vest. 'Da conrack.'

She turned. 'I beg your pardon.'

'Oh my God,' said Russell. 'Of course. The contract. I bet neither of these idiots has had the sense to destroy it.'

Christopher made a sudden movement.

'Stand still.'

Richard's voice cracked like a whip, but the damage was done. Everyone in A&E – and there did seem to be a lot of us – now knew that Christopher had the contract in his top pocket.

Russell smiled down at me. 'Let's see them explain that away.'

Sgt Bates raised her voice slightly. 'Both Mr Kingdoms will be good enough to accompany me to the station, please.'

And as if by magic, Russell and Andrew parted like the Red Sea and two enormous constables, even bulkier in their vests, loomed over everyone.

'Impressive,' said Thomas. *'I wonder how she did that.'*

'Mr Wayland, I'd like a statement from you, too, please.'

'Can you give me half an hour please?' said Bill politely. 'I'd like to ask this lady to marry me.'

We were in A&E on a busy weeknight and yet there was complete silence.

Even Russell, king of the conversational bomb, seemed thunderstruck. That would be only be very temporary.

'Yed,' I said, taking advantage of this rare moment and keen to get him away from the danger zone. 'Ad it'd … afder dark tho we… need to get da chicked do bed.'

Russell allowed himself to be distracted. 'Yes, you're right, Jenny. And what's the betting bloody Francesca's up on the roof again.'

The universe ground to a halt. Everything stopped. Everywhere.

'Uh-oh,' said Thomas.

Her voice reverberated around Rushford. 'YOU NAMED YOUR CHICKEN FRANCESCA?'

'Only one of them,' said Russell, as if that was a matter for congratulations.

'Which one?'

'The pretty one,' he said, his instinct for self-preservation kicking in thirty years too late.

Daniel snorted.

'Language.'

'Never mind all that,' said Mrs Crisp, ruthlessly elbowing aside this irrelevant conversation in a manner which even Francesca herself could never have achieved. 'What did you just say?'

'I said I wanted to ask you to marry me, Lizzie.'

'Have you noticed the doctor has stopped asking people to leave? I wonder if they've thought to charge admission. The NHS is broke, you know.'

'Have you noticed the number of people listening to us? I'm never going to be able to walk down the high street again.'

'Well, at least you'll have the option – unlike your ghastly relatives.'

True.

'Well, Lizzie? What do you say?'

There were tears in her eyes. Clutching at her handbag, she said, 'Bill, I can't marry you. Or that other thing. Look at what's happened this evening. I can't leave Russell. You must see that he needs me.'

'What other thing?' said Russell.

She blew her nose. 'We were…' She ground to a halt.

'What?' demanded Russell. 'What's going on?'

Bill said quietly, 'Lizzie is considering starting up her old catering business. We've been looking for suitable premises.'

Heads swivelled towards the suddenly devastated Russell.

I looked up at him and whispered, 'Ruddell,' willing him to understand.

He looked down at me for a moment. I whispered, 'Ruddell,' again. You could have heard a pin drop at that moment.

He seemed to make a huge effort and in a voice that wasn't quite steady, he said, 'You're right, Auntie Lizzie, of course I need you. I'll always need you, but any day now I'm going to grow up and it's time I started to look after myself and my family. So you go ahead and marry your Bill – if you want to, of course. If you don't, just say the word and I'll happily throw him out – although actually, I do think you should marry him and have a home and a life of your own. It's about time. And, don't forget, he has his own handcuffs.'

She said, 'Oh Russell,' and groped for another handkerchief.

He put his arm around her and kissed her hair. 'I've never thanked you properly for your love and care over all these years, and this is the best way for me to do it. Marry your Bill, Auntie Lizzie. Start your business again, and live happily ever after.'

She was crying. 'Russell ... I...'

He wasn't far off himself. Clearing his throat, he patted her vigorously on the shoulder in a manner rather reminiscent of encouraging Boxer past a menacing butterfly, and said, 'You're not doing this properly at all, are you? This is supposed to be the happiest moment of your life. Doesn't say much for the rest of it, does it?' He turned to Bill. 'You'd better take good care of her, or I'll be around to have a word. Oh, and for your own sake, don't ever let her near a fireman because she loses all control.'

Francesca seemed unable to move on. 'You named a chicken after me? Why would you do that?'

'She has hairy legs,' said a voice that no one was ever able to identify afterwards, but I suspected might be the insurance industry's revenge.

Her bosom heaved impressively. 'You named your chicken Francesca because she has hairy legs?'

'It was a compliment,' said Russell, indignantly.

'How?' she demanded. 'How could having hairy legs possibly be a compliment?'

'Well, two of them dig holes and wallow in the dirt. A couple more sneak under the hen house and secretly eat worms, and the cockerel shits in the water trough. Which one of those do you prefer to hairy legs?'

Daniel winked at me. Neither of us had any objections to the pair of them arguing.

Sgt Bates, however, had obviously decided that lesser mortals could be left to sort out these minor issues and was shunting her charges towards the exit. 'Miss Bauer, tomorrow afternoon, then.' She looked at Russell. 'There will be no need for Mr Checkland to accompany you.'

'Let no one ever accuse me of neglecting my husbandly responsibilities,' said Russell, grandly. 'I shall be there, to facilitate the proceedings to the best of my ability.'

Thomas snorted.

'Language,' I said, possibly a little punch drunk by now.

Bill turned to go. 'Lizzie, I have to go with the sergeant, now. We can talk about this tomorrow, if you like.'

'Yes,' said Mrs Crisp.

How about tomorrow afternoon, then? Shall I call around?'

'No, I said yes.'

'I fear you may have lived with Russell Checkland for far too long,' said Bill gravely, looking down at her. 'No, you said yes – what?'

She clutched her handbag even more tightly, squeezed her eyes shut and said, 'No, I said yes, I'll marry you.'

There was a round of applause from the other side of the cubicle.

261

CHAPTER TWENTY

Russell was right. It did sting the next morning. I awoke to a face like a rainbow.

'*Good heavens,*' said Thomas, ostentatiously not reeling back in horror. '*Aren't you the colourful one?*'

I peered at myself in the mirror. 'Actually, it looks much worse than it feels. I'm looking forward to lots of sympathy today.'

'*I think it would be best if you stayed away from young children, those of a nervous disposition, and horses who panic easily.*'

'That's almost everyone I know, then.' I pulled up the covers. 'I shall stay in bed today.'

'*No,*' said Thomas firmly. '*You should get up and move about. Exercise can be very beneficial you know.*'

'Even for my face?'

'*Especially for your face. Up you get.*'

Grumbling, I showered, dressed slowly and made my way downstairs.

Russell was feeding Joy. He'd collected her last night on our eventual return from the hospital. She'd shown no signs of missing her parents.

'I don't know,' said Russell. 'One rusk and she's anyone's.'

We had a peaceful breakfast. As Russell said, no one had kidnapped his wife in the night, all the livestock were present and correct, and his housekeeper hadn't nipped off and married someone, and what a pleasant change that made, didn't it?

Mrs Crisp put an enormous breakfast in front of him

and he heaved a tragic sigh. 'I'm not sure I have the strength to eat this. Treachery and desertion are so undermining, don't you think?'

I was wiping Joy's mouth and when I turned back most of the breakfast had disappeared and he'd started on the toast and marmalade as well, so I don't think anyone was in any danger of taking him too seriously.

'Right,' he announced, pouring himself another cup of tea. 'Plans for the day. Jenny. I had a quiet word with Mrs Balasana last night. She knows about Bundle and she's coming along later this morning to collect her.'

'But…' I stopped, remembering the last time I'd seen the little dog.

'No, it's all right. I nipped out and collected her first thing this morning while you were still snoring. She's in the stable, wrapped in one of Joy's old blankets. I've tidied her up a bit and she's quite presentable.'

I smiled at him. 'That was a nice … thing to do.'

He shifted uncomfortably. 'Just don't tell anyone. It's bad for my image as a hard-drinking, care for nobody, womanising artist with the devil in his soul and a bottle in his pocket. Is there any cake left over from yesterday?'

With no expression at all, Mrs Crisp placed the biscuit tin in front of him, caught my eye and retired to the sink.

He whipped off the lid, still talking. 'Then this afternoon, of course, we have to present ourselves…' he died away, staring at the wriggling mealworms and then looked up at her.

'Is this your method of giving in your notice? A normal woman would say, "I'm very sorry Mr Checkland, but I'm leaving at the end of the month to get married. While I realise my disloyal behaviour leaves you destitute and alone, I really can't pass up the opportunity to marry a man with his own handcuffs. Please accept my notice to leave your employment and never mind about my last month's salary." *Not* to scatter the table with the larval form of *Tenebrio molitor*. I'll admit I don't have any fond feelings for either the insurance industry or its workforce, but I can't help wondering if I shouldn't take the poor man aside and explain about you and your little ways.'

'*So he's resigned to her leaving, then?*' said Thomas.

'It would appear so. I think he's still very upset about it, though.'

'*I don't blame him. How are the cooking skills coming along?*'

'My cooking is slightly worse than my driving.'

'*My heart goes out to him. How about a short walk? I think we should leave them to have a little chat, don't you?*'

I left Joy with Russell. I think I thought she might be a calming influence. Instead of heading for the gate to the lane, however, Thomas took me around the back of the stables. Past the spot where Russell parks his Land Rover. Past the scorched area where we have our bonfires. Past the manure heap, and on to the crumbling wall that marks the edge of our property. A couple of very ancient apple trees grew nearby that Russell said he remembered climbing in his youth. They were bent and gnarly and covered in mistletoe. One of them had only one working branch left. A few windfalls lay on the ground and I picked them up and slipped them into my pocket for Marilyn and Boxer later on.

The weather was sunny and warm. Fluffy white clouds littered the sky. The air was still and smelled of grass and dust and horses. Everything was very quiet. I sat on the old garden roller, half buried in the long grass and closed my eyes. So long as you sat upwind of the manure heap, this was a very peaceful spot.

Thomas stood beside me, swishing his tail. I thought

265

about everything that had happened yesterday, about how much can change in just twenty-four hours. Russell and Joy were safe. Mrs Crisp was getting married. And I thought about poor Mrs Balasana – the one person who wasn't going to get her happy ending.

I don't know how long I sat there, surrounded by silence, feeling the warm sun on my head and the heat from the metal roller on my bottom. This afternoon promised to be messy, noisy and complicated. I should enjoy this moment of tranquillity while I could.

I heard footsteps approaching and opened my eyes, expecting to see Russell coming around the corner, but it wasn't him. An elderly lady I had never seen before stood only a few feet away, seemingly oblivious to my presence. I could see she wore a scruffy old mac, disreputable wellies, and leaned heavily on an ancient walking stick. I could see her pink scalp through her wispy, white hair. She stood quite quietly, a tatty wicker basket over her arm, seemingly waiting for something.

I stood up quietly so as not to alarm her and said, 'I'm … sorry, I didn't … know you were here. Can I help you?'

She ignored me. I wondered if perhaps she hadn't heard me and went to approach her.

'*Just give it a minute,*' said Thomas softly.

She looked about her, smiled a little, thumped her stick on the ground, and said in a creaky voice, 'Now then, Jack. Where's my boy?'

I heard a gentle footfall behind me and Jack appeared from around the corner. He stood still for a moment, then lifted his head, pricking up his ears. For the first time that I could remember, he made a slight sound of recognition and then trotted daintily towards her. I could hear the sound of his little hooves hitting the ground. Slowly, very carefully, he stretched out his head towards her.

Settling her weight on her stick with one hand, she gently stroked his ears with the other. First the left one and then the right and then back again. He stood quietly with his eyes closed, and it was very obvious that both of them were enjoying every moment of it. If donkeys could purr, then Jack would be vibrating like a sewing machine. Still with his eyes closed, he rubbed his head against her but very, very carefully as if he was aware of her fragility. She laughed and said, 'That's my boy, Jack.'

Opening his eyes, he began to root around in her basket. She stood perfectly still while he did it. I suspected this was a big game for both of them, and one in which they both found a great deal of pleasure. He was gentle but thorough. It was obvious they both knew there was something in there worth finding.

And there was. He found an apple. A big, red, shiny apple.

She laughed softly and held it out to him. Taking it delicately, he began to crunch away.

The sun made a halo around both of them and I squinted into the bright light, eyes watering. What was I seeing here?

'Thomas…'

'Ssshhh…'

Even as he finished the apple, the old lady began to fade. Jack nuzzled her gently, but she was fading in front of my eyes. Leaning forwards, she whispered something I didn't catch. Only Jack heard her final words. And then a small, sharp breeze blew out of nowhere and when I blinked the water out of my eyes, she had disappeared.

I said to Thomas, 'Was that …?'

He rubbed himself gently against my arm. *'Sometimes Jenny, all that's needed is a chance to say goodbye.'*

I stood in that quiet little place and thought of all the hundreds of thousands of people, every day, who never have a chance to say goodbye. Russell to his mother as she drove away, never to return. Or Mrs Crisp to her family. Or Mrs Balasana to her Gerald. Or to Bundle. We all, every day, have the opportunity to say the things that really matter and we never say them. We always think there will be a tomorrow, but tomorrow doesn't always happen. I tried to swallow the huge lump in my throat.

For a long, long time, Jack watched the space where he had last seen her, and then, ears drooping, he slowly turned and plodded back into the yard. Back into this world. Ignoring everything around him, he took up his usual position by the wall, his head hanging low. All by himself again.

We stood together, watching him. I said again, 'Thomas…'

'Hush,' he said. 'Something important is going to happen.'

I held my peace, but it seemed to me that whatever Thomas had done, it hadn't worked. To me, Jack looked even more unhappy than he had before.

I sighed. 'Mrs Balasana will be here soon. Russell went out and found Bundle first thing this morning. He's put her in the stable. She's going to be very distressed. I'm not sure I want to stay for this.'

'Too late,' said Thomas, as we heard the gate click. I looked around to see Russell holding it open for Mrs Balasana.

She looked tired and tear-stained. She wasn't dressed with anything like her usual care. I could see jeans and a plain top under a light jacket, and her hair was loose. I thought it made her look younger and nicer. She was carrying a basket in which, presumably, to take Bundle home for the last time.

'Hello Mrs … Balasana. Ananda.'

Her manners were still intact. 'Good

268

morning … Jenny. I've come to…' she stopped, clutched her basket, and stared at her feet.

I didn't know what to do. Or say. I stared at Russell, who said gently, 'She's just in here,' and held open the stable door. She set down her basket and followed him inside.

I didn't go in. Thomas and I stood in the doorway.

Russell is wonderful. Not only had he gone out and found her little dog, cut her down, and brought her back, but he'd cleaned her up, brushed out her coat and re-tied her top-knot. Then he'd carefully wrapped her in such a way that anyone looking at her would think she was just asleep in her favourite blanket.

'We'll be just outside when you want us,' he said quietly, and I felt a sudden surge of love for him.

We sat on the bench by the back door, enjoying the sun. He took my hand. 'All right?'

I nodded and leaned against him.

Mrs Balasana reappeared a few minutes later, stuffing a tissue back into her pocket.

Russell stood up.

She picked up her basket. 'I've brought something to carry her home in. I wonder, Mr Checkland, if you would be kind enough to…' she stopped, struggling.

'Of course,' said Russell, very gently. 'But would it be easier for you if I brought her up myself, later on? You could take the time to choose a spot … you know, somewhere she liked … and I can bring a spade as well.'

She nodded, staring at her feet again. 'Thank you. That would be … Thank you very much.'

We stood in an awkward silence until she said, 'Well, I should be going.'

I said, 'Would you … like me to … walk with you?'

'Oh, no, but thank you for the offer. You don't look well, Mrs Checkland. Jenny. I should have asked – how are you feeling this morning?'

I was about to respond that, contrary to all appearances, I was very well thank you, when Russell nudged me.

'Could we all stand very still, please?'

I saw Mrs Balasana's look of faint alarm. Best behaviour notwithstanding, this was still Russell Checkland and Frogmorton Farm, and anything could be about to happen.

I peered around Mrs Balasana. Jack was approaching. I could hear his hooves on the concrete. In deference to the solemnity of the occasion, Boxer and Marilyn were in their field and the chickens were firmly shut in their multi-coloured hen house. There was only Jack. And, for the first time ever, he appeared to be initiating some sort of contact.

I stared suspiciously at Thomas who was inspecting the brickwork around the stable door, seemingly oblivious to what was happening over here.

Jack halted a few feet away, pricked up his ears just as he had done before, and stretched out his neck to Mrs Balasana.

All credit to her, she didn't flinch. She patted him gingerly, saying, 'Hello old fellow, who are you?'

'His name is Jack,' I said. 'He likes his ears ... stroked. First one, then the other.'

'Oh.' She stretched out her hand and gently stroked his ears, one at a time, slowly gaining confidence. He closed his eyes and sighed a deep, donkey sigh.

'Well, I'm blowed,' said Russell. 'Jenny, are you seeing this?'

I said, 'Thomas, what's happening?

They have both said goodbye to someone they love this morning. Now they can begin to look to the future.' He looked at me through his forelock. *'What a shame we*

270

don't have an apple.'

Everything fell into place. 'Oh.' I pulled one out of my pocket and slipped it into her basket.

Mrs Balasana gave him one last, lingering pat. 'Well, I suppose I had better … Oh, what's he doing?'

Jack had his head in her basket and was apple hunting.

'It's his … game,' I said. 'It's what he and his last owner used to do. He's looking for his apple.'

'Well, he won't find one in there.'

Very, very gently, Jack removed his apple. To the general astonishment of all. All except two of us, perhaps.

'Good heavens, how did that get in there?'

'I wonder,' I said, looking at Thomas, who had moved on to an inspection of the woodwork, because obviously none of this was anything to do with him.

I know my duty, however. 'Why Ananda, how … clever of you. That's his party trick, and he … doesn't do it for just anyone.'

'Really?' She looked down at Jack, solemnly chomping away at his apple. 'He's a very clever boy.'

'He's a very lonely … boy,' I said softly, nudging Russell before he could queer my sales pitch.

The world seemed to hang in the balance. Even Russell seemed afraid to speak.

Jack finished his apple and rubbed his head very gently against her.

'That's how he says thank you,' I said, around the lump in my throat.

She stroked his nose. He closed his eyes and heaved that deep, donkey sigh again.

I thought of her little orchard next to her cottage. A handsome donkey living in a pretty orchard. Safe and happy to the end of his days. He would love and be loved. Isn't that what we all want? And, because he belonged to Mrs Balasana, he would have the best of everything.

271

'He really seems to like you,' said Russell, without any hint of astonishment. I was proud of him. 'You're the first person he's ever had any sort of interaction with since his owner died. We haven't been able to do anything with him. In fact, we're about to send him back to the sanctuary.'

We weren't about to do anything of the sort, but Russell has his own sales pitch.

'But why?'

'Well, he lost his owner and nothing anyone does seems to get through to him. Until today.'

We all looked at Jack, doing his sewing machine impersonation again.

'I wonder, Mrs Balasana, do you think you would like to take him?'

'What? Oh, no – no, I don't think so. It's so painful when you lose something or someone precious. When they die it's almost unbearable.'

His voice suddenly gentle, Russell said, 'Yes, you're right. How long did you have her?'

'Eleven years. She was the last link with … someone special.'

'Well, you're going to feel pretty rotten for a week or so, but to me that seems a more than fair exchange for the joy she's brought you over the last eleven years. I mean, take Jenny here. Far more trouble than she's worth, and as you've seen, her relatives are a living nightmare, and yet I wouldn't give up one single second of the time we've been together.'

I couldn't look at him. 'Russell…'

Jack looked up at her. She looked down at Jack. The moment went on and on. No one spoke.

She seemed to come to a decision. 'Mr Checkland, I wonder if I might have a word with you…

I had been so involved with Jack and Mrs Balasana, that I hadn't noticed Thomas walking slowly towards the gate. I watched Russell and Mrs Balasana go into the house together, and then chased after him. 'Where are you going?'

'Sometimes Jenny, all that's needed is a goodbye.'

'Thomas, no. You're not leaving again, are you?'

'I am, yes. My work here is done.'

'But I'll see you again?'

Silence.

'But we agreed…'

'I know we did, but you really don't need me any longer, Jenny. You and Russell will have many happy years together. Your daughter will grow to be joyful and your son will be happy. What more do you need?'

'Nothing. I don't *need* anything, but I *want* to see you.'

He smiled. *'You will – but not for a while yet.'* Suddenly, he was mischievous Thomas again. *'You shouldn't have seen me now.'*

Something fell into place. He had told me he was just passing through. 'You're not here for me, are you?'

'No. Although I couldn't resist calling in to see you again.'

'So, if not me – who *were* you here for?'

He said nothing, but looked back at the house.

'You were here for Mrs Balasana?'

'She was so very unhappy, Jenny.'

'Do you – do you do this sort of thing very often?'

'I do it all the time. Some people see me – some people don't. I just do what I can. Shall we walk?'

We stepped out into the lane and began to walk up the lane. The sun shone brightly and the air was hot between the high hedges. Birds sang all around us. Everything was wonderful and Thomas was leaving me again.

'It's always so peaceful here,' he said, over the quiet

273

clop of his hooves.

I made one last appeal. 'Thomas…'

He looked down at me through his forelock, his dark eyes full of love. *'Take care, my lovely Jenny.'*

I knew. I just knew. There was nothing I could say. The time had finally come…

I made myself be calm. I wouldn't cry. I had my world. I had Russell, and Joy, and Russell would need me if Mrs Crisp left, and there was Sharon's cupcake shop to support, and this Christopher business to sort out, and I was learning to drive, and I was pretty sure I now had ovaries straighter than a plumb line. In other words, I had a life. I finally had a voice and a life and I would never take either of them for granted. Every day, I would love the people around me. I wouldn't wait until it was too late. And I would be happy.

I tidied his forelock, gently pulling the strands together and smoothing them straight. 'Look after yourself, Thomas. I shall often think of you.'

'And I of you. Come here.'

He lowered his head and we rested our foreheads together. For the last time, I inhaled the scent of warm ginger biscuits.

'I can never thank you enough, Thomas. For everything you have done for me.'

'You have already thanked me. Many times. Have a lovely life, Jenny.'

'You too, Thomas. Don't forget me.'

I could hear the smile in his voice. *'Jenny, I tell you now, the events of yesterday will live with me for ever.'*

I smiled. 'Me too.'

He stood waiting and I suddenly remembered. Stepping back, I placed one hand on forehead, and said, 'Thomas, I release you.'

'Goodbye, Jenny.'

For the first and last time, I kissed his nose. 'Goodbye, Thomas.'

He turned and walked away up the lane, his hooves sending up little puffs of dust. After a few paces, he turned and looked back at me and I knew he was smiling. And I knew that the next time I saw him he would be taking me with him. But not for a while yet.

Then he turned back, broke into a sudden gallop from a standing start and thundered up the lane, kicking up small stones and clouds of dust. His mane and tail streamed behind him. The lane bent around to the right, but he just carried straight on. Reaching the hedge, he bunched his muscles and leaped into the air. My eyes were blurred with tears, but for a moment – just for one perfect moment – time stood still and he hung in the air, a shimmering golden arc in the sunshine. I ran to a gap in the hedge and watched him gallop away for the last time.

And then – in that final moment – just before he disappeared into the distance, just before he left my life for ever, he kicked up his heels for the sheer joy of living. Then the sound of his hoof beats died away, and he was gone.

THE END

ACKNOWLEDGMENTS

Thanks to Jo Hobbs for the chicken chat. An eye-opening glimpse of the bizarre world of the chicken.

Want to know what happens next?
Catch up with Jenny as she continues to navigate life
on Frogmorton Farm . . .

LITTLE DONKEY

It's Christmas and Jenny Checkland is beset with problems.

The Vicar, who really should know better, has asked to borrow Marilyn the donkey for the nativity play thereby unleashing chaos on the already chaos-laden Frogmorton Farm.

Will Marilyn survive her bath?
Will anyone survive Marilyn's bath?

Robbed of her role as the Virgin Mary, what revenge is the Angel Gabriel plotting?

Why is that sheep so fat?

Will Charlie ever get to say his one line?

Can Marilyn be prevented from eating the Baby Jesus?

Where is Thomas, who promised he would be there?

And worst of all – will Russell, lost on the moor in a blizzard, make it back in time for the birth of his first child? Or even at all?

Available in ebook from

HEADLINE

Discover more from the inimitable Jodi Taylor
in her gripping supernatural thriller series,
featuring Elizabeth Cage . . .

WHITE SILENCE

'I don't know who I am. I don't know what I am.'

Elizabeth Cage is a child when she discovers that there are things in this world that only she can see. But she doesn't want to see them and she definitely doesn't want them to see her.

What is a curse to Elizabeth is a gift to others – a very valuable gift they want to control.

When her husband dies, Elizabeth's world descends into a nightmare. But as she tries to piece her life back together, she discovers that not everything is as it seems.

Alone in a strange and frightening world, she's a vulnerable target to forces beyond her control.

And she knows that she can't trust anyone . . .

HEADLINE

DARK
LIGHT

The thrilling sequel to White Silence

Betrayed, terrified and alone, Elizabeth Cage has fled her
home. With no plan and no friends, she arrives at the
picturesque village of Greyston and finds herself involved
in an ages-old ceremony that will end in death.

And that might be the least of her problems – the Sorensen
Institute would very much like to know her whereabouts.
And Michael Jones is still out there, somewhere, she hopes.
No matter how far and how fast she can run, trouble
will always find Elizabeth Cage.

HEADLINE